CW00407385

STAG PARTY

A PATRICK FLINT NOVEL

PAMELA FAGAN HUTCHINS

SKIPJACK PUBLISHING

FREE PFH EBOOKS

Before you begin reading, you can snag a free Pamela Fagan Hutchins *What Doesn't Kill You* ebook starter library by joining her mailing list at https://www.subscribepage.com/PFHSuperstars.

CHAPTER ONE: BUCK

Patrick

Ice crystals tumbled through the air from the low-hanging clouds above the pickup, dancing to a landing on the windshield. For a moment, Patrick Flint stared at an oversized flake, mesmerized. It looked like a fancy Christmas tree ornament, only prettier, with an intricate pattern of branching arms radiating from a multi-faceted center. So white it was almost blue, so fresh and clean that it was hard to believe it had probably started its life as a particle of dust. But its beauty was fleeting. The heat of the defroster on the inside of the glass melted it, and it turned into a colorless blob that merged with other blobs and became water. *Amazing. And to think millions more are landing all around us.* The ground had been snow-free and the weather unseasonably warm until only a few hours ago. Which meant the snowflakes would be melting on the asphalt, too, then refreezing into something dangerous. He gave his head a shake and cut his eyes back to the road.

"Look at the branches on those plates. Dendrites, I'd say." He drummed his hands on the steering wheel in time to "Frosty the Snowman" playing in his head, but didn't sing it, sparing himself ridicule from his kids. "You get them when the humidity is high and the temperature is just perfect, like today. Five degrees. A little warmer, a little colder, and they'd be smaller. Less humidity, and we wouldn't see all the arms."

"It's like a snow globe." His son Perry leaned forward and peered upward. The boy's football season crew cut was growing back in, a few shades darker than the snow.

"And every one of them unique."

"Do they have different names?" Perry asked.

A heavy sigh vibrated from the lips of his daughter Trish. All he could see of her was her long, blonde braid. She was turned toward the window, but he doubted she was watching the snow. To call her moody and morose right now was downplaying the situation. Her boyfriend Ben was leaving for college at the University of Wyoming in Laramie the next day. It was an early departure for the spring semester, but he was starting a work-study program and had to report to his job.

Patrick played to his appreciative audience. "Well, there *are* names for the different types. Dendrites, plates, columns, needles, prisms. But even those have a bunch of names. Hollow columns, solid plates, stellar plates." He grinned at his son. "Too many variations for me to remember them all."

And Patrick had tried to remember them for the last few winters. He'd visited the Johnson County Library and studied up on the formation of snow during their first year in Wyoming. Living in Texas, he'd thought all snow was just *snow*. But now he'd quickly seen the diversity of it firsthand. Shoveling and plowing had driven the point home. Not all snowflakes—or snowdrifts—are created the same. From tiny pellets to large flakes. Heavy and dense to light and fluffy. Pill-like and differentiated to lacy and seemingly interlocking. He loved them all, until about March fifteenth or so, when he and the rest of the state were ready for sunshine and green grass.

The big dendrite flakes falling today were his favorite.

And they were coming down thick and fast, obscuring the view of the palisades of Crazy Woman Canyon and the greater Bighorn Mountains to their west. Already, a thin, white blanket had settled over Trabing Road. Off the asphalt—its dark color drawing heat from the sun that was augmented by the friction of warm tires—the ground was cooler, and snow was accumulating around the leafless buck brush, rocks, and fence posts. *No dilly dallying at the ranch. These roads are gonna get slicker than goose poop.*

"All I care about is how good they'll be to snowmobile on." Perry's wide smile showed off a slightly undersized temporary fake tooth held in place by a retainer.

Patrick grinned back. Perry was over the moon about their weekend trip. Dr. John, Patrick's boss at the hospital, had invited them to join a group of his friends from around the world—fellow Yale alumni, real movers and shakers—up at a mountain lodge, for guy time and winter sports. Not just snowmobiling, either. Dr. John had promised snow shoeing, dog sledding, and cross-country skiing. They might even go ice fishing on Meadowlark Lake if the conditions were right.

Perry's voice cracked as he joined in with a song on the radio. "You picked a fine time to leave me, loose wheel."

"It's *Lucille*, not loose wheel." His sister shot him the type of cutting look teenage girls do better than anyone, her blue eyes like diamonds.

Perry deflected it in the way thirteen-year-old boys do better than anyone. "I know you are, but what am I?"

"That doesn't even make sense. And you stink like rotten meat. Learn to take a shower like the rest of us, shrimp."

He chanted, "So, so suck your toe, all the way to Mexico."

"Dad, tell him to stop."

Patrick tightened his lips to keep from laughing. "That's enough, Perry." The freckle-faced boy delighted in getting under his sister's skin. Patrick was just happy to see Perry showing some spirit. Since the death of his best friend and football buddy John the previous September, he'd been in and out of a deep, blue funk. Lately, he was showing signs he might have escaped it.

A new-model, mint-green sedan appeared, driving in the opposite direction from the Flints, toward town. Not the usual type of vehicle Patrick saw out on these roads, and not one he recognized as belonging to a local. Most of those were gas guzzlers like his own truck. As it drew closer, Patrick identified it as an Impala with unimpressive tires. The driver was a dark-haired fellow, and the passenger, too, Patrick thought, from the brief glimpse he got of him. He didn't envy them their drive. The roads already didn't favor low clearance and city treads, although the vast distances between filling stations were an advantage of the Impala. Patrick still remembered a few years back, in Texas, when he had to hold off filling his tank more than a time or two because of gasoline shortages. It was hard to believe things happening all the way on the other side of the world could impact him at a gas pump in Wyoming, but they could, if it happened again. How much worse might it be here? Maybe he should get a smaller vehicle . . . except then he'd be in the same boat as these poor saps the whole long winter. He hoped he didn't find the Impala and its occupants stranded later.

A gate and a new wooden O — M sign over it appeared on their left. The recently renamed O Bar M Ranch—previously known simply as the Ochoa homestead—was now jointly owned by the Ochoa and Mendoza families, descendants of Basque that had moved to the area in the early 1900s to herd sheep. Patrick clicked on a last second blinker and made a careful turn, pumping the brakes gently without sliding. The snow was deeper on the dirt entrance road. The depth wasn't a problem yet, though.

The storm had made early afternoon seem like dusk, but visibility was better as they headed east, and he even got a decent glimpse of the property before them. Rugged hills and gullies without a tree in sight, except around the house and ranch buildings fifty feet ahead, where a herd of deer had clustered, foraging behind a wind break. Mostly does and their spring fawns, but also a few bucks of various sizes, including one with a trophy-size set of antlers. Something was running in the field behind them. At first, he thought it was a man, then he decided it had to be a deer. No one would be out there on foot in this weather.

"I can't believe you drug us out here, three days after Christmas. It's not even civilized." Trish pulled her puffy blue coat tighter around herself but didn't zip it.

"Your mom needs a horse."

Cindy—his wife Susanne's horse—had died over a year ago. Been murdered, actually, if that's what you called it when someone intentionally killed a horse for no good reason. She hadn't joined them on any rides since then, even when friends offered her their horses. Patrick's friend, Mayor Martin Ochoa, was looking to sell his father's horse now that the older Ochoa had retired to town with his wife, to be nearer to medical care and their son. Hence Patrick's trip out to the O Bar M.

"She hates horses."

"She doesn't *hate* them. They make her nervous. But if we find her the right horse, she'll get over that. She's missing out on some great adventures."

"And some not so great. Or have you already forgotten about our ride up to Highland Park?"

The ride where mobsters from Chicago had killed Perry's friend John. No, he hadn't forgotten that one, and he hated that Trish had brought it up in front of her brother, but Perry didn't flinch. "Different adventures than that one."

"Like the one to Walker Prairie?" Perry said.

The ride where Trish had been kidnapped by the sons of a patient Patrick had been unable to save. Of all the risks of practicing medicine, it was one he'd never anticipated. "Or that one. We've had plenty of other fun trail rides." He pulled the pickup to a stop next to a blue and white Ramcharger, one he often saw parked in front of City Hall in Buffalo.

"I'll wait here," Trish said.

"I need your opinion."

"My opinion is that this is a bad idea."

"About the horse."

"My opinion about the horse is that it's a bad idea."

Patrick realized debating her was the bad idea. "Noted. And you're coming. You, too, buddy." He smiled at Perry.

A shaft of brilliant sunlight broke through the clouds over a little white ranch house. In its front yard, a nearly vertical shaft of snow rose from the ground and began to rotate.

"Snownado!" Perry shouted, pointing at it as he climbed out of the driver's side after Patrick.

Or snow devil. Snow devils were rare, but less so in windy Wyoming than elsewhere in the world. Patrick had seen a generous handful of them in just a few years. Combine surface wind shear and cold air over a warmer, snowy surface—especially in sunny spots, and most especially before or under a snow squall—and, just as sure as Bob's your uncle, a column of snow particles would whirl skyward. Perry ran toward the ranch house, chasing the snownado, which danced away from him and disappeared. He returned, laughing and pink cheeked.

The three Flints walked toward a weathered red barn, zipping jackets and shoving hands in gloves and hats on heads. The kids, wool caps. Patrick, a cowboy hat, which his ears were already complaining about. The cold wind had a bite to it.

A grizzle-haired woman with a bowed back and bare head waved to them from where she was standing at a hitching post by the barn. She was clad in a long oilskin jacket with the collar up around a black scarf. The get-up made her seem miniscule. She had her hand on a normal-sized dapple gray horse, saddled and ready. The woman stomped the ground with black rubber boots, swishing her wool skirt around her calves. The horse lowered its head, eyes closed, and blew steam from its nostrils.

Patrick lifted a hand. "I'm Patrick Flint. We're supposed to be meeting Martin out here."

She shook her head no.

"I thought that was his Ramcharger back there?"

"It is. It break down. He call earlier today. He not coming."

"What happened?"

"He no say. I show you horse?" She smiled, wrinkling her face into the lines of a topographical map, with her nose a mountain peak.

"That would be great. What should we call you?"

Her lips parted. Her upper gum was bare of teeth. Unable to afford dental care when she was young? By the looks of her clothing, she still couldn't. "Rosa Mendoza."

Patrick hid his surprise. Rosa Mendoza was the new matriarch of the ranch, married to Stefano Mendoza. From what Martin had told Patrick, the Mendozas had bought a half interest in the Ochoa homestead, for cash, which had funded his parents' retirement. Patrick had treated Stefano for bronchitis the previous winter, too, and knew him to be fifty-five years old. Rosa was not the destitute old woman Patrick had thought her to be at first sight. And, despite her diction, she wasn't a newcomer to the state of Wyoming, either. It just went to show you couldn't judge a book by its cover. Not completely, anyhow.

"Nice to meet you." He put a hand on his son's head. Perry ducked out from under it. "This is Perry." He waved his hand at his daughter. "And this is Trish."

"You the doctor?"

"I am one of the doctors from Buffalo."

"You look at my sheeps, yes?"

"Uh . . ." Patrick had filled in for the vet, Joe Crumpton, on multiple occasions, but, so far, he hadn't been pressed into treating any sheep. Sheep dogs, yes. Actual sheep, no.

"Ewes got babies on the way. Some not so good."

"I'm not . . ."

"Come." She motioned him to follow with her hand.

Trish raised her eyebrows at him. Perry snorted. Patrick shook his head and followed Rosa into the barn. *Sheep. There's a first time for everything.* Patrick brushed snow off his face while his eyes adjusted. He looked back at the light streaming in the entrance. Dust motes spun in the air. The interior of the wooden structure was warmer, darker, and stinkier than outside had been. With a light sniff he identified dirty wool and droppings. Sheep weren't known as the sweetest smelling of animals.

"This way," Rosa said. She was standing beside a wooden-slatted stall with two wooly sheep in it, both of their heads down. Above her, stacks of hay in a loft reached to the peaked two-story ceiling. "Them sheeps."

"What seems to be the matter with them?"

She lifted her arms and dropped them. "I think they got the lambing sickness. Yes?"

Patrick had talked to enough ranchers to know she was referring to pregnancy toxemia, which was incident to low blood sugar and occurred most frequently in late term pregnancy with ewes carrying multiple lambs. And that it was often fatal. "Is that what you think?"

She nodded. "I call the hands when I find them in here, but they no answer. It their job to take care of them. Lambs due soon. These ewes dull. Not eating."

"I'm sorry about that." A late term pregnant ewe dull and off her food sounded serious. He leaned into the pen and palpated their sides. Under their thick wool, he found taut pregnant bellies without the layer of fat ewes relied on to make it through their pregnancies. The animals needed nutrition. "I'd call Dr. Crumpton out, if I were you. But in the meantime, do you have corn syrup? We could feed them that with a syringe." They needed electrolytes, too. "And Gatorade?"

She nodded. "I get syrup from the house. I know how to make the alligator drink. I bring it. And I call the lazy hands again. You ride the horse while I gone."

He noted she didn't respond to his suggestion to call the vet. It might be nearly 1978, but, when it came to ranchers, they were by and large old school, preferring to save the money and do their own veterinary work. Not because they didn't care about the animals, but because vet care was an expense that might leave a rancher right side down on an investment. He couldn't force her to do it, even if he thought it was the right thing.

"All right then," he said.

She scurried out of the barn.

"These poor sheep." Trish opened the stall and went inside. She knelt between the ewes and rubbed their heads. They didn't resist her. "Will they die?"

"Maybe. They probably would have if they'd been left with the herd."

"That's so sad."

"Mother Nature can be harsh."

"I've got to stay with them."

"I need you out with the horse and me."

"But—"

"I'll do it. I'll stay with them." Perry slipped into the stall.

Trish started to protest, but then she buttoned her lip. Patrick didn't know what had gotten into her, but he appreciated the reprieve. The wind hit him like a sledgehammer as they exited the barn. The temperature had plummeted, and the sun had disappeared again. He popped the collar on his flannel jacket and wished he'd brought the down one instead. Ice pelted his face, sharp and stinging. Gone was the flaky snow of earlier.

"This isn't very good weather for trying out a horse." Trish walked to the animal's head with her palm down. Its eyes were wide open, whites showing. The horse snorted and jerked back against its line. "He doesn't think so, either."

Patrick grinned. "This is Wyoming. We can't buckle under at the first snowflake."

"Wind makes horses crazy."

Patrick rubbed circles in the rigid muscles of the gelding's neck. "Hey, boy. Martin said you're a big pussycat. We're just going for a short ride. If all goes well, we could move you off this ranch and into our pasture where there's a nice run-in shelter. Would you like that?"

The horse pawed at the ground.

"That didn't seem like a yes," Trish said, her voice dry.

Patrick untied the lead line from the post and led the horse a few steps away. Was it his imagination or had the temperature dropped five degrees since they'd been here? He pulled his hat further down his forehead. He just needed to get this over with. For everyone's sake, including the horse. "Trish, can you hold his lead and unclip us when I'm up?"

She walked over and held the rope, leaning toward one of the horse's ears. "I'm sorry. This will be over soon."

Patrick gathered the reins in his leverage hand, grasped some mane, put his foot in the stirrup, and stepped up. He swung his leg over the saddle. The stirrups felt about the right length. The horse shifted its feet beneath him. "Feels like he's about ready to go."

Trish unclipped the lead rope. "Or something."

A gust of wind rattled the eaves of the barn and sent Patrick's hat flying from his head and past the horse's nose. The horse reared up on its hind legs. Patrick was caught unawares, before he'd set his feet firmly in the stirrups. One of his feet slipped out and he grabbed the saddle horn.

Trish stumbled backward, away from the flailing hooves, and slipped down onto her rump.

After what seemed like an eternity but was only fractions of a second, the gelding leaped forward, landing halfway across the barn-yard, then whirled and ran in the opposite direction, with Patrick barely hanging on. The horse half-galloped, half-bucked for a few steps. Patrick pushed his weight down into the seat with one hand and one foot, desperately searching for the bouncing stirrup with the other foot. After several failed attempts, he found it with his toe. Just as he was about to shove his foot in, the horse came to a stiff-legged full stop.

Patrick exhaled. "It's okay. We're good. Everything's okay."

The horse ducked its head and pumped its back legs skyward with a kick so powerful that Patrick shot out of the saddle like a cannon ball. He sailed into the air. *The snowflakes. I can see them even better from up here.*

Then he landed on his side with a crunch. His head came to rest in the snow, and he wasn't thinking about snowflakes anymore.

***

PATRICK HEARD MOANING AND SCREAMING. For a moment he didn't know where he was—who he was—what had happened to him—why his side hurt so bad—who was making all the darn racket.

"Dad! Dad! Are you okay?" A female voice. The source of the scream. His brain ground a few gears, then caught. Trish. His daughter.

But Trish wasn't moaning. That was him. *Ugh. Must stop it. Scaring Trish.* Real men didn't panic their kids. He slowed his breathing. His brain came up to speed, mostly. He opened his eyes and gasped a response. "I will be. Can you catch the horse?"

Trish was kneeling over him, wide-eyed, face drawn. "I don't think I should leave you."

"I'm fine." He pushed up on an elbow. Pain knifed his ribs. *Don't let her see it.* He clamped his mouth shut so tight it felt like the enamel on his teeth would break. Breathing was a struggle.

Perry's face floated into view beside Trish's. "Dad!"

It was hard to see his kids, not just because of the pain, but because snow was coming down straight sideways. The compact pellets stung his cheek.

Then he heard Rosa's voice. And something else. Hoof beats on the snowy ground. "You okay, mister doctor? I bring the horse. You try again?"

Holding his side with one hand, he answered in spurts around grimaces. "Gotta . . . pass . . . on that." He hadn't even caught the horse's name. *Hell Cat. Or maybe Satan.*

"You lose your hat. I think it blow away."

The least of his worries. "Kids, grab me under each arm and help me up, all right?"

They did as he asked without further comment. Or if they did comment, he didn't hear them, because the pain obliterated every sound except the scream inside his head. But it was just pain. Something to block out, to push through, to get stronger from.

"Thanks." He tried to stand up straight and almost made it, but the excruciating catch in his left side had him seeing stars instead of snowflakes. Closing his eyes, he focused on the sound of his breath. *In with the good air, out with the bad air.* He ran his right hand along his side. Nothing felt out of place. He was as sure as he could be without an x-ray that he'd broken a rib in his seven to ten range—or several. But the break or breaks was closed. He pressed harder into the most painful area, feeling for broken edges, without finding any. *Good.* Either the fractures were partial or at least they were stable. His breathing sounded fine, if short. He'd hear it if he'd punctured a lung. Bottom line, he wasn't dying. If things got worse, he'd get an x-ray. In the meantime, he just needed to suck it up.

Trish whispered into his ear. "Dad, Rosa asked you a question."

"Sorry. What was that?" Patrick looked at the matriarch. Rosa held a plastic pitcher in one hand, a bottle of syrup under an arm, and the lead line of the mockingly docile-looking gray horse in her other hand.

She raised her voice. "I say I call the bunkhouse and they no answer. I knock. Same. Can you go ask them when they do their jobs?" Even yelling into the wind, her words and manner were prim. He understood. Walking into a bunkhouse for men wasn't something he'd wish on most females. Not the mess, the smells, or the possible cursing and nudity.

"No problem."

"Want me to come with you, Dad?" Perry's face was tight, his eyes cloudy and worried.

Patrick wouldn't wish the bunkhouse on his son, either. Some things couldn't be unseen, and if the hands were involved in unsavory activities, well, best that it only be Patrick to roust them. "Why don't you and Trish get some Gatorade and syrup in those ewes for me?"

Perry nodded and bounded back toward the barn. Trish eyed Patrick suspiciously. He thought she'd give him an argument, but she just frowned and shook her head at him.

"See if you can find a plastic syringe so you can squirt it on the back of their tongues."

Rosa nodded at Trish. "In the metal cabinet. You see it in the barn. By the big doors."

"Okay, thank you." Trish ran to catch up with her brother.

Rosa motioned vaguely toward the outline of a long, narrow building, past the barn. "The bunkhouse."

Patrick squinted. He could barely see it through the snowfall. "Back in a moment."

Holding his side, Patrick leaned into the wind, setting his feet down as carefully as if he was walking on glass. Each step was a painful stab to the ribs. The cold was really getting into his bones, too, and he wished he'd worn heavier outerwear. It took him three times as long to reach the building as it should have, four times if there'd been no wind.

With the muscles in his torso and abdominals clenched as tight as he could knit them, he rapped on the door. The contact of his knuckles on the wood jolted his ribs like a high-speed collision with a concrete wall. He groaned and shivered. More high-speed collisions, a series of them. Gritting his teeth, he settled on a mantra, which he repeated to himself in rhythm with his breaths. Inhale. *It's only pain.* Exhale. *It won't kill you.* Inhale. *It's only pain.* Exhale. *It won't kill you.*

When no one answered after a minute, he tried the door. The knob turned easily in his hand. He raised his voice. "Anyone home?"

The interior was dark and quiet.

"Rosa—Mrs. Mendoza—sent me to fetch help for some sick ewes." He paused. "Hello?"

He took a step backward, at first intending to return to Rosa and let her know the hands weren't home. But he was inside already, along with a musty stink that made him think of wet socks in front of a fire and overripe garbage. He might as well get the complete picture. All he really knew was no one was answering. Someone could be lying in bed ill or hurt. Unconscious.

Or hiding, not wanting to go out in the storm.

But first he needed light. He groped along the wall, searching for a switch plate. He found one but flinched. It was sticky. In a bunkhouse of bachelors, especially bachelors who worked with livestock, he didn't want to imagine what substance was now on his hand. He flipped a switch upward. No light came on. He fumbled around for another switch but found none. *Burned out? Great. Now I'll have to find one in another room.* Running into furniture in the dark wouldn't be fun with a broken rib or three. He put his left hand in front of him, moving it back and forth as he shuffled his feet. He could make out a dim glow in what he assumed was the kitchen. An oven clock? A refrigerator ajar? It gave him a target to aim for.

He was making steady progress until his foot bumped into something. *Furniture?* Maybe, but it didn't feel that solid. He shifted to the left and moved forward. His foot hit the whatever-it-was again. He reached down in front of him but didn't find a chair, a couch, a table, or anything except air.

Frowning, he pushed the object with his toe. It gave and shifted. He pushed harder, and it rolled away from him. *What the heck? Not heavy enough to be a pillow. A rolled carpet, maybe?* He definitely needed light. He scooted further to the left until he was around the obstruction and shuffled double time toward the glow. His eyes were adjusting to the gloom. Not much, but enough to confirm he'd found the kitchen and to see the switch plate. He flipped two switches to their on position. The kitchen was immediately bright as a summer afternoon. He squeezed his eyes shut, holding his hand up as a shield. *Darn fluorescent bulbs.*

Turning back toward the entrance to the bunkhouse, he craned his neck to see around a wooden dinette table and chairs he'd skirted, looking for whatever he'd bumped into on the floor, but without success. He stepped out of the galley kitchen for a more direct view. The living area he'd traversed was small. The furniture—a love seat, a threadbare armchair, and the dinette set—dingy. His eyes were drawn to an incongruity beyond them, on the wall by the front door. The switch plate wasn't white like he would have expected. Or not much white, as it was nearly completely covered by a dark residue. His mind went to mammalian body fluids brought in by hands in need of a good washing.

Then his eyes returned to the floor and the lump that had blocked his path. Suddenly, he wished he had listened to Trish. He'd been wrong to come to the O Bar M. Susanne didn't want a horse. He'd busted up his ribs for no reason. And now . . . now he was staring at blood pooled near a head of short, sandy brown hair, with boot tracks leading straight to Patrick. His eyes cut to his feet. *My boot tracks.*

His medical training kicked in. Time would be of the essence in rendering aid. Patrick hurried toward the prone figure, ignoring the pain from his own injury. He found a young man, splayed out, a gaping incision across his throat. *He's been attacked.* The wound didn't look survivable, and the man's chest wasn't rising and falling. Patrick crouched, gasping, and reached for a wrist. He searched for a pulse. Didn't find one. Kept trying. Eyed the blood on the floor. It was still liquid but lighter red than fresh blood. The process of coagulation had begun.

A thready voice called, "Help. Me."

Patrick nearly fell over in surprise and cringed in pain from the sudden movement. He shot a look at the man, even though the sound seemed to come from someplace else, further in the bunkhouse. It wasn't this man who had spoken. This man was dead.

"In. Here." The words were a barely audible hiss. Patrick dropped the dead man's wrist, stood, and spun in a circle, searching for the source of the voice. "Kitchen."

But I didn't see anyone in there. He retraced his tracks. A wide smear of blood, darkened but still wet-looking, led across the tiny kitchen floor to a door, which was open about a quarter of an inch with light seeping out around it. *The glow from earlier.* A pantry? A laundry room? A hallway?

Whatever was behind it, Patrick didn't want to open that door. But he knew he had to.

He sucked in a shallow breath and wrenched the knob, pulling outwards to expose a surprisingly deep pantry. A bare bulb with a pull string hung from the ceiling. It illuminated cans of food and bags of rice, beans, sugar, and flour on the shelves, and a long-legged man with a boot missing from one foot slumped against the base of the wall. He held one hand on his bleeding head, hair color indeterminate. The other pressed into his round, oozing gut.

Patrick drew in a sharp breath. What had he stumbled into? "I'm here to help you. I'll be right back after I call an ambulance."

The man shook his head, revealing broken teeth in what may have been a smile. "Not. Gonna. Make. It."

Patrick squatted to get a closer look at the gut injury. The man's intestines had oozed out around his fingers. What seemed like half his body's blood volume was seeping into gapped wooden floorboards. Patrick couldn't be sure without moving the man's hand, but it looked like he was dealing with another incision in addition to the traumatic head injury. Patrick gave the man a ten percent chance of survival, only because he'd toughed it out so far.

He said, "Just let me . . ."

"He. Got. Away."

Patrick paused. Part of him wanted to discourage the man from wasting his energy on speech. But this was important information. The man in the other room had been murdered. In a few minutes, this fellow would likely meet the same end. Right now, he was a living witness to a homicide. Possibly the only one who could identify a killer. A killer who might attack someone else. Friends, neighbors. His wife. His kids. The murderer might even still be on the ranch, where he was a current threat.

"Who?" Patrick asked.

"Man. Dark hair. Dark . . . skin."

"Indian?" The Wyoming population was by and large either light-skinned or, if dark-skinned, American Indian.

A slight headshake. "Ay-rab."

Arab? Patrick didn't know of a single person fitting that description in Johnson County. Nor all of northeastern Wyoming for that matter. "A man from the middle east did this to you?"

A barely perceptible nod. Then the man's eyes closed.

"Stay with me, sir. I'm calling an ambulance." Patrick heard the rattle of the man's last breath before he'd even backed out of the pantry.

He was beyond any help that could be summoned, other than through prayer. Still, Patrick found a phone on the kitchen wall and made the emergency call. Then he hurried outside to give Rosa the bad news.

CHAPTER TWO: WITNESS

South of Buffalo, Wyoming
Wednesday, December 28, 1977, 3:00 p.m.

Trish

When her dad had discovered the hands dead—*which was awful, of course*—Trish's first thought was, *Who will take care of the poor sheep?* Perry, on the other hand, had wanted to run to the bunkhouse and see the bodies, which her dad had said no to, *natch,* because *um, dead people, you know,* and probably because he was afraid it would upset Perry. The last dead person they'd seen was Perry's best friend John. It was probably weird to think in terms of which dead person it was in the long list from their last few years, but that was their life in Wyoming. Anyway, Perry hadn't handled John's death well, understandably, and she couldn't figure out why he wanted to face those feelings again. Trish had no interest in seeing another corpse for as long as she lived.

"Who dead?" Mrs. Mendoza said, clutching her coat at her breastbone.

"The hands."

Tears welled in her eyes and she crossed herself.

"I'm very sorry, Rosa. County personnel should be here soon." Her dad's blue eyes were somber, and his face was pinched, whether because of the murders or because of getting bucked off the horse, Trish wasn't sure.

"Who coming?" Mrs. Mendoza said.

"People with the sheriff's department. I'll wait for them outside the bunkhouse. Everyone needs to stay clear of it. We don't want to accidentally mess up any evidence."

Mrs. Mendoza chased after him. "Where the killer? He maybe in my house? He hide? My husband in Casper!"

Trish couldn't hear her dad's answer over the wind. Mrs. Mendoza had brought up some valid points. It was creepy as all get out that someone had killed those men on this ranch *today*, with the Flints here. Trish didn't want to go back in the barn by herself. She was in favor of getting the heck out of Dodge, but she was stranded here, wasting Ben's last day in town, while they waited on law enforcement.

She grabbed Perry by the hem of his coat. "Let's go save some sheep, squirt."

"Ah, man. I wanna go with Dad." He scuffed the snow with his boot, but he turned and came inside with her.

For the next half hour in the dingy barn, she tried not to think about the dead men and the murderers. She and Perry took turns holding the listless sheep and squirting fluid into their mouths. Most of it ended up on the floor of the barn. Trish coated her finger with syrup and rubbed it in their mouths, hoping they'd at least accidentally swallow tiny amounts. It was exhausting, smelly work. Sheep had a particular odor. A little bit wet dog, a little bit rancid grease. The ewes' coats left her hands black with an oily grime, too. Still, she liked them, and she decided to ask her parents if she could raise a lamb to show and sell at the county fair that summer. Might as well have something to do with Ben gone.

"I hear somebody." Perry rose from his kneeling position, releasing a sheep. "I think Dad's talking to a deputy."

Trish hadn't heard the vehicles arrive, and for a moment panic lapped at her. Could it be the killer? The wind was so loud in the eaves of the barn that she could barely hear Perry talking right next to her. She cocked her head and moved her hair away from her ear. Voices. One of them her dad's. Yes, just outside. Her tension eased a little.

She rubbed the head of each of the mama sheep and looked deep into their eyes. "You're going to be okay." Her dad was always coaching her about the power of positive thinking. Maybe the ewes would pick up on it and it would help them.

Perry said, "Let's go see what they're doing."

She looked at their supply of Gatorade and syrup. It was almost gone. There was nothing more they could do for the sheep. She felt a squeezing sensation in her chest. *Please be all right, little mamas.* "Okay."

She looked outside. The snow had stopped, the sun was out, and the world was sparkling like the crystal chandelier over her grandmother Mama Cat's dining room table. She'd always loved looking up at the light fixture when she was little, and she paused, squinting, to take in the sight. It was beautiful. She wished Ben was there to see it. That and the snow devil. He loved stuff like that, and he had a theory that the snow devils were warnings from Mother Nature.

She was going to miss him so much.

"Are you coming?" Perry turned, shooting her an impatient look. "I don't want to go by myself."

She ran after him, not wanting to spend a single second by herself in the barn, either. Her breath came in pants after only a few yards. Since cross country season had ended, she hadn't been running much. First because she was burned out. Then because it was winter. She was going to be hating life if she didn't get in shape before track season. The coach wanted her to compete in the mile and two-mile races.

Between the barn and the bunkhouse, Mrs. Mendoza and their dad stood talking to two uniformed deputies, one a very short, very young man with a red birthmark across his cheek, the other one a woman with a blonde French braid hanging halfway down her back. The man was wearing a brimmed hat, the woman, a wool cap. Trish recognized her immediately. The Flints' former next-door neighbor, Ronnie Harcourt. Ronnie and her husband Jeff had adopted a little boy a few months before. Trish had been spending a lot of time in the old neighborhood, babysitting for the Harcourts on the weekends. Baby Will's real parents were awful, but the Harcourts were an adorable family.

Ronnie wore a grim look and was talking in a tone to match it. "How many hands were living in the bunkhouse?"

Mrs. Mendoza said, "Three."

Trish's dad's face furrowed. "There were only two bodies inside."

"You're sure three lived in there, Mrs. Mendoza?" Ronnie asked.

"Bai. I mean, yes."

Ronnie and the male deputy glanced at each other. She continued to take the lead. "And you looked everywhere, Patrick, and there were only two men in there?"

"Yes. I'm positive. Only two."

Mrs. Mendoza wrung her hands together, shaking her head. "So, who dead and who not?"

"I'm sorry," Trish's dad said. "I didn't get their names. But one was young and had light brown hair. The other was older, with a round belly and long legs."

"They white?"

"Yes."

Mrs. Mendoza put her face in her hands. When she looked up again, she spoke, her voice quavering. "Young one Bryan. Fat one Herman."

"When was the last time you saw any of them?" Ronnie said.

"This morning. I fix them breakfast."

"All three men."

"Bai."

Ronnie sighed. "We're going to need to get a name and description out for the one that's missing."

"He go by Muhammed."

The name raised Trish's eyebrows. She'd never known anyone named Muhammed. Not in Texas and not in Wyoming. It sounded foreign.

Perry poked her and whispered, "Like Muhammed Ali?"

"I don't know," she whispered back.

Ronnie's voice sounded surprised, too. "What was his last name?"

Mrs. Mendoza shrugged. "I forget. We just call him Muhammed."

"Okay—where is he from?"

"California, he say."

Trish wondered if the name Muhammed was more common in California.

"Can you describe him for me?" Ronnie asked.

"Like Mediterranean. Olive skin. Dark hair. Lotta hair. Dark eyes."

"The name Muhammed—is that middle eastern?"

"Bai. Maybe."

"Any reason to think he would have done this?"

"No reason anybody do this."

"But was he fighting with the others. Like over money? Women? Work?"

Again, Mrs. Mendoza shrugged.

"All right." Ronnie turned to the male deputy. "Could you radio in a BOLO?" From all the time she spent around Ronnie when she babysat, Trish knew a BOLO was a "Be on the lookout".

The man nodded, jiggling his hat. "I'll check on the ETA of the crime scene techs while I'm on the horn."

Ronnie gave him a crisp nod. "Good." He left at a trot, and she turned to Mrs. Mendoza and Trish's dad. "Did either of you see anybody or anything unusual?"

Mrs. Mendoza shook her head. "Everything same like always today."

Trish's dad put one arm around his middle, like he was hugging it. He'd probably hurt his ribs, even if he wasn't fessing up to it. "Nobody and nothing. It was snowing like mad. You could barely even see the bunkhouse from where we were by the barn."

"Any first impressions from the scene?"

He rubbed his forefingers across his forehead, leaving a red mark. "I'd say it had to have been at least an hour since they'd been attacked."

"Why is that?"

"The blood from the younger man. He was dead when I found him. Probably died almost immediately, I'd say, based on the type of wound." He glanced at his kids, but he continued. "When blood is fresh, it's a dark red. The blood on the floor beside him was a lighter red, and it had started to clot. But it hadn't started to look gelatinous or dried out yet."

Ronnie's eyes showed a spark of interest. "What time did you feed them breakfast, Mrs. Mendoza?"

Mrs. Mendoza didn't hesitate. "Five thirty. Every day, five thirty."

"And, Patrick, you found them at . . ."

Trish's dad said, "Two forty-five. This isn't my area of expertise, but, given the condition of the blood, and how dry and cold it is, that's my guess on timing."

Ronnie said, "The killer can't be too far away then."

Trish moved a step closer to her dad. Was it her imagination, or did it feel like someone was watching them?

Mrs. Mendoza looked around. "What if he come back and kill me? I by myself."

"Is there someone you can call, Mrs. Mendoza? To stay with or for them to stay with you?"

"Yes. But my sheeps."

"Maybe you could get help from people at your church?"

Mrs. Mendoza nodded.

Trish's dad said, "There's another thing, Ronnie."

"What's that?" she said.

"One of the men was still alive for a few minutes after I found them. Herman, I guess. The older guy. He described the killer."

Ronnie raised her eyebrows. "And?"

Patrick waved his hand at the bunkhouse. "He said it was an Arab man."

"Muhammed?" Mrs. Mendoza cried out. "Muhammed do this?"

"Herman didn't give me a name."

Ronnie shook her head. "Have you ever seen another Arab man in the area?"

"I haven't seen one in the entire state."

"Exactly." Ronnie stuck out her hand. "Thanks, Patrick. Hopefully we can keep you out of this one. You and the kids are free to go."

"That would be ideal. But you know how to find me if you need anything else." He motioned for Trish and Perry to follow him and started toward their truck, his strides shorter than usual. He was holding his ribs again, too.

Trish hurried after him. She couldn't wait to get home and call Ben. An Arab murderer in Buffalo, Wyoming. It was horrible, but so . . . so . . . exotic. He'd want to hear all about this.

CHAPTER THREE: WITHER

Susanne

Susanne Flint hurried out of the registrar's office at Sheridan College, her spring class sign-up complete. She shook her head. The political science elective she'd wanted had been full, and she was being forced to take a seminar in geopolitics and international relations. She imagined the papers she would have to write and shuddered. *The rise of opposition to the Shah of Iran. Not my thing.* Other than that, though, it was a schedule she could live with.

She shoved her registration paperwork into her purse as she stepped aside to let a group pass her. Her first semester had flown by. She'd never been as busy in her life as when she resumed classes toward her teaching degree. It was supposed to be easier, now that Trish had a driver's license and an old truck. That *did* help. Susanne ferried her daughter around far less, and Trish taxied Perry to his practices. But somehow Susanne still spent most of her time on the road—running errands, attending sporting events, and commuting to her own classes. It barely left her time to study. Out of desperation, she'd started tape recording lectures and replaying them during her thirty-five mile drive each way, north to class and south back again to Buffalo. The strategy had paid off, by a mere whisker. She'd eked out Bs and Cs in all her classes. No As. She'd hoped for better, but given her reality, she was satisfied. And tired. Beyond tired. Exhausted, honestly. She longed for a break. A real one with actual relaxation.

But she wasn't going to get one. She glanced at her watch. Three thirty. She'd seen the hideous weather through the window a few minutes before. Her drive was going to be white-knuckled and long— she'd be lucky if she was home by five. Dinner would be delayed. For a fleeting moment she wondered if the kids would cook. They were still off school for Christmas break this week and next. Then she snorted. *Fat chance they'll cook without explicit instructions, dire threats, and no better offers.* Maybe, if they were starving. And that was a slim maybe. So, she'd be cooking late and *then* she'd be cleaning like a mad woman. The house had to be spotless because she was expecting last minute house guests.

Susanne turned left down a hallway of unpainted cinderblock walls toward the building exit. Ivy League Sheridan College was *not*. Her thoughts remained on the guests due that evening. Her brother Barry had called the day after Christmas with an announcement. He had a (another) new girlfriend. And he'd already asked this one to marry him. After Susanne had picked her jaw up off the floor, she'd recovered in time to hear him ask if he could bring Esme to meet the Flints.

In two days.

The words, "What's the rush? Is she pregnant?" nearly slipped out of her mouth. She had literally clamped a hand over her lips to hold them in.

Whatever the reason, her big brother and his fiancée had gotten into a car in Austin the next morning and driven straight through to Wyoming, even though Susanne had told them Patrick and Perry were spending a long-planned weekend on the mountain with Patrick's boss, Dr. John. A last-minute spot became available with Dr. John's group, and Barry was going to fill it. *What in the world am I going to do to entertain a woman I've never met before all weekend long?*

She'd better think of something because Barry and Esme were due to arrive that evening. *At least they're not bringing my parents and seven kids,* she thought, remembering Patrick's brother's disastrous visit the previous summer to the Gros Ventre Wilderness. She loved Pete and his wife and kids, and she loved her in-laws. Well, she loved her mother-in-law, anyway, and she tolerated her father-in-law. But hosting a big group was a lot of work. One man and one woman would be far easier.

Oh, who was she kidding. Barry had been treated like a king since birth by her parents and their childhood nanny. Now that he was an adult with an attorney's income, he employed a housekeeper and ate most of his meals out. Barry and his fiancée were going to be as much work as a dozen children.

She sighed. Her moon boots squeaked on the floor. She shuffled through her purse, digging for her keys. She was only looking down for a moment, but that was enough, and she ran pell-mell into another human.

"Oh, I'm so sorry," she said.

"Oomph," the other person said.

Susanne got a heavy whiff of roses. A woman. Wearing a lot of perfume. And when she looked at her, Susanne realized it was a woman she knew, although she couldn't remember her name. She stood a head shorter than Susanne, with short, prematurely gray hair and dewy, youthful skin sans makeup. Susanne became hyperaware of her own long, honey-brown curls, glossed lips, and blusher. In Texas, she considered herself a light touch when it came to her looks, but sometimes she felt like a hothouse flower in Wyoming.

The woman squinted at her. "Susanne Flint?"

Drat. She knows my name. "Um, yes. Hello."

"You don't remember me, do you?" The woman looked her straight in the eyes.

Susanne hated being put on the spot. Southern women didn't confront, except in private. But Wyoming women were direct. Overly, publicly direct. She thought they'd do better with hairbrushes and a little lipstick than with antagonism, but she was outnumbered.

There was nothing to be done but own up to the truth. "Your face, yes. Your name, I'm so sorry, but I do not."

The woman dug in a large shoulder bag and brought out a business card. "I'm Wendy Nelson. President of the Johnson County Women's Club. We met at a parent-teachers association meeting."

The PTA. Yes. Susanne took the card, glancing at it. Half of the front was taken up by a bundle of lilacs tied with a ribbon. The other, Wendy's name and a 307 area code phone number. *Like an old-fashioned calling card.* "Yes, I remember meeting there now."

"Amongst other times and places."

Susanne ground her teeth together behind her smile. "Well, I won't forget again, I can assure you of that. What are you doing up north?"

"Hanging fliers for our big annual fundraiser. You?"

Susanne straightened her shoulders. "Oh, just registering for spring classes. I'm working on my teaching degree." Although sometimes she hated admitting she'd quit college years back, she was proud to be finishing her education now.

"That explains it."

"Explains what?"

Wendy puckered her mouth like she was sucking a sour lemon. "People have just been . . . surprised . . . that as a doctor's wife you aren't involved with charitable work in the community. This must be why."

Susanne's insides turned queasy. *People in Buffalo are talking about me, and not in a nice way?* "Oh, my. Well, yes, with our move and then my kids and the classwork, I've been stretched a little thin. But I've been wanting to get more involved."

"No better place to start than our JoCo Women's Club."

Susanne's smile felt wooden. The last thing she wanted to do was join a women's club. She enjoyed time with friends, but she liked to pick them herself. She forced her smile wider. "Absolutely."

"I can get you signed up. Actually, it's good luck I ran into you today. Your name came up as a potential committee chair for our fundraiser."

"Oh?" She girded herself. This was exactly how she felt riding a horse. A little out of control with a world of bad possibilities out of sight around the next bend.

"Yes. We need someone to solicit commitments from our more well-heeled citizens and businesses. You're a perfect fit for the job."

"Wow. I'm so . . . flattered."

"Great. I'll put your name down for it. Our next meeting is a potluck at the Methodist church. Eleven thirty, sharp, tomorrow. You don't have to bring anything, since it's your first meeting. Unless you want to. Might make a good impression, though. Overcome old ones. See you there." Wendy waggled her fingers and marched smartly down the corridor

Susanne was frozen in place behind her, open-mouthed. *Did she really just suggest I be their money grubber?* Susanne had grown up without money. Talking about money, much less asking for it, made her insides curdle like buttermilk in the sun.

She walked to the parking lot on autopilot. Drove her Suburban in a fugue state through the snow squall back to Buffalo. Parked in four inches of snow in front of her serene, beautiful dream house on Clear Creek in a total kerfuffle.

Learning from Wendy that people were talking badly about her had thrown her into a chasm of self-doubt. She trudged through a little snowdrift toward the house. *Am I making a mistake chasing after a teaching career when we have all the money we need? Should I be concentrating on good works instead?* She believed she could make a difference by working with children. But another thought hit her. *If I become a teacher, am I taking a job away from someone who needs it more?* These things had never occurred to her before, and she wished they hadn't now.

Pausing on the front steps of their two-story home, she looked back and noticed Trish's truck wasn't there. *Ben's last day in town.* Patrick's truck was home, though. Susanne opened the door, expecting to see her husband pacing the kitchen, hungry and help-less. The man could save a life, he could climb a mountain, he could fix a transmission, but he couldn't pour milk in his cereal without a kitchen assistant. She smiled. Her mama had always told her that it was good job security to be needed, and Patrick made it clear to her in many ways every day that he needed her as well as wanted her.

She stepped into the high-ceilinged great room, stopped in front of the towering stone fireplace. No Patrick in there. She peeked around the corner of the dining area. No Patrick in the kitchen, either. Just her beloved heavy walnut dining room set.

"Patrick?" she called, unconsciously stroking the wood of the tabletop.

When he didn't answer, she frowned. Maybe he was in the garage at his work bench. She could check there in a moment. First, she headed into their bedroom to drop her purse.

"Hello, honey."

She startled. In the low light, she could just make out the figure of her husband lying on top of the covers on their queen-sized bed. Patrick *never* napped. Occasionally he accidentally shut his eyes on the couch or great room floor while watching football or golf on Sunday afternoons, but never in an official "in bed" capacity. She left the lights off.

"What's the matter?" She sat down beside him. He was holding an ice pack to his torso.

He cleared his throat. "It's been quite a day. Curl up and I'll tell you all about it."

Their uncooked dinner almost drew her away, but if he didn't mind, she didn't either. Sneaking a break with her handsome husband was a treat. She snuggled up to him, enjoying the feel of his fit, muscular frame, and his masculine scent. Irish Spring soap, sweat, and . . . horses? Maybe he'd been working with theirs. "Mine was pretty eventful, too. Not ice pack eventful, though, so you go first."

He put his chin on her head and nestled it into her hair. "You want me to start with the bucking bronco or the two dead bodies?"

Susanne groaned and dug her face into his shoulder. *Is it just me, or is Patrick a magnet for trouble?* "Tell me everything," she said.

CHAPTER FOUR: RIDE

George

George Nichols kept one hand on the steering wheel and pulled his fingers back with the other, cracking his knuckles. Behind the truck, the trailer was swaying in the high crosswinds, but not as badly as it had on the two-hour drive south. The return leg of his round-trip from Big Horn to Kaycee and back was wearing on him. An electrician by trade, George started working before sun-up. Today he'd knocked off early to make the snowy drive, and he still had another hour left. It was bleary-making stuff. He smiled. And that wasn't even counting the effects of his late night with Lisa, a pretty waitress from the Silver Spur who he'd been seeing for a couple, two, three weeks.

Ahead of him, sun broke through the clouds. He even caught a glimpse of the silhouette of the Bighorn Mountains to his left for a moment. "Come on, come on," he said. "Give me a little clear weather."

Storm driving wasn't fun, and double that pulling a trailer. It had been worth it, though. He'd picked up a 1970 Arctic Cat Panther snowmobile—a sweet sled—for a song. He'd grown up watching Arctic Cat dominate snowmobile racing. This was his first chance to own one. It outshone his Rupp Sprint, the mean red machine he'd learned and fallen in love with the sport on. There was room in his heart for more than one though, with women, and with snow machines.

And as much as he enjoyed women, snowmobiles were his true passion. Clear Creek Resort up in the Bighorns had just started renting snowmobiles to guests, and he'd be guiding tours for them. Not for pay. Just for tips. They'd offered to let him stay over when they had space and to use one of their machines, and that wasn't nothing. He'd turned them down on the sled, of course. He'd be far cooler on his new blue and white Boss Cat. His only problem was the size of the group for the upcoming long weekend. They were bigger than he could handle alone. He'd lined up a buddy to help and sleep on the floor of his comped room, but the bum had cancelled on him that morning. If he didn't find someone soon, he'd have to back out. He planned to start calling everyone he knew as soon as he got home. Lisa, maybe? He was going to miss her. But she was a flatlander with no experience. So, no. He'd just have to survive without female company for a few days.

Ahead of him, movement on the side of Interstate 25 captured his attention. He tensed and took his foot off the gas, expecting an animal to run out in front of him. Despite the lessening storm, visibility was still iffy. But whatever it was didn't look four-legged. In fact, as he got closer, it looked upright and two-legged to him. Human. A man, trudging through the snowy drifts on the shoulder, a cowboy hat jammed on his head, in stark black contrast to the white landscape. *Poor sucker's out in the middle of nowhere—must have car trouble.* There were no houses, no businesses, no nothing on the road until Buffalo, and it was ten or so miles away. After checking his rearview mirror for oncoming traffic, George slowed behind the walker. No vehicles in either direction and there hadn't been for fifteen minutes. He eased his truck up alongside the man.

The man kept his eyes forward.

George cranked down his window. "Need a lift?"

The man pulled up his collar, like he was blocking the wind from his face. He squinted, taking a moment to study George before he answered. "Where are you headed?"

"Big Horn. I can drop you anywhere between here and there."

The man dropped his collar, revealing a swarthy face. *Mexican?* He nodded once, then stomped over to the passenger door. He tried to open it, but it was locked. George leaned across the bench seat and pulled up the mechanism. The man climbed in.

"Name's George." He stuck out his hand.

The man shook it. "Thanks for the ride, George," he said, with a hint of an accent. *Yeah, probably Mexican, via Texas.* He rubbed bare hands together and blew on them. "I'm Abraham."

George accelerated onto the empty interstate, then glanced at his passenger, who was shivering and trying to hide it. Abraham wore cowboy boots and jeans with only an oilskin jacket on top. No gloves. Nothing over his ears. He sure wasn't dressed for a winter hike. "Looks like your ride broke down."

"Something like that." The man jerked his chin back toward the trailer. "Your Boss Cat?"

George nodded. Abraham knew snowmobiles. "I just picked it up."

"It is a wonderful sport."

Abraham had a soft way of speaking that made George nearly hold his breath to hear him. When he was certain he'd processed what the other man had said, he asked, "You ride?"

"I race. Or used to."

George's heart rate kicked up a notch. "Where?"

"The Sierra Nevadas and the Elburz."

The Sierra Nevadas were in California. George had never heard of the other place, although he didn't want to admit it. He only knew the western half of the U.S. anyway. Someday he wanted to travel. Pick up an atlas and start on page one and drive until the last page of the book, camping along the way.

"Far out, man." He also didn't usually talk that way, but he was speaking to someone who had raced snowmobiles in California. He didn't want to sound like a bumpkin. "What did you race?"

"An El Tigre."

George pounded the steering wheel. "That's my dream machine!" It was *just* the premiere Arctic Cat of the early seventies.

"They are finely made."

They approached the outskirts of Buffalo. "Need me to drop you here?"

"I'd prefer to ride as far north as you're going. But thank you."

"Where are you headed?"

Abraham faced the passenger window. His soft voice grew even more muffled. "Where the winds of destiny take me."

It was a weird thing to say. Maybe George had misheard him. "What about family?"

Abraham's voice grew tight. "I have lost my family and wander alone."

Even weirder. But if he was as available as he sounded, and he was a snowmobile ace, George could overlook the weirdness. "I don't suppose you'd be interested in helping me guide some snowmobile tours this weekend? I've got two sleds. This one and a Rupp. We'd head up to Clear Creek Resort tomorrow afternoon and be done by Sunday night. I've even got us a room to stay in."

Abraham turned back to George. "I'm not familiar with the resort. Clear Creek?"

"It's just up Highway 16 from here." George threw his hand in the direction of the mountains. "A nice place. But, uh, we'd be guiding for tips. I'd split whatever we make with you. Seventy-thirty, since we'd be on my machines, and I landed the gig."

Abraham nodded and pulled at his chin. "I don't have a place to sleep tonight."

George grinned. That sounded like a yes. "You can bunk at my place if you don't mind a sleeping bag on the floor. It's warm enough, though. And that would sure make it easy for me to give you a ride to and from the resort."

Abraham held up a hand, like he was asking George to be quiet. George zipped his lip.

Finally, Abraham said, "I accept the commission. It is much appreciated."

"Out of sight, man." George held up his hand to slap a high five, but Abraham didn't lift his in return.

The guy was definitely an odd duck. But George didn't care. He didn't have to cancel. And he'd be guiding with a bona fide California snow sled racer. As far as he was concerned, Abraham was just about perfect.

CHAPTER FIVE: DIVE

Perry

Perry packed another shovelful of snow onto the ramp he was building. It sloped from the deck railing down his back yard, between two tall, bare cottonwood trees, all the way to the creek bank. He missed whacking his dog Ferdinand's head with the shovel by an inch. The wiry Irish wolfhound was barking and dodging, trying to catch the bits of snow that were falling from the ramp.

"Goofball. Stop it, Ferdie." Perry nudged the dog backward with his knee. It didn't do any good, so he turned his attention back to packing snow. Ferdinand's head was so big and hard that he'd barely feel a little tap with a snow shovel anyway.

Perry was pumped up about the ramp. He was going to use it to sled across the creek bed, so he needed to make it high enough that he could get up good speed. The snow had to be packed hard, too, so he wouldn't sink through it. He gave the ramp another whack with the back of the shovel.

He looked around. Ferdinand looked up at him. Perry had used up most of the snow in the back yard building his ramp. It was bare down to brown grass now, except for the ramp to the creek, of course. Since he was out of raw materials, it would have to snow again before he could add to the ramp. He ran his mittened hand along it. It was slick.

A smile broke out across his face. Time for a test ride. He'd use his disc. The creek wasn't frozen and snowed over yet, so he'd have to ditch before he got to it, but that was no problem.

Perry had propped his sled and his disc against the back wall of the house earlier, just in case he finished building the ramp before dinner. He ran for the round piece of metal, with Ferdinand leaping and bounding at his heels. But when he touched it, he stopped in his tracks. The last time he'd used the disc, he'd been with John. They'd been sledding down the hill to the park, coasting to a stop in front of the swimming pool. It was filled with water from Clear Creek each summer and was Arctic cold, but it was kept empty in the winter, with a big fence around it. The hill across from it was the best in town. A bunch of kids from the football team had been there, and they'd had races and snowball fights. Perry had been at a disadvantage because he'd been wearing a cast on his ankle, but he'd held his own, mostly. John had won the final sled race, and afterwards, they'd walked over to Main Street and got vanilla Cokes at the Busy Bee.

It was the best day.

And now John was gone. Perry didn't have a second-best friend. It had just been John and him, ever since the Flints had moved to Wyoming.

Ferdinand sat and watched Perry, his head cocked.

"Mom and Dad said the best way to remember someone is to keep doing the things they loved." Saying it out loud to his dog made his throat tickle. "John would have loved testing the snow ramp, so that's what we're going to do, Ferdie."

The dog barked and bounced straight up in the air off his back legs, landing back in a sitting position.

Perry laughed. "You can be my best friend now." Remembering the need for a backup, he added, "And Duke can be my second-best friend." Duke, his stout paint horse, was loyal and good, but he couldn't play in the back yard or come in the house.

Perry jogged onto the deck and climbed up on the railing. "Geronimo," he shouted, and flung himself and his disc into space over the ramp. Landing knocked the breath out of him, and his chin bounced off the edge of the disc. He shot across the yard and was sliding down the creek bank before he could ditch. The disc bounced across the rocks and landed under three inches of cold, cold water.

A split second later, Ferdinand splashed down beside him, barking and snapping at the water.

Perry bellowed and jumped to his feet. He picked up the disc and ran, stumbling and splashing through the rocks. He tried to scramble up the creek bank, but with his wet feet, it was a lot harder than he'd figured for, and he fell on his hands and knees. The disc slid back into the water. Ferdinand, who'd galloped up the bank with no problem —*claws would be nice about now*—stared back down at Perry.

"Duke is my best friend, dog. You're in second place now."

Perry stomped back to the disc and shook the water off. He was freezing and his teeth were starting to chatter. He put his hand to his mouth, doing a quick check that it was still there. He walked upstream to an easier section of the bank where he made it up on the first try.

He trotted toward the deck. He wanted to get inside to take off his wet clothes, pronto. Maybe jump in a hot shower. Then wrap himself in a blanket in front of the fireplace with a mug of hot chocolate. The thought quickened his steps to a run as he crossed the deck, where he dropped the disc by the door.

It was hard to open the door handle with ski mittens, but he managed. He wasn't going to get his wet skin stuck to the metal. Not after the stories his dad had told him about people ripping all their skin off by touching metal with wet body parts in freezing weather. One about a boy who stuck his tongue to an icy stock tank and lost most of it still gave him the shivers.

Ferdinand pushed inside ahead of him. The first thing he noticed as he entered was the doorbell ringing. He ignored it and made tracks for the staircase, wet ones, which matched the wet pawprints Ferdinand was leaving as he ran in crazy circles all over the room. The bell rang again just when Perry reached the bottom step. *Why isn't Dad answering it?* Then he remembered his dad was hurt and had gone to bed with an ice pack and a bottle of Tylenol. He took two more steps, planning to ignore the visitor until a thought popped into his head. *What if something happened to Mom or Trish?* Before last year, that never would have occurred to him. Their lives had been quiet, with no drama. But he'd learned bad things really did happen to good people sometimes.

He headed to the door, getting there as it rang again. He shouted, "I'm *coming*."

If it was Trish locked out because she forgot her purse and keys, he was going to be so mad. She'd done that once before. She could just stand out there and ring all day this time, for all he cared. He peeked out the window beside the door, over Ferdinand's head. He caught a whiff of wet dog. His mom wasn't going to be happy Ferdinand had been in the creek.

The woman on the steps was too old to be his sister, and she had short hair like his Aunt Patricia and the pretty figure skater who won the Olympics—he couldn't remember her name because he didn't watch figure skating. This woman was pretty, but with kind of a pointy chin. He studied her a second longer. He didn't open the door to just anyone, even pretty women. Coach Lamkin had been a stone-cold fox, but she'd still been a killer, after all. This one didn't look like a killer. She had a scar on the side of her upper lip that was almost hidden by makeup. She seemed sort of familiar but maybe not? His mom's age, probably. Her clothes were a lot cooler than his mom's, though. Not right for Wyoming. High-heeled boots with thin leather weren't warm in snow and didn't look like they had any traction. And a *skirt*, which left her legs bare. He knew firsthand how cold the air was on bare skin. At least she had on a sweater and a down jacket with some mittens.

He decided he'd better open the door before she froze to death. He pushed Ferdinand aside with his hip to keep the dog from greeting her with a take down.

She smiled at him, showing the whitest teeth and widest smile he'd ever seen. Then she frowned. "You're wet."

"Yes, ma'am. And cold."

"You don't remember me, do you, Perry?"

He couldn't admit that. It was rude. "Uh . . . yes, ma'am?"

She laughed. "I'm Dian Griffin. I went to high school with your parents. Your mom is one of my best friends. But I haven't seen you since you were really little."

"Cool."

"Are your parents here?"

"My dad." Then Perry saw the Suburban. "And my mom, too, I guess. You want to come in while I get them?"

"That would be great." Dian—Mrs. Griffin?—stepped into the house. Even with her boots, she wasn't much taller than him. "That's a big dog you've got there."

"He won't hurt you."

"How'd you get so wet?"

"I fell in the creek."

"I'm sorry. I'll bet you were on your way to get dry clothes when I showed up."

"S'okay. You can wait in here. I'll get Mom." He grabbed Ferdinand by the collar and dragged the dog down the hall, his boots squeaky and squishing and water dripping from his pants. Knocking on his parents' door, he said, "Mom. Dad. Dian, er, Mrs. Griffin is here. For Mom." He wished he knew what to call her. It was easy with grown men. They were always mister, while a woman could be a miss or a missus or even a mizz, whatever that was.

He heard rustling in their room, then his mom's head appeared. He could tell she was wearing a robe.

"Who?"

"Um, Dian. Your friend."

His mom looked confused. She whispered, "I don't have a friend here named Dian."

Perry was more confused than she was. Ferdinand whined and strained at his collar, trying to free himself to go show their visitor a proper welcome. "But she said. And she knew my name. You went to high school together."

"Dian Griffin?"

"Yeah."

His mom's face lit-up. "What's she doing here? She lives in Texas." Then her mouth made an O. "Your uncle Barry. He's coming tonight. With his new *fiancée*."

"Yeah."

"Yes, ma'am."

"Yes, ma'am. So?"

"So, before he was engaged to Esme, he was engaged to someone else." She gave him a significant look.

"Your friend?"

His mom nodded. Then she started laughing. "Tell her I'll be out in a minute. But don't tell her Barry and Esme are on their way." More to herself, she muttered, "I've got to think of a way to keep their paths from crossing. And whatever it is, do it quickly." The door shut.

Perry sloshed his way back down the hall with Ferdinand just as the doorbell rang again.

CHAPTER SIX: STRAIN

Ben

Ben pushed the meatloaf across his plate with the tines of his fork, knocking it into his mashed potatoes, which spilled gravy onto his green bean casserole. Only his homemade icebox roll remained unspoiled. Vangie had made all his favorites for his farewell dinner. The smell in the house had been great all afternoon. It had been nice of her, and he felt bad that he wasn't hungry.

The long dining room table—which regularly sat a couple of ranch hands for breakfast and lunch in addition to the regular members of the household—was only half filled. The kitchen occupied a space as big as the dining area. It was quiet except for the crackle of fire in the wood burning stove that Vangie cooked on and used to heat the room. Baby Hank was in a highchair in front of her as she fed him tiny bites of the potatoes. He was making gurgling noises around the food, kicking his feet, and reaching for his mother's dark hair. Henry was watching his wife and son with a goofy grin on his face. His hair was creased from the cowboy hat he'd been wearing all day, and the horizontal line matched the deep scratch across his forehead that he'd gotten when a colt he was breaking had thrown him into a fence that afternoon.

Ben was going to miss the three Sibleys like crazy.

Tears threatened, so he gulped down some of the Tennessee sweet tea Vangie served with every meal. He was nearly nineteen years old, and he'd only lived with the Sibleys out at Piney Bottoms Ranch for nine months, but it had been the best time of his life. The most normal time. Growing up in Cody with his real family, he'd never felt like this. Like he belonged. The Sibleys treated him as much like a son as they did Hank.

And Hank. Who knew babies were so cool? The kid was a pistol. Henry was already taking him out on the horses—the gentle ones— in front of him in the saddle. Hank was crawling and pulling up on things, trying to walk, constantly babbling and laughing, especially when he looked at Ben. By the time Ben came back from school on summer break, Hank would be scooting around on his own two feet, and he'd have forgotten that Ben was his best friend.

A hand reached for his under the table. Soft and small, it squeezed his, then rested on his knee.

Trish.

He could barely look at her. She was so pretty, it hurt his eyes sometimes. Golden hair, bright blue eyes, and the little mole beside her mouth that he called her beauty mark. She was adventurous, smart, tough, and fun, and she made him feel like he could be anything, do anything. The way she looked at him. The way she was looking at him now, which he could only see out of the corner of his eye, because he just couldn't meet hers.

"When is your roommate going to get to Laramie, Ben?" Vangie asked in the baby voice she was using with Hank. She did that a lot lately.

He cleared his throat. He'd talked to Chad only once since they'd been assigned to live together. "He's already there. His parents are on a trip to the Alps, so he decided to stay in the dorm. He's from Los Angeles. It's a long drive there and back, especially in the winter."

"Oh. That's good. So, you won't be too lonely."

Ben doubted that. Without Trish and these people he'd come to think of as his family? He couldn't think about it. It made him too sad. "Yes, ma'am."

Henry held out his finger, and Hank snatched it, coating it in mashed potatoes, gravy, and baby spit. "We got the oil changed in the truck. It's all gassed up. New tires, too. Running like a top and ready for the morning." He paused, wincing. "Ouch, Hank. Let go." Hank didn't release his father's hand. "Let go, now." Henry finally managed to twist his finger out of the kid's grip. "Did you make a note of your license plate number?"

Ben didn't understand why he needed to make a note of something that was on the front and back end of his pickup. "I will."

Trish's voice broke in, musical and sweet, to Ben's ears anyway. "My dad makes us all memorize each other's license plate numbers, in case of emergencies, since we've had a lot of them." She rattled off a series of digits and letters. "Dad's." She recited another. "Mom's." And another. "Mine."

"I like how your dad thinks," Henry said.

"What time are you leaving?" Trish asked.

"I'm not sure." Ben still couldn't look at her.

Henry said, "With these roads, I'd give it six hours for the drive. Then you have to unload. Let's call that another hour or two. You need plenty of sunlight for that. Sun sets before five. That means you should pull out of the driveway here no later than nine."

"Make it eight. You'll want to stop to eat. I'll send you a picnic lunch." Vangie paused with the spoon in midair, sending Hank into a tizzy, kicking and reaching for it.

"Will you stop by and say goodbye to me and my family?" Trish said. There was a quiver in her voice.

Ben squeezed his eyes shut. "Yeah. Of course."

"Seven-thirty, then." Vangie popped the spoon into Hank's mouth. He gurgled, smiled, and drooled some gravy. "I heard you had some excitement today, Trish."

Trish said, "Yes, ma'am. Two ranch hands were murdered at the O Bar M. My dad found them. But I didn't see them."

"Still, that's scary."

"A little. But Ronnie and another deputy got there fast."

She nudged Ben's leg with her knee, a pre-arranged signal. He dreaded saying what Trish had begged him to, knew the response he'd get from Henry and Vangie.

He said, "Okay. Could I, uh—could I take Trish to a movie tonight? Since it's my last night here?"

Vangie put the spoon down. Her eyes met Henry's. The silence stretched out into an uncomfortable wall between Ben and them.

It was Henry who finally spoke. "I wish we could say yes, but you know that's up to Patrick and Susanne."

For four months, Trish and Ben had only been allowed to see each other at school or one of their homes, in the presence of adults. Ben didn't blame Trish's parents. He'd spent time in juvenile detention when his uncle and father had kidnapped Trish. Ben had to go along with it. His father or uncle could have hurt her. She could have died. But in the end, it didn't matter why he'd helped them. The bottom line was, he had. Her parents had been scared to death, and the situation had put her whole family at risk. It hadn't exactly been the best beginning to a relationship. Not to mention Trish could have dated anyone she wanted to. She was a straight A student. A good girl. She'd probably go to college on an academic scholarship, not probationary with late acceptance like him.

If he was her dad, he wouldn't have let Trish date him at all.

He heard Trish swallow. She'd hoped Vangie and Henry would say it was fine with them, so she could use their approval to convince her parents to give theirs. "The meatloaf was delicious, but I'm finished eating. Could I go call my parents?"

"Sure, hon." Vangie's eyes looked sad as they followed Trish to the phone in the kitchen.

Trish dialed, then twisted the phone cord around her finger. Ben couldn't help watching her now. He could feel her anxiety. She ducked her face, turning away from the table. "Mom? It's Trish." She paused. "May I go to the movies with Ben tonight? He's leaving in the morning." Pause. "We're at the Sibleys eating dinner." Pause. "But, Mom—" Pause. Her voice hardened. "Fine. I'll see you by nine."

Ben cringed. He hadn't wanted to push the issue with her parents, but Trish had insisted. Her face was a storm cloud as she stomped back to the table. Trish might be a lot of good things, but she had a temper, and she didn't hide her feelings.

He hoped it didn't ruin their last night together.

But who was he kidding? Of course it would. His stomach sank like a bag of rocks.

CHAPTER SEVEN: SQUIRM

Flint Residence, Buffalo, Wyoming
Wednesday, December 28, 1977, 6:00 p.m.

Patrick

Patrick readjusted his body on the bed, pressing his ear to the telephone. Usually, he avoided any painkillers stronger than over the counter, but he was a cat's whisker away from raiding his medical kit for some Percodan. Maybe later. He breathed deeply. It hurt, but he was pleased that it sounded normal. He palpated the soft tissue below his ribs. Nothing too sensitive there. He decided he'd been right not to inflict his injuries on the hospital staff. Time would heal these wounds.

"Hello?" he said.

A familiar woman's voice said, "Patrick, it's Ronnie. I thought you'd want an update on those murders at the O Bar M."

"I do. I guess you're not calling to tell me you guys caught the killer?"

"I wish. And no progress running down Muhammed. No

evidence from the crime scene that would give us an identity. About the best we found was that blood on the switch plate."

Patrick gazed at his fingers. He'd washed the blood from the switch plate off his hand earlier. "And?"

"We were able to type it. It's the same as Bryan's." The younger of the two hands, Patrick recalled. "We'll try to see if we can match it or if it belongs to someone else, but that's going to take a while. I don't suppose you thought of anything else you saw?"

Patrick didn't tell her about the Tylenol or his long nap. He was still dozy and foggy. "No. I'm sorry. Getting bucked off that 'gentle' horse and taking care of the Mendoza sheep sucked up all my attention."

"The Mendoza sheep?"

"A doctor's free vet work is never done."

Ronnie snorted. "Tell Susanne I said hello."

"Thanks for calling." Patrick held the receiver to his chest, dreading rolling over to hang it up. He hoped Johnson County found the culprit soon, and that they left the Flints out of it.

After he recovered from hanging up the phone, he walked to the door. Susanne had left it ajar when she'd followed Perry out to greet her old friend Dian, seconds before the phone had rung with Ronnie's call.

Dian Griffin, here in Wyoming. She'd been friends with Susanne since they were little girls in College Station, Texas. And Dian still lived in Texas. *What's she doing in Wyoming, and why didn't she tell us she was coming?* Something about the voices in the great room caught his attention. The number of them, for starters. But also, one was clearly an adult male. Perry hadn't said anything about a man.

Uh oh. Were Barry and his new fiancée already here?

Trailing one hand on the wall, he walked stiffly toward the great room, gathering speed as he went. When he got there, he found quite a crowd standing around. Dian. His dark-haired brother-in-law, Barry. A woman who must be Barry's fiancée, but whose name he couldn't remember, *darn it*. Susanne. A crotch-sniffing Ferdinand. And Perry.

Laughter exploded from the group, but it set his teeth on edge. It was the uncomfortable, brittle kind. And it seemed to be coming from everyone except the woman Barry was adding to the family soon.

When there was a pause in the laughter, Patrick announced himself. "Looks like a 1960s Tigers reunion in here." He had attended the same high school as Susanne, Dian, and Barry, and their mascot had been a tiger.

"Patrick." Barry grabbed Patrick's hand and shook it, pulling him in for a shoulder hug and slapping him on the back before Patrick could protest.

Despite his best efforts, Patrick gasped. His brother-in-law wasn't bigger or stronger than him. It just didn't take much to set off a tsunami of pain in his midsection.

"Are you okay?" Barry released him, frowning.

"Broken ribs."

"Fresh ones," Susanne said. She didn't look like she had as much sympathy for Patrick as he thought he deserved. "Got bucked off a horse he shouldn't have been on."

Patrick arranged his face in a painful grin. "How about I skip hugs?"

"Good to see you. Sorry you're hurt." Dian forced cheer into her voice. Of course. This was an incredibly awkward situation for her.

"Good to see you, too. And thanks."

"Patrick, I want to introduce you to my fiancée, Esme Wheeler." Barry put his hand on the woman's waist. He wasn't a giant man, but it emphasized how tiny she was. Fragile even, although her coloring was robust. With a name like Esme—short for Esmerelda, maybe?— and her dark skin, eyes, and hair, Patrick guessed she was probably of Mexican heritage, which wasn't unusual in South Texas. Patrick looked at Dian and then back at Esme. Two Texas fiancées in one Wyoming room. While both women were small, Esme was fine featured, whereas Dian's features were rounded. Esme seemed more reserved, or maybe that was just because of the tense situation. He'd rarely met anyone as outgoing as Dian, anyway. The woman had been born for her role as head Tigers cheerleader, and she'd continued cheering at the University of Texas. Barry continued, "This is the woman who is going to make me a husband and the father, someday, of a couple of rug rats. That's all a man needs in life. Am I right, Patrick?"

Dian's eyes dropped to the ring finger on Esme's left hand. She was sporting a whopper of a diamond. Patrick glanced at the simple gold band on his own wife's hand. It had been all he could afford when they'd married as teens. *That isn't quite true. I couldn't even afford that ring.* His parents had lent him the money to buy it for her a few months later, after they'd confessed about their elopement. His mother Lana had said it wasn't right for Susanne to be ringless. In the years since, his wife had assured him many times that it was all she needed. But sometimes he wondered. Susanne was a treasure, and he ought to do something more substantial to show it.

Patrick nodded and smiled at Esme. "Welcome. A pleasure to meet you. We're so glad to have you here, even if it had to be with this shyster."

Esme frowned. "Barry's no shyster. He's a very successful and highly regarded member of the legal profession."

Patrick clenched his teeth. Teasing had always been a hallmark of his relationship with his brother-in-law. In the silence after Esme's words, the air felt charged, like it did before a lightning storm. There was a strange odor, too. Like adrenaline. Or fear. And it seemed to be coming from his brother-in-law.

Barry cleared his throat. "He's just kidding, honey. I call him a quack, he calls me a shyster."

"Didn't sound like kidding to me."

Heat built in Patrick's neck and cheeks. Susanne grabbed his hand and squeezed his fingers so hard that he winced.

Barry smiled tentatively at Esme. "I appreciate you sticking up for me, Ez. But Patrick is family. And I can assure you, when he needs a lawyer, I'm the one he calls."

Patrick decided he couldn't let Esme strain things any longer. "Only because your price is right."

Barry socked Patrick in the shoulder. He tried hard to hide the jolt of pain, given the circumstances. "What, you mean the double rate I charge you?" Barry's voice sounded de-stressed, like someone had loosened a screw and given him a few inches of room to breathe.

Susanne relaxed her grip on his fingers, but her voice was still tight. "Patrick, Dian is on her way to Billings from Denver. Her flight was canceled. She rented a car so she could drive through here and surprise us on her way north."

"Surprise," Dian said. Her grin looked sickly.

Patrick was glad for a change of subject. "What's in Billings?"

"Work. I was deadheading there for the weekend and flying out with a crew Monday."

"Ah. Great for us, getting to see you." Patrick mulled over her words. The terminology was mostly Greek to him. Dian worked as a flight attendant. He got the part about flying out from Billings on Monday. Nothing else.

Susanne raised her hands to shoulder height, like she was ready to ward off blows. "I hate to admit this, but I haven't started cooking dinner yet. I had it in my mind that Barry and Esme would be arriving later, then time slipped away from me. How does everyone feel about chicken fried antelope steak and mashed potatoes?"

Esme's eyes widened, and her mouth made an O.

Dian stepped backward toward the front door. "I need to get back on the road. I can grab a burger on the way. I just wanted to say hello."

Patrick looked at his wife. She gave a slight shake of her head. It was more than an hour past sundown on bad winter roads. They had to offer Dian a place for the night. She had no business continuing to Billings, no matter how uncomfortable that made things with Barry and Esme already staying here. The situation would be dicey, which put the ball squarely in Susanne's court. In social situations, he was inept where she was easy and sure. In the wilderness, their roles reversed. Patrick nodded.

Susanne said, "Dian, you can't drive to Billings tonight. It's not safe."

She batted a hand. "I'll be fine."

"I've been driving winter roads in Wyoming for three years, and I wouldn't do it."

"Really?" Her expression fell.

Susanne raised her eyebrows at Patrick like she was telling him to get on with it already.

Darn it. Patrick sucked in a deep breath. "Really. You should stay with us."

"Oh, I can't impose with Barry and Esme here."

"Don't worry about that," Barry said. "We're all old friends."

Esme slowly and deliberately stepped on the toe of Barry's tennis shoe, not seeming to care who saw her do it.

Susanne said, "We can make this work. Dian, you'll sleep with Trish in Perry's room. He gets the couch. Esme, you're in Trish's room—it's the nicest—and Barry, we made up a daybed for you in my sewing room." She beamed, like none of this was a problem. Patrick knew she was faking it for all she was worth.

"But—" Dian protested.

Susanne cut her off. "Nope. Your protests won't do you any good here. I will let you help me in the kitchen, though."

Dian paused, looking from person to person, skipping Esme. When her eyes returned to Susanne, she said, "But will there be wine involved?"

Susanne laughed. "I have a box of white zinfandel."

"And I brought a cooler of Lone Star beer, all the way from the Lone Star state. The ice is still frozen," Barry said.

"Everything is frozen up here," Esme muttered.

Susanne turned to her. "White zinfandel for you?"

Barry gave Esme's shoulders a squeeze.

She sucked in a deep breath, then tried to smile, with partial success. "Why not?"

"Great. This way, ladies." Susanne headed toward the galley kitchen.

Dian followed Susanne to the kitchen. Esme stalled but finally went after them, throwing a desperate look over her shoulder as she did.

The phone began to ring. Susanne picked up. "Hello?" She paused. "Where are you now?" Then, "No," and finally, "Be home by nine." She mouthed, "Trish," at Patrick, then grimaced.

Barry didn't seem to notice Esme's unease. He grinned at Patrick. "How about I bring in that beer now?"

Patrick glanced toward the kitchen, watching for signs of smoke or the sound of small arms fire. "I wouldn't say no to one." Or, depending on how things went between the women, maybe even two or three.

CHAPTER EIGHT: RIP

Flint Residence, Buffalo, Wyoming
Thursday, December 29, 1977, 7:30 a.m.

Trish

"Trish, Ben is here." Her mom's voice shocked Trish out of sleep.

Ben? Already? Trish looked at the clock she'd set on Perry's desk. It was seven thirty already. She'd set the alarm for six thirty. Why hadn't it gone off?

"Coming. Tell him to wait!"

She scrambled out of bed. Her mom's friend Dian had slept in the other twin, but the navy comforter had been pulled up and the suitcase on the floor was zipped and standing upright. Trish ripped off her flannel pajamas and threw on the clothes she'd laid out the night before, back when she'd planned to get up early to wash and style her hair. She wanted Ben to remember her looking her best, so she'd picked her newest pair of Gloria Vanderbilt jeans with a light-weight color block sweater tucked into the waist. But where were her boots? She thought back. She'd left them in the bathroom last night. That was her next stop anyway.

She bolted toward the door in her stocking feet and tripped over Perry's barbells. *Dumb bells is more like it.* Muttering a word her parents didn't think she used, she hopped on one foot. When the smarting eased up, she ran into the hallway, hollering. "Wait, Ben. Wait. I'll be down in just a sec."

"Okay," he called back.

She grabbed the bathroom doorknob and tried to turn it. It didn't budge. *Locked. No!* She put her ear to the door. She heard the shower. Her toothbrush and toothpaste. Her hairbrush. Her makeup. And her boots. She couldn't get to them.

She could wear different shoes. She crossed the hall to her bedroom door. The metal sign with her name and a palomino horse on it made her grimace. *Baby stuff, ugh. I need to change that.* The door was shut. She tried the knob. *Locked, too!* The nearest hairbrush and toothpaste were in her parents' bathroom, downstairs, past the great room. No matter what, now she had to walk past Ben barefoot looking like . . . like . . . *this.* This is how he would remember her when he met college girls. Stupid Uncle Barry and his fiancée! She swiped angry tears from her eyes. Then, holding her chin high, she walked down the stairs.

"Hey, Trish." Ben smiled up at her. He was tall and so handsome, with his dark hair, and he looked grownup, but something in his eyes was sad. Was it that she looked so awful? Or that he'd miss her? He met her at the foot of the stairs.

"Ben, do you want some breakfast?" her mom yelled from the kitchen.

"Uh . . ."

"Tell her yes. I have to finish getting ready."

"But . . ." He gave her a puzzled look.

Trish sped up to a run as she went by him without stopping.

"Sure, Mrs. Flint. Thank you," he said.

Trish ducked into her parents' bedroom. The door to their bathroom was open. She hurried into it, then realized water was running. Before she had a chance to avert her gaze, she got an eyeful of her uncle. Completely naked, stepping into the shower. She about-faced, unable to breathe. *Oh my gosh, oh my gosh, oh my gosh.* Cheeks burning, she leaned back against the wall inside the doorway to her parents' room. She'd never seen a fully naked man before, not even her dad. Pictures, yes, when a friend brought a magazine to school that had been confiscated by their teacher when it drew a crowd at recess. But never in real life.

When she'd recovered enough from her shock that she could move, she zombie walked back to the great room, forgetting all about her hair, bare feet, lack of make-up, and unbrushed teeth. Her mom had just set a plate of pancakes and bacon in front of Ben at the kitchen table. Trish stopped and watched him. He scooped margarine out of a tub and plopped it on the stack, then squirted syrup until the bacon was swimming. He carved off a section and stuffed pancake in his mouth, chasing it with bacon, chewing, and washing it down with milk.

Unable to think of a good reason to stall any longer, she plopped into the chair across from him. Outside, she saw Perry wielding a snow shovel by the deck. Behind her, the front door opened and then slammed shut. She turned. Her dad grunted, dropping an armful of logs in the wood box by the fireplace. His face was pasty white. She knew where everyone else was. Behind locked doors upstairs and an open one in her parents' bathroom.

"Good morning, Trish," her mom said.

Trish made an unhappy noise, somewhere between a snort, a grunt, and a whine. "I couldn't get into my room or either of the bathrooms. All of them were being used."

"Sorry, honey."

Trish leaned toward Ben and whispered, "And I just saw my uncle naked."

His dark eyes widened like an owl's. He grinned with his lips closed. "Whoops."

She pouted. "I look awful, and I have bad breath."

"You're beautiful to me."

"This isn't how I wanted you to remember me."

"It's not like it's the last time I'll ever see you, Trish."

"Still."

He stuffed in another bite, then stood, still chewing. He pushed his bangs off his forehead. The C-shaped scar her dad had left when he walloped Ben during Trish's rescue was still noticeable, like a brand. Pointing at the clock, he swallowed and said, "I've got to get going."

Trish felt like she'd been kicked in the stomach. The time she could have spent with him, stolen from her.

Her dad stuck out his hand and shook Ben's. "Good luck in Laramie."

Her mom hugged him. "Study hard!"

"Thank you, Dr. Flint, Mrs. Flint." Ben's expression was serious. Then, to Trish, he said, "Walk me out?"

She felt numb. "Yes." She put her hand in his. Together, they walked to the front door.

He opened it and stepped out onto the stoop. "You're in your socks."

"It doesn't matter." She went outside with him. The sun was shining but it was windy and felt like the temperature was in the teens. She wrapped her arms around herself.

He put his around hers. "Is that better?"

She dropped her forehead to his chest. Nothing could make it better. "Thanks."

"I'm going to miss you."

"I'll miss you, too."

"I, um, I have something for you. I was going to give it to you last night, but then, well, it's not much, but I want you to have it."

She looked up as he backed away from her and jammed his hand in his pocket. "What is it?"

Ben held out a ring. A small, golden ring with a bright purple stone. "It's your birthstone."

Trish sucked in a breath. She reached for it. "It's beautiful." Her hands were trembling. "What finger do you want me to wear it on?"

"Maybe it could mean something."

"Like?"

"A promise? About us?"

Trish's heart hammered in her chest. "Yes." She slipped it on her ring finger. "Yes!" She held out her hand to show him.

"You have such pretty fingers."

"It's perfect." She threw her arms back around him. "Thank you. I promise. Someday. Us."

His exhale rattled her chest. "I'm glad. Me, too."

"Can you call me when you get to Laramie?"

"Trish, calls are expensive. I don't have much money."

"Just to let me know you're all right. One minute."

"Okay. Then I'll write to you every week."

"I'll write to you, too."

She felt him shake his head. "This is crazy. Maybe I should just go work on a fishing boat in Alaska. What if I'm not cut out for college?"

"You are. You're smart and you're going to do great things, Ben Jones." Trish tried to hold back her tears. "With me."

"I'll be home at spring break. Maybe sooner."

"You'd better."

He squeezed her. "I love you, Trish."

She nodded, no longer able to speak. He released her and started backing toward his truck, his hand over his heart. When he got in and closed the door, a sob broke loose from her, and she bolted through the snow. He looked up in surprise and rolled down the window.

"I love you, too," she said, wiping her eyes.

He reached his hand out and touched her wet cheek. "It's going to be okay."

She tried to nod, but her head wouldn't move. She rotated the ring on her finger. It was going to be okay.

Ben drove away, waving to her. She stayed rooted in place in the driveway, oblivious to the cold and her feet, waiting for just another minute, in case he came back.

He didn't.

She went inside, back to Perry's room, flopped onto his bed face down, and cried.

CHAPTER NINE: SMOOTH

Susanne

Susanne sat with her feet propped on an ottoman. She was drinking her third cup of coffee when the guests began arriving for their late breakfasts. *Third shift.* Patrick had eaten before the kids. Dian appeared first—a petite model ready for a magazine photo shoot—followed seconds later by Barry, who looked adorably rumpled. The norm for them both.

"Do I smell bacon and coffee?" Barry said.

"Good morning to you, too. You do."

"Hallelujah."

"Good morning," Dian said.

"Why does she have such better manners than you? Good morning, Dian. Pancakes and bacon in five," Susanne said. She was proud to have guests at her polished walnut table and chairs. Even after all the years Patrick had been a doctor, the table they'd bought his first year out of medical school was still the nicest piece of furniture they owned. "Coffee and mugs are on the counter. Sit anywhere you like."

"Thanks, Tootie." Barry grinned at his sister, or maybe at the childhood nickname he used to torture her with. He poured two coffees. "Still take it black, Dian?"

"Yes, please."

Barry sat across the slab tabletop from Dian, his view into the living room, Dian's of Clear Creek running past the frozen back-yard, and Susanne's of the two of them. Susanne tried not to make it obvious she was eavesdropping as they chatted. Barry and Dian had quite a past. They'd been engaged as high school sweethearts, then broken up during college. Gotten back together at a high school reunion, decided once again to marry, then called it quits. There had to be a story to their ending, but neither Dian nor her brother had ever told it, no matter how many ways Susanne had asked.

"Barry, pancakes for you," she said.

He said, "I like the table service."

"Don't get used to it. Dian, here you go." Susanne set a second plate down.

Patrick, who had been reading the paper in the living room, joined them. "Found yesterday's or last month's coffee cup on the mantel when I was loading the firewood box earlier, honey." He brought a Dallas Cowboys mug to Susanne and winked at her.

"Ha ha. Thanks." Why did it always have to be Patrick who found the mugs she lost around the house? She always seemed to set them out of her own line of sight.

Patrick returned to the dining area. "As soon as you're done, Barry, we have to get ready for the trip."

"When do we leave?" Barry asked.

"This afternoon."

Barry nodded and crammed down a last huge bite, standing as he chewed.

After the men left, Susanne sat down with her own breakfast and caught up with Dian, until Esme joined them, wearing a robe over a long nightgown.

"Good morning." Susanne jumped up. Time to make pancakes. Again. For the fourth time. But who was counting? Guests couldn't be served cold pancakes, after all. But this time, she was finishing the rest of the batter.

"Morning."

Susanne cooked to the sound of Dian's cheery voice and Esme's frosty one. She wanted this to go well. Esme would be her sister-in-law, and Dian would always be her friend. She decided to intervene.

"So, how did you meet Barry?" Susanne raised her voice to be heard as she flipped cakes over in the cast iron skillet.

Esme warmed, turning toward Susanne, and her eyes sparkled. "At a backyard barbecue political fundraiser. I was there with Rick Perry, a fellow I'd gone out with once before."

"Do tell," Dian said, leaning on her hands to get closer.

"I wasn't interested in dating a cotton farmer—that's what Rick is, plus he lives somewhere north of Abilene." She crinkled her nose. "I met Barry in line for the bathrooms, and we enjoyed talking to each other. I gave him my number. Then he didn't call me. I thought he wasn't interested, but it turned out he'd lost it."

"Sounds like Barry," Susanne said, laughing.

Esme's chill returned. "I don't know why you'd say that. Barry is usually very organized."

Susanne and Dian shared a raised eyebrow look. *Boy, has he ever got Esme fooled.* It was well known to all who loved him that Barry was out to lunch most of the time. He came by it honestly, taking after their mother. His life had changed dramatically when he acquired a secretary to handle his schedule, by all accounts. But as for his personal life, Susanne knew Barry was still hopeless.

Esme sniffed but continued her story. "He finally got my number from a mutual friend and called me before Thanksgiving."

"So, you've been together a year?" Dian asked.

Susanne counted the months since Barry's engagement with Dian ended. It had been a little more than a year.

"Oh, no. Six weeks." Esme took a sip of her coffee.

Susanne stared at Dian, who mouthed, "Oh, my gosh." Then Susanne remembered the pancakes. She turned off the burner and removed the pan from the heat, then quickly slipped the cakes and the last slice of bacon onto a plate and took them to Esme.

Dian said, "A whirlwind courtship. When is the wedding?"

"Thank you," Esme said to Susanne. Then, to Dian, "This summer. June."

Dian said, "A June wedding. That's great." Her voice sounded hollow. Dian and Barry had planned to marry in June of the previous year.

Susanne started loading the dishwasher. Esme picked at her food, not seeming to really swallow anything. Susanne didn't think she had eaten more than a bite or two of potatoes at dinner and none of the venison. The wrists extending from her sweater sleeves were small and bony. She was even more slender than Susanne had realized at first. *Starving yourself will do that.*

Susanne glanced into the backyard to check on Perry. He was lying on his back in the snow, waving his arms and legs. *The goofball.* She hadn't seen Trish since Ben had left and wondered what she was up to. *Best leave her be for now.* Susanne predicted a long and serious mope over Ben's departure.

Dian stood. "I guess I should be getting on the road."

Susanne said, "But you just got here. Besides, what will you do in Billings for four days?"

"I have some good books with me. I know how to fill alone time."

Esme cut a miniscule bite of pancake and dabbed it in the syrup. "What are we going to do here while the boys are up in the mountains?"

Good question. "There are some nice museums. And the scenery is beautiful. We could take a drive. Or, I don't know, what do you like to do, Esme?"

"How is the shopping?"

Susanne put a hand to her mouth, glad her mirth was hidden behind the lower cabinets as she leaned down to put a plate in the dishwasher. "Limited. Buffalo is a very small town."

"Denver is only a day away," Esme said.

Footsteps in the kitchen drew Susanne's attention. It was Trish, looking rough, her red eyes circled in black.

"It took me eight hours to drive up from there yesterday, with the storm," Dian said. "But it's a nice city. I've spent many nights and some weekends there between flights. Wonderful shopping and restaurants. And the views of the mountains are spectacular."

"Like our views here." Susanne felt a little defensive of her home.

"But with shopping and restaurants," Esme said.

Trish grabbed a plate out of the cabinet. "Shopping?" She took a few pancakes off the stack that Susanne had accumulated with the last of the batter. Had she not eaten with Ben? "I need clothes."

Esme brightened. "We should go to Denver for the weekend. Book a nice hotel with a pool and a spa. Eat good food. Shop. With the boys on this stag party, we could have ourselves a hen party."

Susanne almost argued with Esme's characterization. The weekend getaway wasn't a bachelor party for Barry. It was men enjoying the winter wilderness. But it wasn't worth the verbal jousting.

Trish sat next to her soon-to-be aunt. "Sounds good to me. What do you think, Mom?"

Susanne's mind whirred with objections. "What would we do with Ferdie?"

"Marcy can keep him. I kept her pugs last time she went out of town. Can we go, please, Mom?"

As long as it's not a hen party. She barely knew Esme. But it had been ages since she'd done something as self-indulgent as a whole weekend away with other women. She rarely spent time just with a group of them, other than once a year with Dian and her other high school friends. Which brought her up short.

She clutched the counter. "I'm supposed to be at a women's club luncheon in an hour!"

Dian laughed. "You don't do things like women's club."

Esme carried her plate to the sink. "While you're gone, I can call and get us some hotel rooms and make a late dinner reservation in Denver."

Susanne felt things rushing out of control. "I—"

"Are you coming, too, Dian?" Trish said.

Susanne was aghast for a moment. Barry's ex-fiancée on a girls' weekend with his new fiancée? What was Trish thinking? But then she remembered it was Perry she had told about Dian and Barry, not Trish. She winced, ready to step in.

But to her surprise, Esme echoed Trish. "Yes, Dian, won't you come, too? You don't have to be in Billings until Sunday night. We could leave for Denver early this afternoon, spend Friday and Saturday there, and drive back on Sunday morning. That would leave you time to get there, wouldn't it?"

Dian shot Susanne a questioning glance. Susanne shrugged. If Esme wanted Dian there, and if Dian wanted to come, who was she to say it was a bad idea?

Dian winked. "I lied about bringing books. Billings will be a drag. Count me in for the hen party, girls."

Trish whooped, seeming to forget about her broken heart. Susanne decided to put away her doubts. It would probably be just fine.

CHAPTER TEN: PUMP

George

George pocketed his change from the attendant at the gas station, but instead of leaving, he leaned one hip against the counter. The store was old and drafty, with sparse offerings on the shelves and only two things hanging on the walls, a poster featuring the iconic Wyoming bucking horse, Steamboat, and a neon Coca-Cola sign. The place had a funny smell to it, too. Molasses, like they'd been selling livestock feed, although he didn't see any sign of it.

The cashier peered up at him from under long lashes, a splotchy blush creeping up her neck. She was freckled, with curly brown hair. And curvy. Very curvy. She couldn't have looked more different than Lisa, but he didn't discriminate. He liked all women.

"Did you need something else?" she asked.

"I was just wondering why I hadn't met you before. I'd remember it if I did. My name's George. George Nichols."

The blush exploded across her cheeks, then faded away. "I'm Gina. Nice to meet you. I just moved here from Hulett."

"Under the shadow of Devil's Tower?"

"You know where it is?"

"Sure, I do. How do you like it here?"

"It's nice, so far, but I don't know very many people yet."

George fished a pen out of a cup. "Well, you know one now. I live just north of here in Big Horn. Close enough to take the new girl in Buffalo for coffee at the Busy Bee, if she'll give me her number."

Gina looked up. She didn't move for a few long seconds. Then she squeaked. "Me?"

He laughed. "If you don't mind." For a moment, doubt flickered. He'd been seeing Lisa. But it wasn't like they were engaged. He'd just get Gina's number, and, if things with Lisa didn't work out, he'd give this cutie a call.

Two men walked in the store. He ignored them and kept his attention lasered on Gina.

"I—I'd like that." She licked her lips.

"I need to write it down." He waggled the pen.

"Right." She printed out a blank section of cash register receipt and handed it to him.

"Ready when you are."

She recited seven digits to him.

He wrote them down with her name and tucked the piece of paper in his wallet. Then he clicked the pen shut and returned it to the cup. "I'm heading up to Clear Creek Resort for a few days with my buddy to guide some snowmobile trips. When I get back to civilization, you just might hear from me." He grinned at her.

Her face reddened like a traffic light. The girl wasn't a poker player, that was for sure. "Have a good trip." She hesitated, then added in a shy voice, "George."

"And you have a nice weekend, Gina." He made a motion like tipping a cowboy hat at her, even though he wasn't wearing one, and he wasn't a cowboy.

He opened the door, setting off a cluster of bear bells tied to it and whistling as he walked back to the truck. When he reached it, he unscrewed the gas cap and started the pump. A familiar truck pulled up at one of the other three pumps, kitty-corner across from him.

Dr. Flint and his son Perry hopped out and headed toward the store. *Nice people.* He'd done electrical work on their house last year. And he'd also gotten Perry and his sister off the mountain when Perry's friend John had been killed up near Highland Park. George had brought the body down on his horse, Yeti, and delivered Trish and Perry to their mother while Patrick had gone back up the mountain to search for survivors from a plane crash.

He waved, but father and son were deep in conversation and didn't notice George.

Abraham rapped his knuckles on the window.

George walked over to him. "What's up?"

"We need to make haste."

Abraham had a funny way of expressing himself. Like he needed some air let out of his tires. "What?" George asked.

"My relations with someone in the station are not the best. I would like to leave before I am seen. If I haven't been already."

"I hear ya, buddy. Gina?"

"Who?"

"Never mind." He put the nozzle up and glanced in the store. Dr. Flint and Perry were at the counter. The two men who'd walked in when he was talking to Gina were still in there, too. He wondered which one Abraham had gotten sideways with and whether it was over a woman. With George, it was always about a woman. The thought made him chuckle. "Let's get this show on the road."

He hopped in his truck and pointed it toward Highway 16 and the mountains.

CHAPTER ELEVEN: BELONG

Perry

Perry squared his shoulders and stretched upward. Standing beside his dad, he felt like his head reached higher up his dad's body lately. Almost to his shoulder. He knew he'd been growing because his jeans were getting too short. The spurt couldn't come a minute too soon, either. He'd been second string wide receiver on the football team last season. His hands were plenty good enough to start next year. What he needed before then was height. Height, plus a better vertical jump. At least his size didn't affect his skiing. The slopes at Meadowlark Ski Lodge had just opened for the winter, and his dad had promised they would go next weekend.

This weekend was all about hanging out with the guys and doing cool things, so Perry didn't mind.

"Ten dollars of regular on pump one, please." His dad handed the woman behind the counter a twenty-dollar bill.

The woman nodded, but she wasn't paying attention to him. She was watching someone or something outside the store. Perry followed her gaze and saw George Nichols pumping gas. He almost snickered. George was popular with the ladies, from what he could tell. His white-blond hair curled just a little over his ears and at his neck and he had blue eyes like a Siberian husky. Perry had blond hair and blue eyes, like George. Maybe when he grew a few inches he'd be a lady killer, too. George leaned into his truck and said a few words to someone, then got in, shut the door, and drove away, pulling a trailer with two snowmobiles behind him.

Perry's eyes wandered back into the store. Two dark haired, bearded men were standing in the rear of it beside a carousel of maps, looking at one they'd spread out and were balancing in the air between them. Something about them seemed unusual. Perry watched them, trying to figure out what it was, probably a little longer than was polite. It wasn't like he never saw people with dark hair and beards around Buffalo. Beards were practically required in the winter. It was the way these two were dressed that made them different. Bell bottom jeans with rectangular denim patches, shiny shirts with big lapels, and corduroy jackets. They were stylish. Trish's old boyfriend Brandon dressed like that, but nobody else around here did.

One of the men stabbed at the map with his middle finger, the impolite one. He said something, but Perry couldn't understand him, either because his voice was too low, or maybe because he wasn't speaking English. Maybe both—Perry couldn't be sure.

The man glanced up and caught Perry staring. He whispered to the other guy, who glared at Perry. Perry turned his head away quickly and pretended to be interested in a display of chewing gum by the cash register.

The woman was still fumbling with the cash drawer. How long did it take to put up a twenty and take out a ten anyway?

Suddenly, one of the men stepped between Perry and his dad.

"How do you get to Clear Creek Resort?" he asked the cashier. He definitely had some kind of foreign accent.

Her eyes made big Os. "Um, I don't know. I'm new in town."

Perry's dad said, "Straight west on Highway 16. It's right off the road about ten miles from town. You can't miss it. In fact, that's where we're headed. Are you part of Dr. John's group?"

The man shook his head. "No." He backed away and rejoined his friend without so much as a thank you.

Rude.

"Here's your change, sir," the cashier said.

Finally.

"Much appreciated." His dad took a used paperback from a trucker book exchange on the counter. *Centennial* by James Michener. He was always carrying a book around, but Perry never saw him reading one.

His dad smiled down at him, and together they walked back to the pumps.

"Where do you think that guy was from?" Perry asked.

"In the station? I don't know, son." His dad started the pump, took off the gas cap, and put the nozzle into the tank. Perry could smell the slightly sweet odor of the gasoline. "Maybe he was Basque?"

Perry remembered Rosa Mendoza from the O Bar M saying, "Bai" instead of yes. "I don't think so. I heard him talking to his friend. Not in English."

"Spanish?"

Perry mulled the idea over. The guys could have been Mexican. But he'd heard lots of Spanish in Texas. That wasn't Spanish. "I don't think so."

"It's a big world, buddy. Lots of countries, lots of languages. And people like to come here. Especially to see Yellowstone and the Old Faithful geyser."

"But it's winter."

"Plenty to do and see in the winter, too."

Perry thought about that for a second. He'd only ever been in the United States. People spoke English here, mostly. But he was okay with that. The United States was great, and Wyoming was the coolest place on Earth. People traveled from all over the world to see it. And it *was* fun in the winter. If he didn't already live here, and he got a chance to come in the winter, he'd take it. Which made him think about everything they were going to do this weekend.

"Can I drive my own snowmobile, Dad?"

Patrick laughed. "Would you like that?"

"Would I ever!"

"We'll see. Is that what you're most excited about?"

Perry gave the question serious consideration. He was most excited about being one of the guys. But he'd sound like a dork if he said that. "Yeah, probably so."

Uncle Barry rolled down his window. "What's a guy gotta do to get a ride to Clear Creek Resort around here? I'm ready to get to this stag party."

The expression didn't make sense to Perry. "We're not going hunting."

His dad laughed. "A stag party is a bachelor party. For a man who's getting married."

"I thought a stag was a buck."

"It is. Although, technically, stag is usually the name for the biggest buck with the largest antlers in a group of bucks."

"Is that the oldest buck? Like the one with the most points?" Perry had seen bucks with everything from one thin antler on each side of its head—called a "spike"—to five points on each side of a rack that was an inch around.

"Well, the size of antlers is partially a function of age. They grow bigger every year until a buck gets old and then they start to lose their size. But mostly size and number of points are about diet and heredity."

Uncle Barry gave a crooked grin. "Exactly. Good breeding. We're a group of bucks, and I have the biggest antlers."

His dad harrumphed, but in a joking way. "I guess we'll see who proves that by the end of the weekend."

"Sounds like you have a contest in mind?"

Perry loved contests. "I want to play."

The gas pump turned itself off at ten dollars, and his dad put the nozzle up. Perry screwed the gas cap back on. The stylish, dark-haired men walked out of the gas station toward the other side of the pump.

His dad grabbed a paper towel from a dispenser and wiped his hands. "Bucks often fight to the death, you know."

Uncle Barry said, "I was thinking of something a little less permanent."

"We'll know when we know."

Uncle Barry shook his head. "Perry, have I told you before that your father is a quack?" Perry laughed. He liked it when Uncle Barry and his dad joked around. "Seriously, Patrick, do you know whether they have beer up there?"

Beer. Never mind that he was too young to drink it. Perry was going on a guys' trip. And there'd be a contest for biggest buck in the group. With beer. It sounded awesome. Then he noticed the man who had glared at him in the store. This time he was glaring at Uncle Barry as he climbed into his car. Not a truck, Perry noticed. But a green car. A sedan as fancy as their clothes.

His dad frowned. "I hadn't even thought about it. Want to stop at the liquor store on the way out of town, just in case?"

"Do bears sh- I mean *poop* in the woods?"

The sedan engine started, its engine revved, and its tires squealed as it pulled out of the station.

Perry chortled. This was going to be the best weekend ever.

CHAPTER TWELVE: READY

George

"We're expecting a full house this weekend. And your group will be pretty big." Debbie Murray scooped another shovel load of snow. The owner of Clear Creek Resort, she was a brunette in her forties with big dimples in both cheeks, and not one to shy away from work. "Dr. John hosts this party every year." Another shovelful. "People from all over the world, important people. Ones he met at Yale, in the Navy, in medical school, and, of course, around here. Most of these folks are used to the very best of everything." Another shovelful. "And this is our first year with the snow machines." She paused to catch her breath. "We're counting on you to give them the experience of a lifetime, safely."

George pulled on the front of his down jacket. He and Abraham were standing to the side of the path Mrs. Murray was clearing to the snow machine shed, which was uphill from the lodge and on the edge of a clearing. Tall, snow-covered pines loomed all around them. "Yes, ma'am. I will. I'm very excited about it. I've brought Abraham with me, so we'll have two guides every time we take a group out. We gave the trails a light packing this afternoon, the ones I broke last weekend. They're in good shape. Two sleds, two passes on each. I don't anticipate any trouble."

Abraham dipped his upper body. "Ma'am. Nice to meet you. We will take excellent care of your fine guests."

Debbie narrowed her eyes at him. "I haven't seen you around town."

"I am from California."

George puffed up his chest. "He raced El Tigres in the Sierra Nevadas."

She raised her brows. "You're not planning on racing with the guests, are you?"

"Oh, no, ma'am. We'll take it nice and easy with them. Abraham just has a lot of skills and experience, that's all."

She grunted. "I only have the one room for you. It's a single with a twin bed."

Abraham nodded. "I brought a sleeping bag. The floor will be more than adequate and much appreciated."

"Good. Food is family style in the dining room at six thirty, a.m. and p.m."

George glanced into the building behind her. The snowmobile shed matched the wooden barn on the far side of the clearing, only smaller, and it was so new you could get splinters just from looking at it. Yellow and black Ski-Doos were lined up in rows of three each inside. He breathed in the scent of fuel and sawdust. Almost nothing better. "We'll just be testing the machines until then. If any need a tune-up, we can do that after dinner."

"First group is booked for nine in the morning, weather permitting."

"We'll be ready."

"Great." Debbie went back to shoveling.

George was itching to test the machines, especially with her working like a dog while he and Abraham were not, but he couldn't go without asking one more question. "I haven't seen Jenelle lately. How's she been?" George had always thought the Murray girl was a looker. She even had her mother's dimples. He hadn't known her well —she went to high school in Buffalo, while he'd graduated from Sheridan High. But what he'd known, he'd liked.

"Living in Gillette these days, working for the city in Planning and Building, but she's coming up for the weekend tomorrow."

A spark flickered in George. He wasn't leaving until Sunday. Given a chance, he wouldn't mind getting to know Jenelle a little better.

Down in the parking area, a line of vehicles pulled up in front of the lodge. The building was single story, built in the log cabin style, with wings branching out like an octopus' legs. The place had been around forever so far as George knew, but it shined like a new penny. *New coat of sealer*, he guessed. Nestled up in the trees along a narrow road were additional, smaller guest cabins, mostly used in the warm months.

Mrs. Murray tented a hand over her eyes. "Looks like the guests are arriving.

"Permit me to finish for you." Abraham gestured toward the shovel.

She frowned, then handed it to him. George frowned, too. He should have offered first. "Thank you. I guess there's plenty for me to do back at the lodge. Hang it on the hook there outside the door and strap it down when you're done." She pointed to the outside wall of the building.

"With pleasure." Abraham began shoveling.

With pleasure. That was laying it on a little thick.

Debbie walked back to the lodge. George started to head into the snow machine shed, then paused when he saw a blond-headed kid that looked familiar. Debbie stopped to greet the two men with the boy. Suddenly, he was racing up the incline toward the snowmobiles. As the kid got closer, George recognized Perry Flint.

"Young Mr. Flint." *Twice in one day.* George waved.

Perry shouted, "George! What are you doing here?"

"I'm in charge of the snowmobiling. But I could ask you the same question."

"Cool! Me and my dad and uncle are with Dr. John and his friends for the weekend."

"You're running with the big dogs, buckaroo." George socked him in the shoulder.

Perry grinned. "Heck, yeah."

"This is Abraham," George said. "He's helping me with the snowmobiles. Abraham, this is my buddy, Perry Flint."

"Yo, Abraham," Perry said in a deep voice, his eyes sparkling.

George grinned. The kid had butchered the "Yo, Adrian" quote from *Rocky. Rocky* had been one of George's favorite movies the year before—he'd seen it twice—so he caught the reference from Perry's phrasing and intonation.

Abraham's face wrinkled in confusion. "Hello, Perry Flint."

"Which snowmobile am I going to be on?" Perry asked.

"Which one do you want?" George said.

Perry walked over to the two snowmobiles parked by George's trailer. He patted the seat of the blue and white Boss Cat. "This one is sweet."

"You've got good taste. But that's what I ride. You can have anything inside the building, though."

Perry trotted inside. "They're all the same."

George pointed at one on the back row. "Yeah, but this one has a little bit more get up and go than the others." In all honesty, he had no idea if it did or not. But it would make Perry happy to think he got the best one.

"Dibs!"

"It's all yours then."

Perry climbed on the seat and pretended to rev the engine.

"What's new with you, kid?"

"Not much. I don't have to go back to school for another week."
He manhandled the steering on the snowmobile and moved the skis
to the right and then the left. "Oh, one thing."

"What's that?"

"Yesterday we went to look at a horse at this ranch—my dad got
bucked off and broke some ribs. He's going to try to pretend like nothing's wrong, but I thought you should know."

"Ouch." Snowmobiling was going to be tough for Dr. Flint.

"That's not even the most exciting part, though. While we were
there, two of the hands were murdered. Sliced up with a knife. There
was blood everywhere. Or, that's what I heard anyway. My dad
wouldn't let me go see it."

Abraham drew in a sharp breath. He lost his grip on the shovel
and it fell into the snow. George glanced at him as the man leaned
over to pick it up.

"Where was that?" George said.

"The O Bar M. And get this. One of the guys told my dad who
did it right before he died. Now there's like a massive manhunt."

"Don't keep us in suspense. Who was it?"

"An Arab." Perry hopped off the snowmobile. "One of the hands
that worked there, Muhammed, he's an Arab, and he's missing, so it's
probably him. Deputy Harcourt is going to catch him."

Abraham put the shovel up on the building and strapped it into
place. Without looking at them, he said, "I'll be moving our things
into our room now."

"If you wait, I'll come help," George said.

He lifted a hand. "It is no problem."

"Then I'll start testing the machines. Come on back after you get
us set up if I'm not there yet."

"I will be sure to do so."

George turned back to Perry. "Now, where were we on those
murders you were telling me about, kid?"

CHAPTER THIRTEEN: TREAT

Denver, Colorado
Thursday, December 29, 1977, 9:00 p.m.

Trish

"I adore room service." Dian patted her belly and flopped back against the pillows stacked at the headboard of one of the beds.

They'd arrived in Denver too late to eat out. Trish, her mom, and Dian ordered cheeseburgers and fries from the hotel restaurant instead. Esme only wanted a chef salad. Trish thought Esme needed to eat about ten hamburgers. She was way too skinny, and it seemed like it was on purpose.

Trish liked the décor. A million different blues with shiny gold and silver accents and paintings of mountains on every wall. Dian had gotten them the flight attendant rate, so they were sharing a room in one of the fancy chain hotels. Esme and Trish in one bed. Dian and her mom in the other. *Maybe someday when Ben and I are married we can stay in a hotel like this one.*

Trish pushed the comforter back with her feet on the other bed.

She'd folded it down so she wouldn't get ketchup on it. But she couldn't eat. She picked up a French fry from her plate then set it back down. She was too worried about Ben. He should have arrived in Laramie a couple of hours ago, and he'd promised he'd call her. Just one quick minute to let her know he was all right. But no one was home at the Flint residence to take his call. Perry and her dad were in the mountains, and she and her mom were in Denver. Ben would be worried about her. Maybe he'd think she had gone out with her friends instead of waiting for his call. What would he do on his first night of freedom from rules and adults if he thought his girlfriend had ditched him? Especially after Trish had been a complete mess that morning.

She didn't have the phone number for his dorm room yet, so she couldn't even call him and let him know where she was. If her mother would have let her, that is, which was a big "if". She'd already lectured Trish about hotels charging an arm and a leg for local calls, much less long distance.

"Oh, Trish, turn that up." Her mom was seated at a small round table with Esme. Her plate was empty. Esme's salad bowl was still half full, like Trish's plate.

Video of a reporter in front of a familiar courthouse filled the screen. The one in Buffalo? What was big enough in Buffalo to make the news in Denver?

Trish walked to the TV and dialed up the volume.

"...near Buffalo, Wyoming. The police are asking you to call the number on the screen if you see an Arab man with olive skin, dark hair, and dark eyes, about five foot ten inches tall, who goes by the name Muhammed, and was last seen at the O Bar M ranch prior to the murders. An update on this story, and more of the news that matters to northern Colorado, at ten."

"Isn't that where you were yesterday, Trish?" her mom asked.

"Yeah." Her mom narrowed her eyes at her, but Trish didn't change her answer to yes ma'am.

"Did you see the guy they're talking about?"

"No."

Dian sighed. "I've gone my whole life and never met a person from an Arab country. I don't think I've ever seen them except on TV. What would one be doing in Wyoming?"

Esme put her fork down. "My daddy is in the oil business. We're not even allowed to mention Ay-rabs in our house."

Dian sat up and away from her pillows. "They're the reason it took us seven hours to drive here at fifty-five miles an hour."

"Don't be fuelish," Trish's mom said, and the other women laughed.

Trish frowned. "I don't get it."

"Don't they teach you current events in school?" Esme asked.

"Uh, some."

"Well, a few years ago, OPEC raised their prices and quit shipping oil to countries that supported Israel in the Arab-Israeli war. The United States was one of them. And we didn't produce enough oil here to meet our own energy needs. We needed the OPEC oil. When supply was cut off and demand remained high, it led to high prices and severe shortages."

"Long lines at gas stations in Irving, when we lived in Texas," her mom said. "Do you remember that?"

Trish thought back. "Yeah. Kinda."

"A lower national speed limit," Dian said. "Conservation campaigns."

Trish felt dumb, but she really did want to understand. "What's oh-peck?"

Esme said. "O-P-E-C. The Organization of Petroleum Exporting Countries, most of which are Middle Eastern countries." She nodded. "Ay-rabs."

Which explained why OPEC sided against Israel and its allies in the Arab-Israeli War. "We don't talk about this stuff at school. Why aren't there people from those countries in the U.S.?"

The women looked at each other. Her mom shrugged.

Esme said, "We have pretty restrictive immigration policies. Not everyone who wants to come is allowed in. My mother's family is from Mexico, although I was born in the U.S. It took her parents many years to get permission to move here."

Trish decided that even if Esme wasn't very smart about her body size and food, she knew a lot of other things. "But Muhammed worked at the O Bar M. He was here."

Esme nodded. "Some Ay-rabs are here, definitely. I had class-mates at the University of Texas who were from Middle Eastern countries. Iran and Egypt, I think."

The way Esme said it made Trish think of a song. "Ahab the Arab." One of the many songs her dad used to sing at the top of his lungs, usually about the time he pulled up in front of her friends, windows down, to give her a ride to or from school. Her mom had made him stop, though. That song, not all the rest of them. Trish said, "There are none at my school." Thinking about her school turned Trish's thoughts back to Ben. Everything turned her thoughts back to Ben. "Mom, Ben was supposed to call me when he got in and give me his phone number. Can I call Mrs. Sibley and get it from her?"

"He hasn't even been gone a day." Her mom made a sour face.

Dian laughed. "Says the woman who married in high school when her boyfriend moved away to college."

"Bite your tongue," her mom said.

"Let the girl check on him, Susanne."

"But it's long distance," her mom said. "Plus, a surcharge per minute by the hotel."

"I know, Mom," Trish said, trying not to whine. "You already told me all that. I just need his number. And to know he's okay. You can even make the call to Vangie so it's short. One minute. How much does one minute cost?"

"Come on, Mom," Dian said.

Her mom frowned. "Okay. I'll make the call. But only one minute."

"Can you do it now?" Trish said.

"Fine." Sighing, her mom picked up the phone and dialed. After a few moments of silence, she said, "Vangie, it's Susanne. I'll make this quick since it's long distance. I need Ben's phone number, if he's called with it yet, and Trish wants to know if he's okay. He was supposed to check in with her, but we drove to Denver to go shopping, so she hasn't been reachable." Her mom grabbed a pad of hotel stationary and a pen from the desk and started scribbling. She repeated the number back. "I'm glad he made it safe and sound. If he calls, tell him Trish is fine but we're not home. Thanks. I'll talk to you when we get back."

"Well?" Trish said.

Her mom handed her the note pad. "Romeo made it before dark and is unpacked. He starts work tomorrow. All is well. Okay?"

"Okay."

"And you're welcome."

"Thanks, Mom." Trish stood and rubbed her hands on her hips, nervous energy seeping out of her. Ben was fine. Everything was fine.

Dian crawled across the bed and reached for Trish's left hand. "What a beautiful ring, young lady. On your *ring finger*."

"What?" her mom said. "Where'd you get a ring?"

Trish jerked her hand away from Dian and put it behind her back. "It's my birthstone."

"Who gave it to you?" her mom demanded.

"Ben."

Dian laughed, high and tinkling. "Susanne, your daughter is wearing a promise ring."

Her mom shook her head. "It's her birthstone."

Dian snorted.

"What?"

"Ask her."

Trish wanted to duck under the bed and hide her head, like Ferdinand did sometimes, with his big body sticking out.

Her mom turned on her. "Is that a promise ring, Trish?"

Trish studied the toes of her boots. "Um . . . sort of, I guess?"

The silence hurt Trish's ears.

Finally, her mom said, "When were you going to tell your father and me about it?"

"He just gave it to me this morning." Trish saw her mom's throat working.

"We'll talk about this later, young lady."

Or never if I can help it.

Esme winked at Trish, which was sort of surprising, but Trish guessed they'd bonded over the OPEC discussion. "Now that we have that settled, who's up for watching a movie?"

"Me, me, me!" Dian said.

Trish's mom said, "Patrick would not approve. We're shopping, ordering room service, and charging movies to our room."

"Remember when he used to sneak people into the drive-in in the trunk?" Dian giggled. "He's always been cheap. But loveable. You married a good one, Susanne."

Her mom smiled. "And with a cute tush, too."

"Mom!" Trish shouted.

The women laughed. While they selected a movie, Trish ripped the page with Ben's number off the pad, folded it, and put it in her pocket. She hated not talking to him, but knowing he was safe would have to do for now. Until she could sneak a moment to call him herself when her mom wasn't around. Trish wasn't sure when that would be, but, where there was a will, there was always a way.

CHAPTER FOURTEEN: PARTY

Laramie, Wyoming

Thursday, December 29, 1977, 11:00 p.m.

Ben

Hank Williams and "Your Cheatin' Heart" blared from the juke box. *So loud it hurts.* Smoke clouded the air, and the place stank of cigarette smoke and stale beer. This was Ben's first experience in a bar. He guessed this one would be called a honkytonk. Plank walls. Scuffed wooden floors. A pool table in one corner, popular from the looks of the people waiting for a chance to play. Bare walls. A long bar worn smooth.

The men outnumbered the women two to one in the place. That was fine by Ben. He wasn't here for the women—he was only humoring his new roommate Chad, who insisted they celebrate Ben's first night as a University of Wyoming Cowboy. He'd even bought Ben a beer, which was a good thing, since beer wasn't in Ben's budget. Maybe after he got his first paycheck from his work study job in the cafeteria, he'd have a little for extras. If he did, though, he'd use it for gas to visit Trish.

He nursed his beer. So far, he'd made it last for an hour. Chad was chugging down his sixth and chasing each one with a shot of tequila.

"See that girl over there?" Chad pointed with the bottom of his empty Miller Genuine Draft bottle, holding it close by his pink-skinned face and hawkish nose. He was a head shorter and fifty pounds lighter than Ben, and he didn't look like he'd ever done a lick of physical work in his life. Probably never did more than ride the bench in any sports, either. Ben's first impression was that Chad's family had money and that he must have a pretty mother, because he had long eyelashes and lips so red it was like he was wearing lipstick.

Ben followed the bottle to the juke box, where a dark-haired girl with a curvy bottom was studying the choices. "Yeah."

"Five bucks says she comes back to our room with me tonight."

Ben flinched. He didn't have five dollars to bet, and girls weren't allowed in their dorm rooms. "Uh—"

Chad didn't wait for his response. "Watch and learn, country boy." His new roommate popped the collar on his shirt and sauntered across the bar, flashing a mouthful of teeth.

Ben leaned back against the bar and shot looks in both directions. No one was paying them any attention. Chad reached the juke box and said something to the girl. She turned around just as he tossed his wavy brown hair off his forehead. She was laughing. Watching them made Ben uncomfortable, so he turned around and propped his elbows on the bar top.

"You want another?" the bartender growled.

"No, thank you."

"Then do me a favor and let the paying customers through, sport."

Ben glanced over his shoulder. People were lined up three deep behind him. "Sorry."

He scooted away and found an open spot on the wall. He leaned back against it, picking at the label on his beer bottle. He was tired. It had been a long day, and he was out of sorts. He'd called Trish like she'd asked him to. No answer. After she'd made him promise to call, she wasn't home, even though she'd known when he was due to arrive in Laramie.

It was a bad beginning to their separation.

Up until now, he'd been the one who'd insisted it would be no big deal. The truth was he'd been trying to talk himself into believing it more than Trish. He had a deep fear that Trish would wise up and find someone better than him. Someone good enough for her. That's why he'd wanted to put the promise ring on her finger. He didn't want to drive her away by being jealous and possessive now. But jealous and possessive was exactly how he was feeling. His stomach churned. He'd expected it take a little longer for her to disconnect from him than this. And it would be too late to try calling her again when he got home. Her parents would be asleep. He'd have to wait for the morning, which he hated, and then he'd be forced to keep it short and within his budget, which he hated even more.

"There you are." Chad lurched into Ben, knocking him sideways. The brunette from the jukebox was tucked under his arm. "Sophie, meet my upstanding and somewhat square roommate, Ben. Ben, meet Sophie, the future mother of my children."

Square? Chad barely knows me.

Sophie rolled her eyes at Chad and held a limp hand out to Ben. Ben took it, but he wasn't sure whether he was supposed to kiss it or shake it.

"Hi, Ben. You're tall. And kind of cute."

Ben froze. "Uh, hi."

Chad thumped Ben in the breast pocket. "We're going to take it offsite, Ben-jammin. That'll be five dollars, please."

Ben gaped. Chad was bragging about the bet right in front of Sophie? Then his mouth went dry. He hadn't agreed to the wager. He didn't have five dollars to spare. But he wasn't the kind of person who welched, even on bets he'd never agreed to.

Chad laughed. "Just kidding about the money, man. But let's get out of here. This party's moving to campus."

Just like that, Chad was taking Sophie to their room? Had he even met the girl before tonight? Ben tried not to let the judgment he was feeling show. "I have work in the morning. Orientation. My first day."

Chad smirked at Sophie. "What did I tell you? S-Q-U-A-R-E."

Sophie looped her arm through Ben's. "Come on, Benny-poo. I can't stay long anyway. You'll get your beauty sleep."

Ben frowned at the silly name and the situation. Trish wouldn't like this. He wouldn't like it in her shoes, either. For that matter, *he* didn't like it. He needed his job, and he didn't know these people. Didn't know if he liked Chad, who he had to live with. "I, uh—"

She pouted. "Don't be a dud and ruin our night, Benny-wenny."

Enough with the nicknames. He should keep the peace with his new roommate. Compromise. With a heavy sigh, he said, "Okay. One hour." He'd kick them out if they were still partying after that. He'd have to.

Sophie squealed and hugged him. "Yippee."

Chad held up a hand for a high five. Ben gave him a tentative slap. "That's my man."

But Ben had a strong feeling Chad wasn't going to be his.

CHAPTER FIFTEEN: WAKE

Clear Creek Resort, Bighorn Mountains, Wyoming
Thursday, December 29, 1977, 11:30 p.m.

George

A thrashing noise woke George from a deep sleep. He sat up, disoriented, his heart pounding, his nostrils filled with the smell of dust and sweat. He'd had most of a six pack after dinner. He felt cotton mouthed. A little lightheaded. On the floor, Abraham was moaning and writhing in his sleeping bag.

George gulped in a breath. It appeared the man was having nightmares. Nothing more.

He flipped over, rubbing his face against the scratchy wool blanket he'd piled on top of the comforter. He'd had nightmares, too, since last summer, when he'd taken the wrong clients up Little Goose Trail in the mountains, and they'd turned on him and the Flints. He'd never forget hearing the shot, the scream of Perry's friend John, and then the sound of a silence so heavy that he knew the boy was dead. Knew it deep in his bones.

Imagining it had been even worse than seeing John's lifeless face and the blood pooled on the ground. But the worst part had been hours later, when Perry's shock had finally given way to grief. His sobs. His horrible, wracking, snot nosed sobs. The memory of them still twisted George up in knots, especially around three in the morning.

That must be why I have such a soft spot for the young Flint.

Even though he felt empathy for him, he hoped Abraham fought his demons off quickly. They had a big day tomorrow. He sighed. Abraham's thrashing continued.

What time was it? He'd brought a travel alarm clock that glowed in the dark. He fumbled for it on the bedside table, found it, and held it in front of his face. Only half past eleven. George had stayed in front of the fire chatting with the guests after dinner. When he'd come back to the room to tuck in around nine thirty, Abraham was already zonked out.

George set the clock down. Abraham punched and muttered. If that dream got much worse, George would have to wake him up before he hurt himself.

A few seconds later, the man stilled.

Hallelujah. But now George was wide awake. A drink of water would settle him and help with the cotton mouth. He flung off the heavy comforter, tiptoed into the bathroom, shut the door, flipped on the switch, and blinked his eyes to block the light. When he could stand the brightness, he came face to face with himself in the mirror. White-blond hair spiking upward. Blue eyes squinting. Skin tanned and wind-burned from breaking trail earlier with Abraham. The man hadn't lied about his snowmobiling skills. He could ride rings around George, and the job had gone much faster with Abraham in the lead, fighting the heavy powder. They'd have an easier time of it with the guests, since they'd done such a thorough job, if they could just keep everyone *on* the trail.

He turned on the cold tap and filled a Styrofoam coffee cup with water, thinking back over his conversation with the guests. Only a few had significant experience on snow machines. Mostly the Wyoming natives, Dr. John and Wes Braten, who would arrive tomorrow. Of the rest, Patrick, his brother-in-law, and Perry were complete novices.

One of Dr. John's buddies, Cyrus, was a tall and athletic New Englander who mentioned playing hockey in college decades before, but he'd only snowmobiled once or twice. George was curious about Cyrus. Mrs. Murray had told him that the man was some big mucky muck in the Carter administration, but George had never heard of him. Cyrus had barely been around the entire evening. He'd made so many calls on the lodge phone that at one point he handed Mrs. Murray a hundred-dollar bill and told her it was prepayment for long distance for the weekend, and that she should keep the change.

The last guy in the group said he had decent experience from a vacation to the Alps the previous year. George figured he would be a lot of fun on the trail. He had wild, curly gray hair and a booming laugh, and he'd been the center of attention most of the night with loud stories about his days in the Israeli army. *Ari. Ari Something-or-Other.*

George sat down on the toilet lid and drank his water in a series of gulps. The room was so tiny, he could have brushed his teeth over the sink from where he sat. But he figured it had everything it needed. Toilet. Shower. Sink. Anything else was a waste of space and money.

A scream from the bedroom pierced the air. George dropped the cup, which landed in the sink. He had to rouse Abraham from his nightmare before he woke the other guests. Mrs. Murray might fire them if there were complaints.

He hurried back into the small bedroom. Abraham was standing in the half-light from the window, tangled in the sleeping bag, but arms up and legs bent in a fighting stance. His eyes were open, whites showing, pupils enlarged.

"I won't tell anyone," he hissed. Then he said something George couldn't understand. Something in a foreign language. Then he switched back to English. "You know I only wish the best for my cousin."

George held his hands out, palms down. In a calm voice, he said, "Abraham, wake up. You're having a nightmare."

Abraham lunged at George. George scrambled backward, shocked, but he wasn't fast enough. Abraham's hands found his neck and squeezed as he fell on top of him, knocking him to the floor. George's head hit with teeth jarring force, but the edge of the sleeping bag cushioned the blow just enough. He found the man's fingers with his and clawed at them. He couldn't draw a breath. His face felt tight, his eyes bulged.

George kicked and bucked. He could barely choke out words. "Wake. Up."

Abraham lifted his head and stared into George's eyes. "Don't make me kill you." Then, again, he spoke in the language George didn't recognize.

"George. Your friend. Help. Stop."

George's words were little more than gasps, gasps that wasted the precious air in his lungs. Abraham's eyes were stone-cold crazed. When the man didn't loosen his grip, George scuttled his fingers around on the floor, looking for something—anything—to use as a weapon. He got a handful of fabric. In the scuffle, they'd pulled the comforter from George's bed. It was of no use to him, and he pushed it aside. Then his fingers bumped into something that dinged. Something with hard edges. The alarm clock! But when he reached for it, he found he'd knocked it out of reach.

George's vision was alternating now between shooting stars and patches of utter darkness. Abraham's scent was overpowering. Testosterone and sweat, like a bull. He was going to pass out. If he did, and if Abraham didn't snap out of it, George was dead.

He wriggled frantically under Abraham, scooting his body fractions of an inch closer to the clock. He stretched his arm and touched only air, floor, and bedding. He twisted and bucked again, and this time, the sleeping bag slid along the floor, moving both men several inches closer to where the clock should be.

George's hand groped like a pouncing spider. The clock wasn't there. It had moved with the bedding, too. He pounded the floor with his palm, desperate. On the third strike, something solid under the sleeping bag dug into his palm. The clock? How could it be under the bedding? He dug with his nails, crazed, getting nowhere, until his fingertip caught a fold. He jerked the fabric toward him, and on his next smack, he was rewarded with cold metal and a ding. *Thank God!*

His fingers closed around the little clock. He twisted his arm over and swung at Abraham with everything he had left in him, hoping to connect with his head. The clock glanced off Abraham's elbow with a pathetic ding. *Short.* Abraham didn't even react. George reeled the clock back in. If he couldn't reach his head, he needed to aim for the next best target. All he had to do was wake him up.

But then a horrible thought entered his brain. What if Abraham *was* awake? What if he had attacked George on purpose? George had picked him up on the side of the road. A hitchhiker. No, not even that. A man who hadn't wanted to meet his eyes or even talk to him.

But he pushed the thought away. Doubt and fear were a waste of energy. He swung. Smashed the clock into Abraham's ribs. The man grunted and froze. *Yes.* George reared back and hit him again. And again. And again.

Abraham's hands relaxed. Then the weight of his body lifted off George.

George rolled over and struggled onto his hands and knees, gagging and coughing.

"What is going on? What have I done?" Abraham cried.

George crawled away from the sound of his voice. His vision was still spotty, but he felt Abraham's presence as the other man leaned over him.

"I won't harm you." Abraham groaned. "Not—not anymore. I am so sorry."

George bumped his head against the nightstand. He rolled over onto his behind and scooted backward toward the bathroom. In his disoriented state, he found himself pressed instead against the heavy pine leg of the bed. He put a hand to his throat, then he pushed upwards, trying to sit. He fell back to the floor, uncertain whether to trust Abraham, weakened and unable to get away.

"I had a nightmare, yes? I was sleep walking. I—I—I am overcome with guilt and anguish. Please, allow me to assist you." Abraham stood. "A glass of water will be of benefit to you."

George heard the faucet turn on and the water rush out, and then the flow stopped. The fight or flight response ebbed out of him. Abraham returned with the Styrofoam cup. He put one hand gently behind George's head, tilting it up, then held the cup to it with the other.

"Sip slowly. It will soothe your throat."

George stared at Abraham. The man he'd spent the day with had returned. His eyes were brimming with tears. Actual tears. The hands that had nearly killed him weren't weapons anymore. George nodded, then sipped. The water burned on the way down. George had never been choked before, and the pain in his throat was sharp. He cleared it.

"You've got a grip on you, that's for sure." His voice was raspy.

Abraham whispered. "I am so sorry. That man was not me. I thought I was fighting for my life."

"Who were you fighting? That guy from the gas station?"

Abraham didn't answer.

"And what language were you speaking?"

"There are some things I cannot disclose. I have—I have made some enemies while spending time in another country."

George wondered if the issue with the guy from the gas station earlier was about more than a woman. "They aren't here in Wyoming, are they?"

Abraham frowned and looked more closely at George's neck. "To my shame, I think you will have bruises. Significant ones."

George tried again to sit. His head swam, but this time he made it. "I'll be all right."

"People will notice."

George tried to grin. It hurt. "That's why God invented collars. No one will see."

Abraham's face was solemn. "I will understand and comply if you wish me to leave."

George gave it some serious thought for a moment. He didn't want a repeat of this tomorrow night. But he needed the help. Maybe he could find a Sunday replacement for Abraham and send the man down the mountain at the end of the day Saturday. If he was unsuccessful, Abraham would have to sleep somewhere else. That was all there was to it. The hallway. A car. In the snow machine shed. He didn't care. Just not in George's room.

"Let's see how it goes today. Help me up?"

Abraham clasped George's hand and hauled him to his feet. "I will never forget your kindness."

George steadied himself on a bed post. "Noted. Now, let's get some rest."

Abraham nodded.

George grabbed his pillow and comforter and went into the bathroom. "But if it's all the same to you, I'm sleeping in the bathtub."

He locked the door behind him.

CHAPTER SIXTEEN: ARREST

Laramie, Wyoming
Thursday, December 29, 1977, 11:45 p.m.

Ben

Ben shuffled across the parking lot to Chad's car. It was slick. Very slick. Biting snowflakes pelted his face. Behind him, he heard the laughter and slurry whispers of his companions.

"I'll drive if you want, Chad," Ben said. He might not know his way around town yet, but at least he was sober. He'd have trouble showing up for his first day of work if Chad wrapped them around a telephone pole.

Keys jangled. "Sure, man. Sophie and I can hold down the back seat."

Sophie giggled. Ben heard a soft slap. "You're bad."

When Ben reached the back bumper, he turned. Chad tossed the keys toward him. They fell short, into a few inches of snow. Ben sunk to his knees, pawing for them with his bare hands. Sophie's peals of laughter set his teeth on edge.

"Sorry, dude," Chad said, not sounding sorry at all.

Ben came up with the keys. "Yeah, *dude*. It's fine."

A bright light popped on, spotlighting the snow a few feet away from Ben. The beam redirected into Ben's eyes. A deep, nasally voice said, "Good evening gentlemen. And lady. You been drinking?"

Panic clawed inside Ben, a wild thing fighting to get out of his chest. A cop. Checking for drunk drivers. He wasn't drunk, but after six months in juvie, he didn't take any interaction with law enforcement for granted. The last thing he wanted was to get on the wrong side of the Laramie police. "Uh, not really, sir."

"He's driving, not us." Chad released Sophie, who teetered against the side of the car.

"Are you okay, ma'am?" the cop asked. With the light in his eyes, Ben couldn't see the man's face.

Sophie burst into tears. "I just want to go home. I don't want to go with him. And I'm c-c-c-cold."

"With him who?"

Sophie gestured at Ben and Chad. Chad threw his hands up in a "not me" gesture. She moaned, then turned and vomited on the ground. The stench was immediate, but Ben didn't recoil.

The officer took a step closer to him. "Sir, I need you to turn around and put your hands on the trunk of the car."

"But, I—"

"Now!"

Ben complied. "Yes, sir." He'd learned some lessons in juvie, and one of them replayed now in his head. *Never argue with a cop. Never argue with a cop. Never argue with a cop.* Everything would be okay. He wasn't drunk, and Sophie wasn't with him.

"Why won't you let this girl go home?"

"She can do whatever she wants. She's not with me. Ask Chad."

Sophie's crying escalated. Chad remained silent.

"How much have you had to drink?"

"One beer."

The cop snorted. "All you college punks from out of town think you can come to Laramie and do whatever you want. We'll see about that when I give you a sobriety test.

"But I haven't been driving. Plus, I'm not even drunk."

"And now you're resisting. Drunk and disorderly. Ma'am, why don't you run back inside with your friends. You're going to be okay. I think you've had enough for the night, though. Is there someone who can drive you home?"

"Y-y-y-yes."

"All right, then."

"Can I walk her inside, sir?" Chad asked.

There was a pause. "Just to the door. Then come right back."

"Yes, sir."

Ben heard footsteps and whispering as Chad and Sophie started their trek back to the bar.

"I'm going to pat you down and look in your pockets," the cop said to Ben. "Any weapons or contraband?"

"No, sir. Just a pocketknife, in the front pocket of my jeans." Everyone carried pocketknives. It wasn't against the terms of his release from juvie. He swallowed and tried to relax. He hadn't done anything wrong. This would be over when the cop figured that out.

The officer pulled the knife out. Then he resumed his search, starting with Ben's heavy coat. Ben knew those pockets were empty. He usually kept his gloves in them, but he'd forgotten them in the dorm room. So, he was shocked when he felt the cop pull something out of one of the pockets.

"Well, well, what have we here?"

Ben turned to look, and the cop shoved him face down on the trunk. "I didn't tell you to move, punk." The officer pressed Ben's mouth into the icy cold metal.

Snow melted on Ben's lips and he tasted metallic dirt. "Sorry, sir."

"Want to tell me why you would have a big bag of weed in your jacket?"

"I wasn't carrying any weed. I don't do drugs." Ben's pulse accelerated. Where had a bag of marijuana come from?

The cop dangled a baggie in front of Ben's eyes. "Huh. I guess it must be someone else's jacket, then?"

"No, sir. The jacket's mine, but that's not my bag. I've never seen it before."

The cop straightened up. Ben heard a jangle, and then cold metal snapped around one of his wrists. The officer jerked his other arm behind him and cuffed it, too. Ben's cheek was still smashed into the trunk. It felt like his lips were starting to stick. His wrists and shoulders hurt. He didn't dare move, though. Didn't dare make a sound.

What the heck is going on?

The officer pulled Ben's wallet from his back jeans pocket. A few seconds later, he said, "Ben Jones from Story?"

"Yes, sir."

"I'm using your keys now to search your vehicle."

"It's not my vehicle. My truck is back at the parking lot near my dorm. I just got here today. This is Chad's car. The other guy."

Ben tracked the crunch of the officer's footsteps as he went to the door of the car and unlocked it. Ben heard muted sounds from inside the vehicle. Snow fell on his face. He moved his lips away from the metal, feeling a sickening tearing sensation and a sharp pain. He wondered if it was okay to stand back up. *No. He couldn't.* Not without permission. He stood, trembling, bent over the car, his face hovering half an inch over it. He tried to think, desperate to figure out what was happening. How things had spun out of control so fast.

Drugs in my pocket. Had he grabbed the wrong coat? *No.* He'd never taken it off. Someone had to have stuck them in there. Someone in the bar, maybe? Someone ditching them, afraid to get in trouble? Because who would spend money on drugs only to stick them in a stranger's pocket unless they were scared of getting caught with them?

Chad. Chad or Sophie.

Then the cop leaned in Ben's face. He had a big grin on his face, fetid breath, and pockmarks and sparse beard hairs across his cheeks.

"I suppose the other bag of weed and all the pills aren't yours, either?"

"I don't know what you're talking about. I swear."

"I found the stash in your glove compartment."

Ben's voice went up in pitch. "Ask my roommate Chad. He'll tell you. I'm a square. It's not my car. They're not my drugs." With a lurch of his stomach, Ben realized Chad hadn't come back from the bar.

His new roommate had set Ben up to take the fall for him.

The cop laughed. "Welcome to Laramie, Ben Jones. You can kiss college goodbye. You're under arrest for possession of marijuana and methamphetamines, with enough on you to deal to half the people in the bar tonight. The only place you're going is prison."

Ben felt his legs giving out and his weight slumped onto Chad's car. How was he ever going to explain this to Trish?

CHAPTER SEVENTEEN: TENSE

Susanne

Susanne jostled her sleeping daughter. "We're leaving for IHOP in ten minutes, Trish. I'm not going to wake you again." She picked up Trish's dirty jeans from the floor. The girl was smart, she was hard working, she was too pretty by far, but she was an absolute slob. Her closet. Her truck. And now this hotel room.

She looked at the head of her daughter on the pillow and the hand beside the face, the purple of the stone in the little ring standing out against the white of the pillowcase. Purple, yes. An actual amethyst, Susanne doubted. Ben didn't have two spare nickels to rub together. So how had he gotten the ring? She wondered if he'd stolen it. Or if the Sibleys had known about the ring and given him the money. She didn't know which was worse, Ben compounding his crimes, or her own best friend betraying her. She'd have a heart-to-heart with Vangie as soon as she got back to Buffalo.

Trish lifted her head. One side of her face was lined with creases from the bedding, the same side drool was running out of her mouth from. "Bring me back something."

Susanne swatted Trish gently on her backside with the jeans. "That's not how it works, young lady, and you know it. If you miss the bus, you miss the breakfast. And we'll only swing back to pick you up to go to the mall one time. After that, you've bought yourself a lonely, hungry day in the hotel."

Trish flapped a hand. Not the one with the ring. "Go without me."

"Get up."

"I can't."

"Brush your teeth and throw on your clothes. Now."

Trish growled and sat. Susanne held in her own return growl. Trish was nowhere near mature enough to be thinking about lifelong commitments. She couldn't even get herself out of bed. She argued with her mother. She was a mere child. *And I was only a year older when I married Patrick.* Which is exactly what had Susanne so terrified.

Dian came out of the bathroom, her hair perfectly styled, and a full face of makeup painted on. Susanne touched her own ponytail.

Dian said, "You're making my ovaries shrivel, Trish Flint."

Trish barely gave her a glance as she lurched into the open bathroom.

Susanne walked to her purse and got out a lipstick. She rubbed some into her eyelids and onto her cheeks. Inside, she felt like she was a train flying off a trestle, but she couldn't let that be what she showed on the outside. "And to think I tried to talk Patrick into four kids. What if I'd had three girls?"

Esme turned from where she was gazing out the window. "I can't wait to have a daughter."

Dian laughed. "Have you heard a word of this exchange?"

Esme clutched a handbag to her chest. "I won't put up with that kind of nonsense. My mother kept a firm hand on us, and my sisters and I turned out all right."

Susanne's hand slipped and she drew a stripe of lipstick from her lips to her ear.

Dian gripped her shoulder as Susanne rubbed off the worst of it. "I'm sure you're right. I hope you have a whole houseful of girls."

Esme turned back to the window. Snow was falling in a sheet, almost like white rain. "It will be dreamy."

Dian held out her hand to Susanne. "I'll bring the Suburban around if you'd like."

Susanne dug in her bag, returning her lipstick, and coming out with keys, which she gave to Dian. "Thanks. I'll be ready in a jiffy."

"I'll come with you, Dian," Esme said.

The two women walked out together. Dian peered back in the door and mouthed "help me" to Susanne before it shut. Despite herself, Susanne smiled and laughed softly. Trish wasn't the only problem child on this trip.

Her daughter came out of the bathroom, looking slightly more alert. "What's so funny?"

"I'm not sure that Esme knows Dian used to be engaged to your uncle."

"What? When?"

"Once, in high school. Then again a year ago. I sure wouldn't be buddying up to your dad's old flame if I were Esme."

"Dian and Uncle Barry were engaged in high school?"

"Yes." And aren't together now. Susanne knew she and Patrick were the exception, not the rule, and she hoped Trish understood it, too.

"That's just weird."

"Isn't it?" Susanne slipped into the bathroom.

She wet a washcloth and scrubbed the remains of the lipstick slash. The cloth left an abraded red mark of its own, making it hard to tell if she'd gotten it off or not. It would have to do. She had been looking forward to eating out and shopping in good stores since yesterday. She hoped Trish didn't ruin it for her.

She locked eyes with herself in the mirror. "Then don't let her," she said, imitating Patrick's voice. "Be the stronger person. Be the parent." Nodding at herself, she walked out.

Trish was holding the phone receiver to her ear.

"Trish, I didn't give you permission to make a phone call."

Her daughter held up her hand. "I just need Ben to know where I am."

"Which Vangie will tell him."

Trish slammed the phone down.

"Thank you. Now get ready."

Trish dove onto the bed and rolled herself into the covers. Her voice was muffled as she replied. "He didn't answer his phone. And I'm not going anywhere."

Susanne sighed. "Be the parent."

"What?"

"I said I'm going to breakfast. See you in an hour."

CHAPTER EIGHTEEN: BREAK

Ben

"Hey, you," a voice said. It came from outside the cell where Ben was being held along with a few other men brought in during the night.

Ben didn't look up. His eyes felt like he'd rubbed sand in them. His fingertips were stained red from biting hangnails until they bled. He hadn't slept all night. His butt hurt from the metal bench he was sitting on, and his hand was numb from propping his forehead in it.

"I'm talking to you, Ben Jones."

Ben stumbled to his feet. A man in a uniform was standing outside the bars. Not the one who'd arrested him, but the same man who'd checked him into what he'd called the drunk tank the night before. Whatever they called it, it smelled like piss, body odor, and vomit, which meant Ben did now, too. The officer—guard?—talking to him was tall and heavy. The fat kind of heavy. His clean-shaven face was so white it was almost pink.

"Sorry."

"We were able to reach law enforcement in Johnson County."

Ben tensed, preparing himself. He knew what was coming.

"They said you did time in juvie."

Heads swiveled toward him. *Not just another college punk sleeping one off with the big boys*, the other men's interest said.

"I was released early for good behavior."

"Kidnapping. That's intense."

Ben flexed his hands to keep from balling them into fists. Around him he heard intakes of breath. One of the guys tutted. *Why did he have to announce that in front of everyone?*

"I was . . ." He trailed off. *I was saving the girl I was in love with from my dad and uncle.* But who would believe that? Explaining wouldn't do any good. "This is all a misunderstanding. Did you check the registration on that car? It wasn't mine. The drugs weren't mine. The girl wasn't with me."

"If I had a dime for every loser who said they didn't do it. You're just another case of history repeating itself."

Ben wanted to scream, but he knew he needed to keep his cool. The guys in uniform loved to get under your skin. Why else would they want these cruddy jobs? If he gave in to his feelings, if he reacted, it would go worse for him. He'd learned that lesson from the jump in juvie. In his first week, a guard had asked him what he'd done to Trish when he had her to himself. Ben had rushed him and tackled him to the ground. He probably would have beat the guard half to death if other kids hadn't pulled him off. He'd been confined to his room for a week and lost all privileges for a month for it.

He'd never made that mistake again, no matter how bad the uniforms egged him on. He'd figured out a strategy that worked for him—never look into their eyes. Just stare at their uniforms and not their faces. Imagine them as less than human. As not mattering to anyone, because that's how they thought about him. His control had gotten him out of there early, too.

He wouldn't lose his cool now.

The uniform cocked his head. "Nothing else to say?"

Ben shook his head.

"You want your phone call?"

Ben walked to the bars, nodding.

"What's the magic word?"

"Please."

The uniform winked. "That wasn't so hard, was it?"

Ben pushed his lips up into a smile he didn't feel. *You have no idea.*

The uniform fastened cuffs around Ben's wrists, then opened the cell for him to exit. Ben kept his eyes down and shuffled behind him down a hall and into a small room with a pay phone on the wall.

"Have at it." The guard stood back, arms crossed.

Juggling the cuffs out of the way, Ben picked up the receiver and cradled it to his ear. He dialed the zero.

"Operator, how can I help you?" a woman said, her voice bored.

"I'd like to make a collect call. From Ben." He gave her the number.

"Hold please."

Ben listened as the phone rang and rang. *Pick up, pick up, pick up.*

"Hello?" Vangie's Tennessee accent was unmistakable.

"Collect call from Ben. Will you accept the charges?"

"Yes. Thank you."

"You have a nice day." The operator dropped off the line.

"Ben? You miss us already?" Vangie teased.

More than she could ever know. *I hate making this call. Hate it.* "I'm in trouble and I need your help." Ben dropped his forehead to the wall and a tear slid from his eye.

CHAPTER NINETEEN: PANIC

Denver, Colorado
Friday, December 30, 1977, 8:00 a.m.

Trish

Trish thought she'd never get rid of her mother, but, once she did, she made up for lost time, calling Ben's dorm room phone line over and over. She sat in a swivel chair at the desk, rocking back and forth. No one had answered so far. She dialed it for the tenth time. Her stomach was in knots. Why wasn't he answering? She knew he had to report to his new job today, but surely, he hadn't started this early. She thought he'd told her he had to be there at nine for orientation. She'd been calling since seven.

Had he been out partying all night? Had he already met a wild college girl? All the bad possibilities played repeatedly in her head.

Or it could be he hadn't picked up for an innocent reason. He'd given her a promise ring. He was a good person. He wasn't cheating on her. He couldn't be. The phone might have come unplugged. She knew it wasn't off the hook because she wasn't getting a busy signal.

But something might have happened to him. Had he been in a wreck? He probably drove somewhere to get food. The roads must have been bad. The storm had made a mess of the interstate near Cheyenne, and that was only about an hour away from him.

Come on, Ben. Come on.

On the fifteenth ring, someone answered. "Hello?" a guy said. Not Ben.

Trish was so surprised she dropped the phone receiver.

"Hello?" the guy said again. "Is anyone there?"

Trish said, "Me. I'm here. I'm calling for Ben."

Silence on the other end.

"Is this Chad?" she said.

"Let me guess. You're Trish."

"Yes! Where's Ben? I've been calling and calling and—"

"He's not here."

"Where is he?"

"I hate to be the one to tell you this, sweetheart, but he's in jail."

The way he said sweetheart sounded like an insult. "What?" Trish knew her voice was shrill and too loud, but she couldn't help it. "Why?"

"We were out, and he got busted by the cops."

"For what?"

"It's a long story."

"How long will he have to be in there?"

Chad sounded exasperated. "How would I know? But I'm sure someone will post his bail soon."

Ben was an orphan. He was broke. He was alone. There was no one in Laramie to help him. "Can you help him?"

Chad snorted. "I don't think that would be such a good idea."

"Why?"

"Listen, Trish?"

"Yes?"

"You need to call his parents if you're worried about your little Ben. Count me out."

Trish heard a click and then a dial tone. "Hello? Hello?" *He hung up on me! I'm practically Ben's fiancée, he's in jail, and his roommate hung up on me!*

Trish stared at the phone. "He doesn't have any parents," she screamed, to no one.

She tried calling back, but, after thirty unanswered rings, she gave up, slamming the phone down over and over on the hotel desk, imagining it was Chad's stupid head. The only thing she could think of to do to help Ben was call the Sibleys. She couldn't get hold of her own mom and dad, not that she would have wanted to involve them anyway. But what if Ben didn't want the Sibleys to know he was in jail?

It didn't seem like she had a choice. Someone had to help him. She dialed the Piney Bottoms ranch number by heart.

"Hello?" Mrs. Sibley answered on the first ring. She sounded upset.

"Mrs. Sibley? It's Trish."

"Oh, honey, did you talk to him?"

"No. But I just got hold of his roommate and he said . . . he said . . ."

"I know. Ben got arrested. Someone planted drugs on him, and his roommate ditched him. And then there were more drugs in the roommate's car. Ben was driving."

"Oh, no," Trish wailed. "Ben!"

"Don't worry, honey. Henry's college friend is an attorney in Laramie, and he went to help Ben the second we called him. He's going to get this straightened out. And as soon as we drop Hank with the Harcourts, we'll be on our way, too."

"With his juvie record . . ."

"It certainly doesn't help."

"Can I do anything?"

"Just pray for him, honey. He's had a tough time."

"And his job. He missed his orientation for his job."

"He'll have to worry about that later."

Trish wiped away tears. "He doesn't do drugs, Mrs. Sibley. I promise you, he doesn't."

"I know, honey. I know. I hate to do this to you, but we have to leave. Try not to worry too much."

"How will I know what's happening?"

"What hotel are you at?"

Trish found the number on the phone, then gave it to her along with the room number and hotel name.

"I'll call you when we know something. But it's not likely to be until much later today."

"Thank you," Trish whispered.

They ended the call, and Trish sank to her knees on the floor of the hotel, head in her hands.

The door opened. An explosion of chattering entered the room ahead of her mother, Dian, and Esme.

Dian saw her first. "Trish?"

Trish held a fist to her mouth. Her shoulders heaved as she sobbed with no sound.

"Trish," her mom shouted and ran to her side. She pulled Trish into her arms. "Trish, what's the matter? What happened?"

All Trish could do was shake her head, grinding her face into her mom's shoulder.

CHAPTER TWENTY: PREP

Clear Creek Resort, Bighorn Mountains, Wyoming
Friday, December 30, 1977, 9:00 a.m.

Patrick

A battalion of snowmobiles was parked in formation by a barn-like structure behind the Clear Creek Resort Lodge. Most of the machines were bright yellow. To Patrick, it looked like a swarm of killer bees. George Nichols was standing in front of them in a white snow suit like the beekeeper.

Patrick strode to him and shook his hand, covering up a wince as pain shot through his ribs. He owed George the world for saving the life of his kids, and he would never forget it or be able to repay the debt. "Great to see you, George. Perry said you'd be our captain today."

"I am. I can't wait for you to try snowmobiling, Dr. Flint. You're going to be hooked," George said. "Take your pick from the yellow machines."

"It's an expensive sport, Patrick. You'd better protect your wallet with one hand." Dr. John was walking around the sleds, occasionally leaning in for a closer look. He moved with a noticeable limp—a military service injury—that didn't prevent him from leading an active Wyoming lifestyle.

Patrick groaned. He moved to the snowmobile Perry was sitting astride. "Is it too late to back out?"

Barry's cheeks were apple red in the cold, matching his borrowed coveralls. He winked at Perry. "It's a well-known fact that my brother-in-law is so tight he can pinch a penny between his cheeks and it comes out a dime."

"Gross!" Perry shouted. "But true."

"I consider it one of my best qualities." Patrick squeezed Perry's shoulder. "I can't afford for you to take up this activity, too. Between skiing and football, you're already bleeding me dry, son."

"Ha ha, Dad."

Patrick walked forward and wrapped his fingers around the hand grip on the machine in front of Perry. Sensory memories flooded through him. Wind in his hair. Bugs on his sunglasses. Dirt in his teeth. For one shining month, he'd owned a motorcycle when he was in college. He'd loved every second of it, too. He'd bought it on a whim as a newlywed and justified the purchase to Susanne as his cheapest and best option to commute to campus. She hadn't liked it, but it wasn't until he'd laid it over to avoid being hit by a car running a red light that she'd put her foot down.

"I'm too young to be a widowed mother," she'd yelled at him, with tears running down her face.

He'd thought she'd been overreacting. "It would be nice if your first thought was how much you love me and would miss me if something happened to me."

When he walked outside the next morning, the motorcycle had a for sale sign taped to it, in Susanne's handwriting.

In retrospect, he probably shouldn't have spoken his thoughts aloud to his pregnant young wife. It remained to this day the only major expenditure he'd ever made without consulting with her ahead of time. Patrick squeezed the brakes on the snowmobile. If he had to guess, Susanne wouldn't be onboard for one of these, either.

Ari grinned at Perry. Gray curls rimmed the bottom of his black wool cap, and his eyes twinkled. He'd traveled all the way from Israel for the get together. "Young Mr. Flint, I believe you should have no fears in this regard. Your father will give you the world if you only ask him."

Perry took Ari seriously. "I'll settle for a snowmobile."

Everyone laughed, even Cyrus, the quiet one in the group. The tall man had a pale, serious face, athletic frame, and ears that stuck out like they were reaching to catch words. If they had flapped, it would have put Patrick in mind of Dumbo. *Oh, heck, yeah, they remind me of Dumbo, whether they flap or not.* Patrick was pretending he had no idea that Cyrus held a cabinet level position at the White House, since Dr. John had told them Cyrus was trying to remain incognito. But it had been hard the evening before when Cyrus was in and out on mysterious work phone calls. Patrick was curious about what it was like to be on the inside, politically. He didn't have any political aspirations. He just couldn't understand why anyone else would willingly put themselves through it, either.

Two men approached. One was a muscular man of medium height, the guide working with George. He'd met him briefly the night before. The other—a praying mantis figure—Patrick knew well.

The long, lean man called out, "Hey, Sawbones. Dr. John. Perry. George. How is everyone?" It was the jack-of-all-trades medical tech Wes Braten, one of Patrick's best friends. He was up for the day rather than the weekend.

"I guess they'll let anyone on this ride," Patrick said.

Wes replied in his droll voice. "Lucky for you, I guess. I tried to talk George out of letting you come along."

He made the rounds, with Dr. John introducing Ari and Cyrus and Patrick doing the same with Barry.

"And this is Abraham," George said to Wes. "He'll be the other guide today, and he's a far better rider than I am. He's even done a little racing out in California."

"At the beach?" Perry asked. "Is there even snow there?"

Abraham smiled. "In the mountains. They're called the Sierra Nevadas. They are stark and very beautiful. You should visit them if you get the chance."

Suddenly, a cone of snow lifted from the ground not fifty feet away from them. Patrick pointed. "Another snow devil, Perry."

"You mean a *snownado*." Perry smiled.

"Either works."

"Out of sight," Barry said. "I've never seen anything like that."

"They're rare elsewhere, but we get them fairly regularly, when the conditions are right."

The sun was almost shining through the snow fall, for now, but that could change quickly, and the temperature was barely up to five degrees. The sparse flakes were tighter, smaller. *Prisms*, he thought. *Like needles.* The whirling snow danced around the edge of the trees for a few more seconds, then disappeared.

George clapped his hands to get everyone's attention. "All right, then. If everyone could gather close, I'll explain the rules of the trail and show you how to operate these snow beasts." Patrick noticed that George's voice was hoarse. He hoped George wasn't coming down with something. "The most important thing to remember is to stay close to the machine in front of you and always on the trail. It's deep powder on either side of it in most places. You're likely to get stuck in it, and then we'll spend our whole day digging machines out of drifts."

Ari raised his hand. "I am too old and too fat for digging."

And my ribs hurt too bad, although I won't let that stop me. Patrick had bound his midsection tightly with lengths of Ace bandage before he'd gotten dressed. And he'd taken more Tylenol. That would have to do it.

George laughed. "Everyone digs. Also, the wildlife out here is wild. And moose are cranky in deep snow. Give them a wide berth if we see them."

Wes patted his hip. "Is everyone armed, in case we have to scare something off?"

Everyone from Wyoming answered in the affirmative. Patrick didn't get dressed without his knife, and he didn't go anywhere in the mountains without his .357 Magnum.

Cyrus said, "I missed the memo. But all I have back east is a deer hunting rifle."

Ari crossed his arms. "And out here it's the wild, wild west."

Dr. John waffled his hand. "In the west, it's every man for himself, against the wild. We all carry, but we rarely have reason to use a gun, except for hunting."

Speak for yourself. Patrick wished there'd been less cause for him to use his. He heard a vehicle engine and glanced down the hillside to the lodge. A green sedan had pulled up out front. *Terrible vehicle for the mountains in winter.* Was it the same one he'd seen at the gas station the day before? He turned back to George. As he did, his eyes passed over Abraham. The man looked almost scared. But of what, and why? Abraham backed up and worked his way to the far side of the group, where he donned a balaclava. When he had it adjusted over his face, he put on goggles.

He's just getting ready, Patrick realized.

He gave himself a mental shake. Time to tune back into George's talk. Patrick wasn't going to be the one who ended up needing to be dug out of a drift today.

CHAPTER TWENTY-ONE: SPEED

Perry

Perry wasn't sure when the sun had disappeared, and the snow had started falling harder. *Gradually.* It sure was pretty, even if it was getting harder to see. The tall pines were wearing snow caps, the rocks were like cupcakes with fluffy white frosting, and the terrain was endless marshmallow fluff. He'd barely looked around earlier. All of his attention had been on his snowmobile and the rooster tail thrown up by George's machine in the trail in front of him. He didn't even mind the exhaust smell that went with it. Now that he'd gotten the hang of it, he could look around more.

Man, he'd only thought he loved football and snow skiing. Snow-mobiling was better. Literally, it was the *best sport ever*. And the more it snowed, the cooler it got. With the way the stuff was coming down, tomorrow would be uh-mazing.

George raised his fist, a pre-arranged signal each of them was supposed to pass down the line to tell the group to stop. Perry raised his and hoped everyone else did the same, so they wouldn't crash into a pile-up. He brushed snow off his face shield and flipped it up as he slowed his snowmobile. The end of his scarf whipped him in the face. The flakes were hard, like pellets. He stuck out his tongue to catch them and they stung just a little. He had to work to keep his eyes open.

The gap between him and George grew smaller. Perry released pressure with his thumb on his throttle. After a few seconds, he gained ground on George again. He backed his speed down until his thumb trembled in the awkward position. When no one plowed into him from the back, he let off the gas altogether. George came to a complete stop. Perry goosed his snowmobile just enough to park neatly behind him. One by one, the engine noise of the snowmobiles quieted as all the riders shut them down.

George climbed onto the seat of his fancy Boss Cat and stood up. He made a megaphone around his mouth with his hands. "Is everybody having fun?"

The group cheered. Perry pumped a fist.

"Okay, then. Huddle up where you can hear me."

Everyone gathered closer. Perry waited on his seat but swiveled around to watch them. The other guys were being careful to walk single file on the packed trail. Those that had stepped off it during breaks earlier had ended up in snow to the knees. Or, in Perry's case, the waist.

He turned back around, admiring the blue and white Boss Cat. It really was a sweet ride. He wondered if George would be willing to let him take it for a spin. Not yet of course. The more practice he got in first, the better. It couldn't be later today, though. A musher was taking them dog sledding that afternoon. The next morning wouldn't work, either. They'd be going ice fishing at Meadowlark Lake. Personally, Perry would be more than happy to just fish from the shore. It seemed like winter had barely started, and he didn't trust that ice not to crack open and give him a deathly cold dunking. But tomorrow afternoon, they planned on doing more snowmobiling. That's when he'd ask George about trying the Boss Cat.

His dad sidled up and gripped Perry's shoulder. His Uncle Barry leaned against the sled from the other side.

Perry grinned at his dad and whispered, "Race ya back, old man."

His dad shook his head, eyes twinkling, but put a finger to his lips as George started talking again.

"It's time for us to head back to the lodge. The snow is coming down thick, so I need us to stay even closer together. Maintain eyesight of the person in front of you." George was raising his voice to be heard over the wind. "We took a lot of breaks on the way out here, but we'll be driving straight through on the way back. It should take us an hour. If you need to answer the call of nature, now is the time. Anyone?" He paused. Perry glanced around. No one raised a hand or headed for the woods. "Okay, yesterday, Abraham and I packed a turnaround loop in the park ahead of us. You can't see it because of the storm, but if you stay in line behind me, you'll be on it."

Ari raised his hand. "Do we call this a storm, or do we call it a blizzard? We do not have these in Israel. I am thinking blizzard."

Cyrus rolled his eyes at Dr. John. "He hasn't changed a bit since college. Still never shuts up."

Wes laughed. "This is nothing. Stick around through April." He and Ari had really hit it off. Ari was always clowning around, and Wes was one of the funniest people Perry knew.

Uncle Barry shivered in his ketchup-red coveralls. "Why does anyone choose to live in an unhospitable place like this?"

Why wouldn't they? Winter sports are the best. Perry sat a little taller, feeling proud to be Wyoming tough.

"Getting engaged has made you soft, shyster," his dad said.

Uncle Barry raised his hands in front of his chest. "Guilty."

"Any more questions?" George said. Ari opened his mouth, but

George held up a hand. "Any more *serious* questions?" Ari made a zipping motion across his lips. "We'll maintain the same order, with me first, and Abraham last." He put a thumb up. "Got it?"

Perry gave him a thumbs up. There were more thumbs and a few "got its" in reply.

"Great. Next stop, hot lunch at the lodge!"

Perry turned on the ignition, grasped the pull start, put his foot up on the runner of the snowmobile, and jerked as hard as he could. It took him five pulls to start it, but he didn't have to ask his dad for help, which was the best he'd done so far. George had started his machine in one pull but was standing on it again, watching the group get ready. He made a big O with his arms over his head, then nodded. Perry had seen George and Abraham signal each other this way before. It meant they both thought everything was okay, he guessed. George lowered himself onto his seat and hit the gas.

Movement caught Perry's attention, to his right near a stand of trees. It was hard to see what it was through the falling snow. Three, no, *four* big-eared mule deer bucks, walking toward the snowmobiles. *What are they doing here in the winter?* It seemed to him like every deer in the mountains had moved into the foothills down near Buffalo. There was a sign in the lodge that said the elevation was 7,700 feet. The bucks were close enough to him now that he could tell two of them were little more than spikes, a third had a decent enough rack, and the fourth had a monster set of antlers. The big boy —the stag—suddenly whirled and ran into the white gloom. The smaller bucks followed him. As quickly as they had appeared, they were gone. *Stag party.* Perry smiled.

He lowered his face shield and squeezed the throttle. The snowmobile jerked forward too fast, so he decreased the pressure. When he seemed to be about the right distance behind George, he followed him into the invisible turnaround loop, easing the skis to the right, then back to the left. Even though the loop was big, because of the low clouds and heavy snowfall he never saw the trees around the edge of the park, other than as dark shadows that felt like they were closing in. It was disorienting. He lost his sense of direction. Suddenly, they were crossing behind Abraham as he started the loop and George and Perry got back on the trail to the lodge. Perry was glad George was in the lead and knew where he was going.

Keeping a steady following distance wasn't hard, and Perry's mind soon wandered. There was nothing to see anymore because of the weather. The ride was strangely quiet, even though the machines were loud. Or maybe because they were. Usually when he went on hikes or drives or trail rides with his dad, there was lots of singing involved. His dad *loved* to sing. But with snowmobiling, all he could hear was engines. He kind of missed the singing. Maybe next weekend they could snowmobile one day and ski the other. His dad would sing on the ski lifts. Perry had gotten skis, boots, and poles for Christmas—from "Santa Claus," who his parents still insisted was real even though he and Trish were way too old to believe in that whole rigamarole anymore—and he was definitely asking for a snow-mobile for his birthday. A used one. He snorted. Like his cheapskate dad would ever get him one. But the kids at school would think Perry was so cool if he had a snow sled. John's smiling face flashed into his mind. Would he have liked snowmobiling? He hadn't liked horseback riding in the mountains, so Perry wasn't sure.

John's face was replaced by another. One that made his cheeks hot. Kelsey, the prettiest girl in their class. So pretty that John had a whopper crush on her. After he died, she and Perry had been sadder than any of their friends. Talking to each other had helped. He'd tried hard not to notice her silky hair or dark brown eyes, or the smile that made his stomach flip over. It had been a losing battle. Now, he had a hard time keeping her out of his head. She'd pop in there at weird times, like now, when he was snowmobiling in a blizzard. Truthfully, her last name kind of freaked him out, too. It was Jones. Like Ben's, but they weren't related. At least he didn't think they were. Maybe he should ask Trish.

His snowmobile suddenly hit a bump and caught air. It landed hard, jerking the handlebars from his hands. With his thumb off the throttle, the machine came to a quick stop. He lost sight of George instantly. Behind him, he heard another engine. His dad, too close. He was going to run into Perry. Perry grabbed for the handlebars and squeezed the throttle. The snowmobile surged forward, but with the handlebars cattywampus, the skis were pointing off trail. He let off the gas—too late—and tumped sideways in a huge snow drift. He had a sensation of falling.

After a moment spent in stunned silence, Perry laughed. The fall hadn't hurt him. He couldn't see anything, though. His face shield was full of snow. He pushed it up, dropping the snow out of it onto his chest. His laughing ended quickly when he realized his machine was sideways and in so deep, it was like being under water. He started swimming away from it. By the time he got uphill of the sled and had his feet on the ground, he discovered that the way back up to the trail was steep. It would have been hard to walk it even if he wasn't in three feet of snow, much less dragging an upended snowmobile.

"Dad?" he yelled.

There was no answer. Had his dad not seen him go off the trail? Was Perry by himself? Maybe it was just that no one could hear him. His machine was still running. He went back—not easy—and turned it off. Without its noise, he heard a thump and a crack and the engines of the other snowmobiles. They sounded close. *That's good.*

"Dad? George?" he shouted.

"What are you doing down there, bud? The trail's up here." It was Wes's voice, back up the trail a little way.

Perry saw his dad's and Wes's forms silhouetted above him. He waved. "I went over a bump and lost my grip on the throttle. Then I worried Dad would run into me, and I couldn't see George ahead of me. I hurried, and I think I gave it too much gas."

His dad said, "I'd say so. Are you okay?"

"I am. My snowmobile's stuck, though. Who all is up there?"

His dad sighed. "Well, I've caused a pile-up, so my guess is everyone."

"A wreck?"

"Kind of like bumper cars. Nothing bad, though."

Wes rotated his neck. "Says you. I think I have whiplash."

"Luckily you know a good doctor."

Wes guffawed. "Where's Dr. John when you need him?"

Perry hoped people weren't mad at him. "Sorry. Is George with you?"

"I don't see—actually, wait a second. I think I hear his snowmobile coming back. Yeah, here he is."

Perry was relieved. He didn't want to admit it, but he had more faith in George getting him out of this mess than his dad.

Within a minute, George, Ari, Dr. John, and Cyrus had joined Wes and his dad on the trail. There was lots of head shaking, teasing of Perry, and laughter. But it wasn't everyone. Abraham and his uncle Barry weren't there. Maybe they'd smashed up their machines and were too upset to look at him.

Perry had to know. "Um, where are Uncle Barry and Abraham?"

"I'm not sure," Wes said. "They were behind me going into the turnaround loop, but I don't know after that. Can't see sh-, uh, I mean anything in this storm."

"I hadn't even realized they weren't here. Abraham hasn't said a word all day," Ari said.

George peered back up the trail, then back at Wes and Perry's dad. "You need my help with Perry?"

Wes shook his head. "Nah. I've got it. Half of snowmobiling is digging out. I've got lots of experience."

"Thanks. You know there are shovels under the seats."

"Except for mine," Perry's dad said. "I took it out to make room for my medical bag."

George nodded." I'll just go find the others real quick. Gotta keep this group together. I'll be back in five."

Within seconds, George had disappeared back the way they'd come with a roar of his snowmobile.

Perry said, "Should I start digging or something?"

Dr. John shucked off his backpack. "Let's get you up here with us. I imagine we'll want to get your machine on its skis so we can tow it out." He unzipped his bag and dug around, then held up a rope. "Never leave home without a tow rope."

"I'll get the snowmobile righted and attach the rope," Wes offered.

"I defer to the younger and stronger man," Ari said.

Wes flexed his arm. His bulky coat made it look huge.

Dr. John sighed. "Ari has always had a talent for getting out of real work."

Cyrus said, "That's why he went into diplomacy. All jawing, no heavy lifting."

Perry wasn't sure what Cyrus meant, but Ari didn't argue with him or Dr. John.

"Perry, can you grab my hand?" his dad said.

"I can try." Perry scrambled as high as he could, then reached up. Their fingers were only a few inches apart. They clasped hands, until Perry's feet slipped out from under him. His glove came off in his dad's hand. Perry slid down a few feet.

His dad held up the glove. He was sort of bent over, and his face had a funny color to it. "Whoops."

"It's really steep at the top." Perry blew on his hand. He moved a few feet over and climbed as high as he could, then tried again.

"I've got you, Patrick," Wes said, grasping the back of his jacket.

Perry's dad leaned over the edge. He took a deep breath, but the color didn't come back to his face. This time, he was able to clamp his hand over Perry's wrist. "Gotcha." He grimaced.

Perry scrambled against the slope. It was a lot easier that time. He got a face full of snow, but in a few seconds, he was standing by the men, shoving his stiff, damp hand back into his glove. It was kind of scary how fast it had gotten cold. His dad put an arm around him. Perry was surprised to feel him shaking. Then he remembered. His dad's ribs were hurt.

Wes picked up a small shovel in one hand and the end of the rope that was now attached to the back of Dr. John's snowmobile in the other. "Tally ho." He stepped off the hill and slid down on his behind. When he found his footing, he tied the rope to a ring on the front of Perry's machine.

"Don't worry about me down here digging your kid's snowmobile out, Doc." Wes waved the shovel at Patrick. "You just stay up there and keep those expensive physician mitts safe." Snow started flying behind him as he shoveled.

Perry's dad shook his head. "Har de har har."

Dr. John said, "As hospital administrator, I approve of Patrick's role in this salvage operation."

Ari hefted a thermos in the air. "Cyrus and I will continue the important job of testing the hot chocolate. Me, because I can provide no additional value. Cyrus, because there's no telephone around."

Cyrus was the kind of guy everyone listened to, even though he didn't say much. He reminded Perry a little of his Grandpa Joe, only less grumpy. He held up a hand. Perry's dad, Dr. John, and Ari all turned toward him. Perry, too. "There's chatter out of the middle east. I'm lucky to even be able to break away for this weekend."

Ari snorted. "There's always chatter. You're on vacation. Give the job a rest."

"My job started the second I took the President's phone call and hasn't stopped since."

As was becoming the norm with everything Cyrus said, Perry had no idea what he was talking about, but he could tell Ari, Cyrus, and Dr. John really liked each other. They joked around like his dad and Uncle Barry.

Ari poured some cocoa. He offered it to Cyrus first, but Cyrus passed it on to Perry.

Perry took a sip. It was warm and sweet. "Thanks."

Cyrus smiled at him. "You looked like you could use a hot sip to warm you up."

He took the cup back and passed it around to the others.

Wes shouted up at them. "I've got it upright and pointed in the right direction. The rope is attached. Looks like if we can get about ten yards down the trail there's a section that will be easier to climb out of. Let me just start her engine and you can give me a tow, Dr. John."

"Got it," the older man said.

Perry scrambled to the edge of the slope and stood beside his dad. Wes was standing on the uphill runner of the Ski-Doo. He signaled with his hand to move out. Perry passed the signal to Dr. John, who gave his snowmobile some gas. The yellow snowmobile below started up, wallowing toward the downhill side, but Wes leaned his behind away from it uphill and pulled on the handlebars. The machine's engine whined as Dr. John pulled and Wes maneuvered it. It leveled out and lumbered forward.

"Now," Wes shouted.

"Now," Perry shouted. He pointed his thumb in the air, jerking his hand up and down.

Dr. John had been watching over his shoulder. He nodded. The engine noise increased. With one hand squeezing the throttle, Wes started jumping up and down on the uphill runner. The engine sounded stressed, but it kept going. Suddenly, the belt gained traction and the snowmobile jerked forward. The machine dug in and launched itself up, up, up, catching a little air as it crested the incline. Perry, who had followed the men down the trail without even realizing it, jumped backward out of the way.

"Yahoo," Wes shouted. He swung over the saddle.

Dr. John stopped pulling as soon as Wes landed. Wes positioned the snowmobile in the center of the trail.

Perry was on his rump and holding his breath. It came out in a rush. "Yeah." He jumped to his feet and threw his fists in the air. Behind him, he heard whoops and cheers from the rest of the guys. *I could barely get myself out of there, but Wes made that look easy.*

When the engines had been shut down, Perry ran up to Wes and slapped him a high five. "Far out."

Wes lifted his face shield. "Piece of cake."

A snowmobile engine approached from the trail behind them. It was George and the Boss Cat. He dismounted and trudged over to the group.

"Did you find them?" Perry's dad's voice had an edge.

But Uncle Barry and Abraham weren't with George. *Dad's worried.* Tingles ran up Perry's spine.

George's expression was grim. "Looks like they took a wrong turn. Dr. John, could you lead the group back in? I need to round up our strays. Neither of them know the area. Can't risk them getting stuck out overnight in this storm."

"By yourself?" Cyrus asked. "That doesn't seem safe."

"I can accompany you, if you wish," Ari said.

George shook his head. "I'll come back for help if I need it. We're not far from the lodge."

Perry was dying to be at the lodge in front of a big fire with a full belly, but not with Uncle Barry lost in the wilderness. Despite the weather, he'd felt mostly warm all day, but his tingles turned into a cold chill deep in his bones. Perry remembered the moment he'd lost sight of George before he went over the embankment. It wasn't so difficult to get separated. Uncle Barry had Abraham with him, though, and Abraham was a snowmobile expert. They'd be fine. Wouldn't they?

"I'm going with you, George." Wes climbed off Perry's snowmobile and crossed his arms over his chest.

"I agree. Wes should go with you, George. I'm fine with leading the group back to the lodge." Dr. John looked calm and confident. In Perry's experience, though, he always did.

George nodded. "That'll work."

Dr. John said, "Ari, you're my sweeper. The rest of you stay closer to me and each other than ever. We're going to ride in slow. Got it?"

Everyone answered in the affirmative. Perry snuck a look at his dad. He was mumbling something to himself and holding his helmet under one arm. His forehead was bright red where he was rubbing it with the other hand.

Wes walked toward his own snowmobile but turned back to Perry. "Keep it between the lines this time."

Perry nodded. He was planning on tailgating Dr. John big time. Getting stuck or lost out here like his uncle was *not* an option.

CHAPTER TWENTY-TWO: YEARN

Trish

Trish sat on her hands, trying to keep from biting her fingernails. She bounced a little on the hotel bed, eager for the women to leave.

"The stores are open, ladies. Time to shop." Dian stood and crossed her arms. "Who's with me?"

Trish pulled one of her hands out from under her thigh. She bit at the nail, but it was too short. She switched to a cuticle. It ripped. *Ouch.* A bright red drop of blood oozed up from the torn skin.

"Stop chewing on yourself, Trish," her mom said.

Trish snapped back before she could stop herself. "It's not like I'm not trying, *mother.*" She braced herself for a rebuke, but none came.

Her mom rolled her lips back and forth, like she was working lipstick into them, even though she hadn't put any on since she'd gotten back from IHOP. "There's a JC Penney at the mall. I thought we could get you clothes, shoes, and makeup all in one stop."

Trish's hand flew to her mouth for a chomp, but she stopped it in time. "I can't go to the mall. I'm waiting on Mrs. Sibley to call me back. You know that."

"Come on, Trish."

Esme put her purse strap over her shoulder. "We came to Denver to shop. Those that want to shop should leave now. The others can shop later."

"I'm not going." Trish shook her head. "I can't leave."

"I'll stay with you, then," her mom said.

Trish jumped to her feet. "I'm not a baby, Mom. I can wait for a phone call by myself. Go. Just go."

"But you're upset."

And having you here staring at me and questioning me won't help. "I'm fine."

"You haven't had anything to eat."

"I won't starve to death in one day."

Her mom rolled her lips again. "You can order room service for lunch. But do it like you would if your dad was here."

How could she eat when Ben was in jail? But she sat back down. "Okay."

"Good," Esme said. "It sounds like we have a plan."

Dian came over to the bed and sat by Trish. She put her arm around her and squeezed, then tipped her head against Trish's shoulder. "Let us bring you something. Would it be okay if I bought some makeup for you?"

Trish nodded. "That would be great."

"And a pair of Sasson jeans, maybe?"

A weak smile worked its way to the corner of Trish's lips. "That would be great, too."

"And could I pick you out a couple of tops? I'm good with color."

Dian had always been the most fashionable of her mother's friends. Trish laughed and nodded.

"Don't go overboard." Her mom's voice was dry, but she didn't say no.

Dian stood and smoothed her pleated pants. "I've always wanted a daughter. You know that. And yours is having a tough day. Let Aunt Dian spoil her a little. It will make me happy."

Dian would have been the perfect mother. But no, Trish was stuck with her own mom, who was so uncool and drove her crazy.

Her mom laughed. "Has anyone ever been able to tell you no?"

"Only one person." A shadow crossed Dian's face. "Now, are we ready?"

Trish's mom leaned down to whisper in her ear. "Are you sure you're all right alone?"

"Yes. Please, just go." Then Trish squared her shoulders. "Have fun. I'll see you guys later."

The three women grabbed their purses and walked out. Trish's mom turned around one last time, her face a worried frown.

Trish waved. The door shut behind them. She got up, threw the lock, and picked up the phone.

CHAPTER TWENTY-THREE: RESCUE

George

George stopped his snowmobile and got off, ignoring his growling stomach. By now, the group was probably back at the resort. Mrs. Murray would be ushering them into the lodge, where they'd be shedding boots, coats, hats, scarves, and gloves. The smell of her spicy chili and sweet cinnamon rolls would be filling the air. She'd serve them lunch in front of the enormous fireplace, which would be so hot it would make their faces red. Jenelle Murray might even be with them by now.

He pictured her pretty face and groaned. Meanwhile, he and Wes had been driving blind in the middle of a storm, with two of their party missing on the first guided snowmobile tour George had ever led. It was a nightmare. He'd never forgive himself if something had happened to Abraham or Barry. As it was, he wondered if Mrs.

Murray would give him another chance taking a group out. He wasn't sure he would in her shoes.

Wes walked up and stood beside him. George lifted his face shield and examined the tracks in the snow. Skis and belts.

"Two sets," Wes said.

"And definitely veering off the trail and creating one of their own."

George could follow them, even though visibility was bad. What he couldn't do was understand. Abraham was experienced with snowmobiles. With snow. With judging distance and following trails. With mountains. Even if he didn't have experience in the Bighorns specifically, it should have been no big deal for him to sweep the rear and keep Barry on track. If they had fallen behind, following the trail and tracks of the others shouldn't have been difficult for him. If nothing else, he would have noticed the difference between the packed trail and the fresh powder. It seemed impossible that he would have veered off the trail. But if he had, he was carrying a compass and should have been able to orient himself back in the right direction.

Wes echoed his thoughts. "Makes no dang sense."

"Maybe one of them is hurt." If Abraham was ill or injured and Barry was in charge, that could account for the disorientation. Maybe. Abraham would have to be seriously out of commission, though.

"I hear something."

George heard it, too, although sound was muffled through his balaclava and helmet. Snowmobile engines, heading toward them from a different direction altogether. Barry and Abraham coming back? If so, they'd driven in a circle, because their tracks clearly led in the opposite direction of the sound he was hearing. He turned toward the noise, squinting, then lowered his face shield again. "They're coming from behind us."

Bright yellow snowmobiles emerged through the white. *Both yellow. Ski-Doo.* Not Abraham, at least, as he was on George's Rupp, a red Sprint. The machines stopped just short of where George and Wes were standing. George lifted a hand in greeting. He couldn't identify the riders through the balaclavas and the face shields of their helmets. When the snowmobiles started up again and went around them without the men even speaking to them, he knew it wasn't anyone from their party. Or anyone that followed back country etiquette. *Didn't even say hello or ask us if we need help. No chance to ask if they'd seen Abraham and Barry.*

Wes broke the silence. "They aren't the friendly sort."

George snorted. "They better hope we don't find them on the trail needing our help later."

George and Wes returned to their machines and re-started them. A sense of urgency was building in George. He'd been sure they'd find Abraham and Barry on the trail. But it was clear now that the two could be anywhere. It was a vast wilderness with hazards he didn't want to think about. They'd just have to catch up to them and bring them back before they got themselves so lost or injured that they froze or starved to death. He shuddered as he climbed back on his machine and gunned it into the face of the storm.

And before they get Wes and me lost or in trouble out here, too.

CHAPTER TWENTY-FOUR: DESPAIR

Laramie, Wyoming
Friday, December 30, 1977, 1:00 p.m.

Ben

Ben picked at the empty Styrofoam cup between his hands. It had held water, which he'd gulped down. He felt out of place in a fancy lawyer's office, especially after where he'd spent the night. Here, there were overstuffed armchairs. There, hard benches. Striped wallpaper instead of iron bars. The smell of warm banana bread on a plate in front of him versus the horrible animalistic smells in the jail.

Possibly the biggest contrast of all: the attorney with the kind eyes across the desk from him—Les Packer compared to the taunting guard. Packer had sprung him and taken him to get his truck. He was speaking in a calm, friendly voice to Ben now. "My friendship with Henry goes back a long way, to our freshman year together here at U-Dub. You're a freshman there now?"

It was hard to picture the two men as friends. Henry, a rough and tumble rancher, and this attorney with soft, white hands and a moon-shaped face. Packer's body was doughy. His face, while unlined, was red-nosed and looked years older than Henry's. But Packer had proved the friendship was real when he'd shown up for Ben on nothing but Henry's say-so.

"Haven't started school yet. Just got here," Ben said.

"Henry filled me in a bit." *That's code for "I know all the bad stuff about you."* Packer's voice turned serious. "We need to talk about what happened last night. Can you tell me your story from the beginning?"

Ben didn't want to think about it, but he was afraid it would be something he'd never forget. He had to face it. It was hard to get himself to force the first words out. He didn't know where to begin or what to say. After a long silence, he finally found a starting place. "It was my first night here. My roommate Chad insisted on taking me out to welcome me to town. We had a hamburger somewhere, and then we went to a bar. I had one beer. Chad was drinking a lot."

"Drunk?"

"I'd say so." Ben stopped.

"Go on."

"He started, uh, talking to a girl. Sophie."

"Had you ever met her before?"

"No. And I barely met her last night. Chad and Sophie said they wanted to go back to the dorm. Chad was my ride. I told them I had to start my new job in the morning, but they promised not to keep me up long. On the way out to the car, I took Chad's keys because I didn't want him driving us."

"Were you drunk?"

"No, sir. I only had that one beer." He shrugged. "I didn't have money for another. The bartender was disgusted with me. He might even remember me as the guy taking up space and not buying anything."

"Then what?"

Packer asked a lot of questions, but Ben didn't feel badgered. It was helping, some. "Then a cop pushed me up against Chad's car.

Sophie threw a fit about not wanting to be with us, which the officer decided meant I was forcing her to come. The cop let Chad walk her back to the bar, and then he never came back."

"Chad didn't?"

"Right. The officer found drugs in my coat pocket and in the glove box of Chad's car."

The attorney drilled Ben with his eyes. "Were they your drugs?"

"No, sir. I'd never seen them before. To tell you the truth, I'd never seen *any* drugs before. I've been in trouble—I'm sure you know that—but it wasn't because of drugs. Since I've lived with the Sibleys, I work and go to school or hang out with my girlfriend Trish at one of our houses, with her parents or Vangie and Henry. I'm, well, pretty square." He remembered the sting when Chad had thrown that word out about him.

"Chad said the drugs weren't his."

Ben slumped forward and put his head in his hands. "I don't know about the stuff in my pocket, but it's hard to believe the drugs in the car weren't his. And he had plenty of chances to put something in my coat pocket, too."

"Could anyone corroborate that?"

Ben frowned. He didn't want to seem dim, but the word was new to him. "Corrobo—"

"Did anyone see Chad with the drugs, or see him put them in the car or your pocket?"

"I'm not sure how I would know that. I didn't even see it myself."

The attorney pushed back from the table and stood. "Henry vouches for you."

Ben nodded. His eyes felt prickly dry and yet wet at the same time. *Don't you dare cry. Don't you dare.*

"But I've got to be straight with you. The drugs in your pocket are a problem. The car, not as much. Unless your fingerprints are on the bags or the glove box."

"They won't be on the bags. Not any of them, even the one in my pocket."

"That would be good."

Ben wiped his forehead. "But I might have put my hands on the door to the glove compartment. I rode in the passenger seat. I don't remember one way or the other."

Packer walked slowly back and forth in his office, in front of a wall of diplomas and photographs, then by the window with the view of the red brick buildings on the other side of the wide downtown street. "If it wasn't for your juvie record, this would be a first offense. Unfortunately, kidnapping is considered a violent crime, which means your record is fair game in adult court. But that was your only brush with the law, correct?"

"Yes, sir."

"No prior drug arrests?"

"Never."

"That will help."

"And my girlfriend, Trish. She's the one—"

He held up a hand. "I know, son. I know. I'm not sure how a judge will look on that. Your release for good behavior is a positive, though."

"Trish would testify for me. She'd tell the court my dad and uncle made me do it. And that if I hadn't, they would have hurt her."

Packer took a chair beside Ben, no desk between them, and leaned toward him. He put his hand on Ben's shoulder. "I'm not judging you. But I wouldn't be doing my job if I didn't help you face what you're up against."

Ben's hand contracted and smashed the cup. Embarrassed, he tried to return it to its original shape, but couldn't. He looked up. "I know. And it includes a roommate who's a liar and a user."

Packer nodded. "If we're lucky, we're going to find he has a record for drug offenses. And that your prints aren't on the bag in your pocket. With those two things, we might get you off clean. I just can't make any promises."

"Because of the kidnapping thing."

"Well, yes, and because the drugs were in your coat and there aren't any witnesses that saw someone else put them there."

Ben bit down on the inside of his lip.

"Do you have any questions for me?"

He had a million. *What happens next? How will I get my job back? Will I be expelled? How do I get out of living with Chad?* But he shook his head. "Not right now."

Packer stood again. "I'm sure you'd like a shower and a nap before Henry and Vangie get here."

"I don't want to go back to my dorm room. I never want to see Chad again."

Packer walked to the office door. Ben realized he was supposed to follow him and did. "Fair enough. Why don't you grab some things from there, though? I'll call my wife and let her know to expect you at our house. You can get something to eat and shower there. Then when Henry and Vangie arrive, you can figure out how to handle the roommate situation together."

Heat rushed into Ben's face. He hadn't expected the kindness. "Thank you," was all he managed to get out.

"Let's meet back here at four, then. All of us." He stopped Ben with a firm handshake. "No matter what, son, you're going to be okay. This is just one moment in your life. You'll get past it."

Ben couldn't even muster a thank you. If he said anything, he'd cry. So, he nodded, swallowing down the huge lump in his throat, and bolted for his truck, which was parked out on the street. He jerked the door open. The meeting had gone as well as it could. The attorney was nice, he was just wrong. This wasn't only one moment in Ben's life. With his history, he'd never get past it. If he stayed here, this is how it would be for him forever.

CHAPTER TWENTY-FIVE: PLUG

Patrick

The falling snow closed around the dog teams and mushers like a heavy curtain, giving Patrick a touch of vertigo. He could barely see the lead dog's black and white body. Just a few days ago he'd been raving about the properties of snowflakes. *What was I thinking?* They all blended now. Too many for too long. And dogsledding, which had seemed like a good idea after lunch, didn't anymore. Not just because the motions of the dog sled—the turns, the bumps, the swoops, the tips, the jerks, and the jolts—were stronger than the four extra-strength Tylenol he'd downed with lunch for his aching ribs, but because Barry hadn't returned yet.

One of the snowmobiles probably broke down. My worrying from here doesn't help. Wes and George have got this.

But Patrick wasn't buying the empty assurances he was dishing out to himself.

Nine ecstatic dogs threw themselves flat-out around a curve on the forest trail. The snow-covered trees leaned inward, making the trail seem like a tunnel. He shifted his weight on the sled runners and his grip on the basket. The centrifugal force pulled at his ribs, messed with his sense of up and down, and sent a churning through his stomach. He prayed there wasn't a moose twenty feet in front of the dogs. If there was, he'd never see it in time to set the anchor brake. They'd be after it, dragging him either to bounce along in rough terrain or to fall out of the basket and do more damage to his side.

What had the musher been thinking giving Patrick his own sled?

From the basket, Perry whooped. His son was almost as ecstatic as the dogs. Patrick was happy that Perry was happy, but he just wanted the sledding to be over. To try it another day when it wasn't so painful, and he wasn't so worried about Barry.

The dogs bounded down a straight section of trail, the homestretch to the lodge. Patrick drew in a shuddering, relieved breath. The outbuildings appeared first, dark shadows behind white static, looming ever closer. Behind him, he knew two more teams had to be careening down the trail, too, but he couldn't hear them. Couldn't hear anything except the wind rushing past his ears and the runners sliding over the snow.

The dogs shushed up to a big wooden barn that saw heavy summer usage in trail riding season. Patrick and Susanne had taken the kids on a ride with Clear Creek when they had come up for Patrick's original job interviews several years before. The resort horses wintered off the mountain, and the barn doors were open, revealing a dark, empty cavern. The owner of the dogs had staged them there prior to the sledding, and it was where they were to disembark as well.

"Whoa," Patrick stepped on the foot brake two times, signaling to the dogs. After they'd slowed, he set the anchor and added his weight to it.

Perry was already scrambling out of the basket before it had come to a complete stop. "Whoa, fellas. Whoa." When he turned to

Patrick, his eyes were full July fourth sparkle. "I can't believe we just did that. Like *Call of the Wild*." Patrick and Susanne had taken turns reading the book aloud after dinner in front of the fire the previous winter, and their teens had loved it, although Trish would never have put it in those words. "Do you think Ferdie could pull a sled?"

Patrick glanced back at the others. All three teams had been silent and focused on the trail, but the chaos of their high-pitched barks and leaping beforehand had made Patrick a little edgy, and the pandemonium of stopping compounded the feeling. He needed more order from life and animals. And he'd learned a few things about sled dogs in the last hour, or at least these Huskies in particular. They lived to run. Most of them had arresting blue eyes, while several had one blue eye and another of a different color. They loved to "talk," mostly in howling "woos." And commands were more like suggestions, hence the dual braking system.

The two other sleds were approaching fast, one after the other. Dr. John was driving the first team with Cyrus in the basket, and Ari had the other with the musher riding. Dr. John's team stopped, but Ari's dogs broke the anchor free and ran forward, yelping.

"Set the brake," the musher yelled.

Ari stomped on it again, putting his entire body weight into it, and the dogs gave in, but not before they'd overtaken Dr. John's sled. They loudly and enthusiastically tangled themselves with the other team in a thrashing of zero body fat and fuzzy hair of black, silver, red, and white.

Cyrus jumped off his sled and shot Ari a look. "By my count, that's the third time in our friendship you've tried to kill me." He ticked on his fingers. "Motorcycling during summer break from college. Skiing in the Alps after your fourth wedding. And now this."

Ari said, "Quit complaining and start helping."

The musher groaned. His assistant, who had led the way via snowmobile and arrived first, came running out of the trees, hitching up the straps of his coveralls and dragging his coat by one arm. He headed straight for the happy scrum of animals.

Patrick raised his eyebrows at Perry. "Ferdie'd be out of control. Just like those guys."

"Maybe he could pull me by himself on our snow disc." His son breathed out his next words with reverence. "Or on skis."

The musher clapped his gloved hands for their attention. He pulled up his goggles, revealing his droopy eye. Patrick had been wondering about it since seeing it earlier. *A stroke? Myasthenia gravis? A tumor? Diabetes? A simple stye?* "The first thing a musher does after a run is take care of his team. Everybody needs to pitch in to secure the dogs and get them fish and water." He lifted the lid of a huge cooler. It was filled with ice and intact, halved frozen fish.

Two yellow snowmobiles burst into their midst, narrowly avoiding the dogs. One of the riders unbuckled her helmet and wrestled it off. Long brown hair tumbled out and over her jacket. Patrick pegged her age at early twenties. She yelled something, then switched off the ignition on her machine and motioned for her companion to do the same. The cessation of their roar gave way to the yipping of the dogs.

"There's a man hurt. His friend sent us to get help." She pointed. "Out there."

"Who is it?" Patrick said.

"I don't know. But he's hurt pretty bad."

"I'm a doctor. I can go."

"You can't go alone. I'll come, too," Dr. John said, joining Patrick in two strides.

"We can show you the way out to them if you want to grab snowmobiles from the shed," the young woman said.

Cyrus frowned. "Should I call for an ambulance?"

The woman nodded, saying, "Yes," at the same time Patrick and Dr. John did.

Cyrus wheeled and started high stepping through the snow down the path to the lodge.

"What do I do, Dad?" Perry sounded steady and mature.

Patrick squeezed his son to his side, ignoring the pain. "Help with the dogs, son."

Ari raised a hand. "I'm on dog duty, too."

Patrick turned to Dr. John. "I'll grab my medical kit and meet you at the snowmobiles, then?"

The young woman said, "And I'll help you with the machines. I'm Jenelle Murray, by the way. My parents own this place. That's my friend, Mandy." Her face dimpled, although she didn't quite smile.

The other snowmobiler lifted a hand in greeting.

Dr. John nodded at her. "Thanks, Jenelle. I'm Dr. John. This is Dr. Flint. Between us, you'll have half the doctors from Buffalo with you. Patrick, see you at the machines."

Patrick was wading through the snow, stymied by the depth of the accumulation and the grade of the slope down to the resort. Cyrus, with his long legs, had made it look easier. Patrick pumped his knees higher and spread his arms wide for balance. Soon, sweat was trickling down his back and his breathing grew ragged. But he didn't stop. Couldn't stop. No matter who it was out there, they needed his help.

He had a horrible feeling, though, that it was going to be someone he knew and cared about very much.

CHAPTER TWENTY-SIX: FLEE

Vangie

Vangie tapped her foot and hugged herself. She was waiting for Henry at the front door of Ben's dormitory. He'd run up to get Ben, who hadn't answered his phone, and hadn't been at Les Parker's home or office when they arrived in Laramie. What a horrible start to what should have been the most exciting time of his life. One that might have serious long-term repercussions. She wished she'd insisted on helping Ben with his move the day before. Everything would have been different. Navigating the space between friend and parent-come-lately with a nineteen-year-old foster son was tricky. This wasn't the first time she felt like she'd gotten it wrong.

Back in high school in rural Tennessee, she'd known a kid like Ben. One from a bad family whose members disappeared one by one on him. Rooster, that had been his name. She and her friends had shunned him, like Rooster had a contagious disease instead of just a funny name, and their parents had encouraged them to keep their distance. Yet she couldn't recall a single thing the boy had done to put them off. He'd been shy. Courteous. Clean, if poorly dressed. Hungry, with sad, hollow eyes.

By the time they graduated, he'd been arrested a couple of times for theft. For stealing *food*. A year later, she'd heard he was in prison for armed robbery. She wondered where Rooster was now, and whether she could have made a difference for him, even a small one, if she'd tried.

It wasn't what had driven her to ask Henry if they could provide a home for Ben. She hadn't even remembered about Rooster until recently, after she'd grown to love Ben. Rooster's story had come back to her like a nightmare. *Not Ben. Not on my watch.* Despite her vow to herself, she was starting to see, though, that there was much she wouldn't be able to protect Ben from. Some things that she could have. Wished she had. A tremor rocked her. *There will be much I can't protect Hank from, either.*

She wiped a tear from the corner of her eye. Ben and Henry could be down any second. She couldn't let Ben see her cry. She had to show him confidence and strength. But what was keeping them? She just thought the drive from Story to Laramie had been hard, worrying about Ben the whole way and unable to get to him any faster.

Vangie leaned against the brick wall beside the door. To her, college had been the time of her life. After two years in Vanderbilt in Nashville, she'd taken a summer road trip to Yellowstone with her roommates. They'd stopped for gas in Laramie, where she'd met a good-looking cowboy at the next pump over. The trip would have been fantastic, even without meeting him, but it was a huge bonus to discover Wyoming and Henry Sibley at the same time.

Henry had pretended he was on his way to Yellowstone, too. He'd caravanned across the state with them, and they'd hung out together over the next week. It wasn't until the trip back to Laramie— with Vangie now riding in his truck—that he'd confessed to her that the trip had been a spontaneous one on his part, just to spend a little more time with the cute, brown-eyed girl with the Tennessee accent that tickled his ears and made his head spin.

She'd transferred to the University of Wyoming for her senior year, and they'd married and both gone to work on Piney Bottoms after graduation. She couldn't help but smile at the memory.

But Ben was starting his time in college with a stint in jail, fighting drug charges. She wished she could turn him around and take him home. Away from this mess. Give him a do-over somewhere else. Instead, they were going to meet with Les about Ben's defense. After that . . . she wasn't sure. But they'd have to figure something out.

She pushed up her jacket and glanced at her wristwatch. Henry had been inside for ten minutes. What was taking so long? Maybe Ben was packing. Or was in the shower.

Then the glass door swung open. Vangie straightened and turned toward it, widening her smile for Ben's benefit. It was a kid about Ben's age, but not Ben. Short, with skin like an English milkmaid, rosy to the point of pink. It looked like he had his hand over a bloody nose. She felt a flash of sympathy for him, but he wasn't her problem, and a bloody nose wasn't fatal.

She sighed and turned her waiting eyes back on the door. It was cold. She was coming unglued from the energy bursting out of her. Pacing the sidewalk sounded like a better option than just standing there, until she tried it. When she came out of the shelter of the building, the frigid wind buffeted her back.

She turned away from it and saw Henry. He was alone.

She ran to meet him. "Where's Ben?"

Her husband's mouth was a grim line.

When he didn't answer fast enough, she grabbed his arm, jerking it and him toward her. The Tennessee deep inside her came out in her stricken voice. "Where is Ben, Henry?"

He held out a piece of paper. "His roommate gave me this. That, and some lip."

"What is it?" She took it from him and unfolded it.

Henry said nothing.

Vangie read it, starved for information. *I can't do this. I have to go. I'm sorry, but I'll be fine. Thank you for everything. You are the best. Tell Hank I love him. Ben*

The paper fluttered from her hand into the breeze and tumbled across a snowy patch of grass. Henry ran after it and snatched it up.

Vangie sank to her knees, put her face in her hands, and sobbed.

CHAPTER TWENTY-SEVEN: REJECT

Trish

Water had run off the ketchup leaving a red mound on the edge of the plate. Trish dunked a room temperature French fry in the gooey part. It didn't stick, but she stuffed the fry in her mouth anyway. She chewed and swallowed without tasting anything, then pushed the plate away. She'd choked down half a cheeseburger and a handful of fries since lunchtime, more out of nerves than hunger. In the background, the television had been droning all day. Cartoons. Soap operas. Now some sort of after school special, even though school was still out for Christmas break. It didn't matter. She wasn't paying any attention to it.

All her energy was directed at the phone, willing it to ring.

She inspected her fingers. The cuticles were ragged, red, and swollen. She had nothing left to gnaw on. Her eyes roamed the walls. The hotel room had seemed so luxurious to her before. Now it felt claustrophobic. The windows wouldn't even open—Trish had tried. She needed fresh air, but she couldn't leave.

And then the phone rang.

Finally! It had only rung once since her mom had left, and that time it had been her checking in on Trish. *Please don't let it be Mom again.*

She snatched it up. "Hello?"

"Trish?" It was Mrs. Sibley. Clearly, recognizably Vangie Sibley. But Trish had never heard her voice sound this high-pitched before or stretched this tight. A section of barbed wire fence in one syllable.

Trish sprang off the bed like she'd been cattle prodded. "Yes. It's me. What is it? Is everything okay?"

A long pause. "Have you talked to Ben?"

"No. Is he out of, um, jail?" Trish hated the taste of the word in her mouth.

"He hasn't called you?"

I already told her I haven't talked to him. Was Mrs. Sibley insinuating Trish had done something wrong? "No. Why?"

"You didn't call him?"

"I've tried his room, but there's been no answer."

"I need you to think carefully about this before you answer me. I need the absolute truth, no matter what it is."

"I've been telling you the truth. I swear." Trish's voice broke. "You're scaring me."

Mrs. Sibley barreled on. "Do you know where he went?"

Trish pressed her palm against her forehead. She'd thought she was all cried out, but the tears were coming again. Mrs. Sibley didn't know where Ben was. "N-n-n-no. Where is he?"

Mrs. Sibley didn't answer.

Then Mr. Sibley's voice replaced hers on the line. "Hello, Trish. Ben met with our attorney earlier, after he got out of . . . custody. We're at the lawyer's office now. Ben was supposed to pick up some things from his dorm room and head over to the attorney's house."

Trish's voice came out a hoarse whisper. "Mr. Sibley, what happened? Is Ben missing?"

"He left a note at his dorm room. For us. It sounds like he's left town, but he didn't say where he was going. Or when he was coming back. We were hoping you'd know."

Trish staggered along the wall, propping herself off it with one hand. "I haven't talked to him since he left Buffalo. He doesn't even know how to reach me in Denver. But I don't understand. Why would he leave?"

"The attorney said Ben was really upset when they met."

"But Mrs. Sibley told me he didn't do the things he was accused of."

Mr. Sibley sounded tired and sad. "None of us believe he did. The attorney had to explain to him that that doesn't mean he won't still be convicted, though."

"Why? How?"

"Even though we believe someone planted drugs on him, the police found them on him. And he has the juvenile record."

"I could testify. It wasn't his fault."

"I know you would. Bottom line, though, we don't know where he is. If he contacts you, will you let us know, please?" Henry recited the attorney's phone number. Trish grabbed the hotel note pad and pen and scribbled it down. "In the meantime, we'll be staying here a day or two in case he comes back."

After promising she'd call, Trish dropped the phone without hanging up the receiver. She pulled at her hair and paced back and forth from the window to the door. *What have you done, Ben?* To the window. *Where have you gone?* To the door. *And why, why, why would you just leave?* Back to the window, where she stopped and twisted the promise ring on her finger. He'd only given it to her yesterday, and now he was gone. Unless . . . unless he was trying to find her? And he had to be. He wouldn't take off somewhere without telling her, without telling the girl he intended to marry someday.

At least, she hoped not. Hoped against hope.

And then she stiffened. She might not know *why* he would disappear, but she did have an idea about where he'd go. It was wrongheaded and crazy, but if she was right, she had to move fast. Get back to Buffalo. Because first, he'd go home. He'd think Trish would be in Buffalo. He'd go to her house, but she wouldn't be there. She tried to think like Ben. Would he wait? He hadn't waited on the Sibleys. Then what would he do? Grab his things from Piney Bottoms and . . . leave?

Her heart was racing, and if she'd had on her track shoes, she would have already been running down the hall and out of the hotel. She had to get home. Get her truck. Go after him. Catch him before he did something stupid.

But how would she get there? Her mom wouldn't be back for an hour or two. Maybe more if she went out to dinner with Dian and Esme before they came back to the hotel. That would be too late, even if Trish could convince the others that they had to leave Denver immediately.

If she had enough money, she could take a bus. Buses stopped in Buffalo every day.

After a few frantic minutes—like Ferdinand searching for a lost ball in the house—she found her purse on the counter in the bathroom, then rifled through it and dug into her wallet. Her Christmas money. This year she'd asked for contributions to the "Trish Flint gas fund" for her truck, and both sets of grandparents had sent perky giftwrapped boxes of cash, through the mail, which her mom had said was nuts. But Trish was happy they'd done it because that meant she had forty dollars.

Forty whole dollars.

Would it be enough to get her home? She hefted the Yellow Pages off the desk and plopped down with it on the bed. Found a number for Greyhound. Called them. Asked about their prices, schedule, and location.

She pumped a fist. She had enough cash. Way more than enough to get to Casper and from Casper to Buffalo. No need to pack up her suitcase and take it. It would be a hassle on the bus, and her mom could bring it home. She grabbed her purse and put on her coat.

Then she stopped. How was she going to get to the bus station? It was too far to walk.

A taxi, she decided, and felt very mature and cosmopolitan. She would call a taxi.

And in Buffalo, once she arrived—how would she get from the bus to her house, where her truck was parked in the driveway? It was two or three miles in winter weather. Walking would cost her time she didn't have. Running was an iffy idea. The roads and sidewalks might be slick. She didn't have her running shoes. And she wasn't in tip top shape after taking her post cross country season break.

She'd have to find a ride. A year ago, she would have been comfortable asking her friend Marcy for any favor. They were BFFs. But things between them hadn't been the same since their basketball coach had gone to prison for murder, with Trish one of the people who had testified against her. Added to that Trish spending more time with Ben than she did with her friends and Marcy wanting a boyfriend of her own more than anything, and the two of them had drifted apart.

I'll call her in Casper. And I'll make it up to her.

Trish crossed her fingers and headed for the door.

CHAPTER TWENTY-EIGHT: FIND

Bighorn Mountains, Wyoming
Friday, December 30, 1977, 4:00 p.m.

George

Yellow against white. A snowmobile. Abraham was riding on a red one, but could the yellow machine be Barry? Between the speed of the machine and the weather, as soon as George had glimpsed it, it was gone.

He and Wes had been searching for the missing men for hours now. Who knew how many—he'd quit checking his watch and he'd stopped paying attention to his growling stomach. The storm. It didn't just make it harder to find the men. It made the search for them more dangerous, and the probability that they'd find them in trouble higher. They'd been through this park earlier, and there had been nothing and no one here, but they had decided to retrace their paths. The lost men could be driving in circles. If they didn't find them soon, they were going to have to call the search off for the night. Sunset was coming quickly, in less than an hour, he'd expect. By now

Mrs. Murray would have reported the situation to Search & Rescue. They'd have reinforcements when the search continued.

If it had to. Because he wasn't giving up until he had to.

He accelerated, jumping to his feet on the runners and craning his neck to see over a rise that snuck up on him. In the near distance, he spotted two mounds. No red. No yellow. Just the mounds, and they were almost upon them. The snow-covered ground between them looked like a terrible place to park their own machines. He braked and lifted a fist in the air for Wes, hoping he was close enough to see him, before one of them or both barreled over the mounds. George vaulted off his snowmobile without waiting to find out.

It was hard going in the thigh-deep snow, but he fought his way forward. The closer he got, to the mounds, the more certain he was that he'd found people. And when he was thirty feet or so from them, Abraham leaned around one of the mounds, his helmet on and his face shield lifted. He waved George toward him. The look on the man's face was pinched. Pained.

George drew closer. He could see Abraham kneeling over something on the ground behind the mounds. Not something. George saw a prone figure near or under one of the mounds—which he knew now were the snowmobiles, buried in snow—a patch of scarlet around his body. Someone. And not just any someone. A dark-haired man with a familiar profile and recognizable red coveralls. Barry. One of his tour customers. Dr. Flint's brother-in-law. From a distance, it looked like his eyes were closed, and he wasn't moving. *Please God let him be alive.* The silent prayer was heading up before George realized it had entered his mind. He'd been raised in a praying household, but he'd gotten away from it in the last few years. This seemed like a good time to resurrect the practice. He did it again, this time on purpose. *Please God let him be alive and let us get him out of here safely.*

"See them?" he shouted to Wes, even though the lanky man had caught up and was standing next to him. The wind seemed to catapult voices into a soundless void.

"Yes!" Wes didn't stop, just kept wading through the snow toward Abraham and Barry.

When George had agreed that Wes would accompany him on the search, he'd done so because of the man's strong snowmobile and mountaineering skills. As they approached Barry, though, he thought of Wes's medical expertise, which he knew about firsthand after seeing him in action during the weeks George had worked on an electrical project at the hospital. George knew the man pitched in with whatever, whenever. The doctors relied on him heavily. It would have been even better to have Dr. Flint or Dr. John out there, but Wes was a godsend. For George, and for Barry.

Wes reached the men first, but George wasn't far behind. Barry's eyes fluttered open. George heard him groan. He still couldn't tell if he was pinned under the snowmobile or simply close to it.

Wes knelt beside the men. "Tell me what happened."

Abraham shot a glance at George, but the man couldn't hold George's gaze. George glared at him. They had an injured client to take care of right now. But, later, Abraham had some serious explaining to do.

Abraham spoke in his formal, clipped tone. "He flipped. The snowmobile landed on him. The mirror broke off. The metal arm impaled his side."

That sounded bad, and from the horrified expression on Wes's face, George got the confirmation he wasn't looking for.

"How long ago?" Wes said.

Barry wheezed. "A lifetime, feels like."

"Half an hour. Forty-five minutes at most. Two young women came by on snowmobiles from the resort only a short while afterwards. They went back for help at my request."

Wes cocked his head. "You left it on him. In him."

Abraham closed his eyes. There was a grayish white cast to his nose. George wanted to punch him in it. "I didn't have anything I could use to close his wound. I was afraid that if I lifted it—removed it—he'd bleed to death. There's been a great deal of blood. And I'm quite worried about shock."

Wes's forehead wrinkled into a stack of lines, like books with blank spines facing out. "Good call. I think he looks shocky, too."

George wasn't sure what shocky looked like, but Barry's skin was pale and seemed a little damp. His breathing was fast and shallow. None of that was good, but then the man did have a piece of metal jammed into him.

"Are you a physician?" Abraham asked.

Wes held the back of Barry's wrist in his palm, his fingers on the exposed veins. "No. But as far as Barry goes right now, I'm close enough."

Abraham nodded slowly. "With the three of us working together, we might be able to move him."

"A place out of the wind and snow where we could build a fire would be good," Wes said, pulling Barry's coat sleeve over his wrist. "His heart rate is on the high side."

"I'm right here," Barry said. His voice was weak, but his sense of humor was intact. "Not dead. Not unconscious."

Abraham ignored him. "In my opinion, it would be best to find the shelter and build the fire before we attempt to move him from this location. Start some water boiling. Possibly we might find materials with your machines or on your persons that we could use to slow the bleeding and for these other purposes."

"I'll check," George said. Returning to his Boss Cat for his backpack, George kept an ear on their conversation. He had matches, kindling, a small pot, a canteen, extra outerwear, and a shovel in the bag. And maybe some other things that Abraham and Wes would find helpful. He'd bring Wes's pack, too, while he was at it.

"I see some rocks over there." Wes stood and waved an arm. "I'll go check it out on foot. I don't want to waste time digging out the sled."

George lugged the backpacks over. "I've got what we need to get a fire going and water boiling. Matches, fire starter, paper."

"Give them to me. If I find us a spot, I'll get everything going before I come back to help with Barry."

Abraham rubbed his chin. "What about tape?"

George frowned. "A roll for the snowmobiles, for burst hoses and the like."

"Good. When you return, we can lift the snowmobile and pack Barry's wound with fabric and wrap his torso in tape. It is better than nothing, I think."

"Now? Or when I come back?" Wes asked.

"When you return. I will surround the wound with the cleanest and most absorbent fabrics while you are gone."

"10-4. I'll hurry."

George fished the supplies from his bag. Wes stuffed them down the front of his jacket and zipped it up. He saluted Abraham and George with two fingers, then hunched over and plowed toward the rocks. The white park looked like a bowl of whipped cream, peaked in spots, wavy in others. Wes took one step, stomping it all the way down, then took another and another, slowly moving across the park. Soon he was thigh-high, which was saying a lot for a man with legs like a stork.

George turned away from Barry to question Abraham as soon as he thought Wes was out of earshot. Abraham was searching through the backpacks. He had pulled out George's hooded Sheridan Broncs sweatshirt.

"How in Hades did you get yourself and Barry separated from the group?" George hissed, whispering.

Abraham stood, sweatshirt trailing from his hand, his eyes on Barry, his voice even lower than George's. "I tried to slip away unnoticed, but Barry kept turning back to look for me. He saw me leave and followed. I didn't intend for that to occur."

George hadn't expected that answer. A hollow opened inside him that was quickly filled with burning fury. "You left us on purpose? On my snowmobile?"

Abraham's eyes flicked up. They looked as tortured as the night before when he'd woken from his nightmare to discover he'd attacked George. "They're here. They followed me here."

Was Abraham crazy? "What do you mean?"

Abraham's mouth opened and shut several times. He looked away for a moment. When his eyes returned to George's, they had gone blank. "I—never mind. I became discombobulated. It is humiliating to admit, for someone of my experience. I am sorry for all the trouble I have caused."

George gaped at the man, as angry—and confused—as he'd ever been in his life. "Whatever, man. Just keep it together from here on out. Okay?"

"Of course. And now I must pack around Barry's wound. He is bleeding profusely, and I am quite worried."

George turned away from Abraham. *I'll never get another guiding gig after this.* He just hoped Barry would survive.

CHAPTER TWENTY-NINE: PANIC

Denver Colorado
Friday, December 30, 1977, 5:00 p.m.

Susanne

Susanne stalked down the hallway ahead of Dian, who was speed walking to stay well in front of Esme. The day had gone well enough. Good even. Until they'd taken a break for a mid-afternoon coffee an hour before. Esme had asked one question too many about their youth in College Station, Texas, and Dian had given too much truth in her answer.

Not that it was Dian's fault. Not entirely. Susanne had been in serious need of a pick-me-up. The mall had worn her out. *No. Worrying about Trish has worn me out.* As they passed by a cluster of food and beverage outlets, she'd spied a bakery with a sign by the cash register. HOT COFFEE ALL DAY. *Praise the Lord and pass the biscuits.*

"Would anyone mind stopping for a coffee at that bakery?" she'd asked, pointing to the cute sign in forest green lettering. It had a

French feel to it, with a picture of a croissant on one end and a tall, layered cake on the other. Of course, it was a counter in front of a display case in a mall. For all she knew, the baked goods were Sara Lee from the frozen food section of a grocery store. But there could be a gourmet kitchen and a pastry chef back there somewhere. Or maybe there wasn't.

"I thought you'd never ask." Dian was half Susanne's body weight but twice her size in shopping bags. Without waiting for Esme to weigh in, Dian began shedding bags beside a little round table in front of the bakery.

Esme sniffed. "I don't drink coffee after noon. But a chamomile tea wouldn't hurt."

Within minutes, the women were seated at the table—with a third chair they'd borrowed from the Orange Julius next door—hot drinks in front of them and, in Susanne's case, fork buried in a slice of carrot cake with cream cheese frosting.

"You'd better be planning on sharing a bite with me." Dian was emptying packets of artificial sweetener one after another into her coffee.

Susanne moaned as she chewed her first bite. She handed the plastic fork to Dian.

Esme dunked her tea bag. "You and Barry seem to be good friends, Dian."

Dian's eyes widened. Her mouth was full. She made an agreeable noise, nodding.

"Did he date much in high school?" This time Esme addressed the question to both Susanne and Dian.

The old friends looked at each other. *Hadn't Barry talked to her about his past? About Dian?*

Susanne swallowed her carrot cake and reached for her coffee. She waffled her hand.

"He certainly dated half the women in Austin before me." Esme's laugh was brittle. "But no one serious, he said, except for one ex-fiancée."

Esme doesn't know! She doesn't know about Barry and Dian.

"One, but two times," Dian blurted out.

Susanne kicked Dian's shin under the table.

Esme cradled her paper teacup with both hands. She leaned toward Dian. "Two engagements? He didn't tell me that. What do you know about it? About her? About them?"

"Oh—" Dian said.

Susanne cut in. "Gosh, Esme, those are questions for Barry."

Esme's eyes narrowed to slits. "I'm going to be family. Your sister."

Susanne faked a laugh. "I'm already his sister. And he'd kill me if I talked about him behind his back."

"Fine. Not him, then. Her. Tell me about her."

"Esme . . ."

"Her name, at least." Esme's voice rose. "Just tell me her name. You owe me that much."

Owe her?

Something in Dian's posture changed. *Uh oh.* Her voice was firm and unapologetic. "Dian."

"Excuse me?" Esme said.

Susanne squeezed her eyes shut. *This is going to go badly. Why couldn't Dian have let me handle it?*

"Her name was Dian."

For long, silent moments, Esme didn't speak. Her eyes flitted from Susanne to Dian, back and forth like a metronome. Finally, she said to Susanne, "Is she saying that she was his fiancée?"

Dian answered for Susanne. "Both times. We were slow learners."

"I'm spending my hen party weekend in Denver with my fiancé's old girlfriend?" Esme screeched. She knocked her tea sideways. Susanne caught it and kept it from spilling.

Dian smiled. "His old fiancée. But one who couldn't be happier for the two of you."

"Have you two been laughing at me this whole time?" Esme was staring daggers at Susanne.

Susanne reached out and put a hand on Esme's arm. "No, of course not. This whole weekend has been lovely." *Except for right now. And my daughter's boyfriend being thrown in jail.*

Esme's lips pressed into a straight line. She clutched the V of her blouse collar. Her voice turned venomous. "When exactly were you going to tell me?"

Dian wasn't known for having a lot of rope, and her patience had run to the end of it. "Honey, that is a question you should be asking of our sweet Barry-boy."

"Barry-boy? Is that your pet name for him?"

Susanne didn't know how to defuse the situation. It had turned so ugly, so fast. She was going to give her brother the business for not telling Esme before he let the women go away together for the weekend.

She smiled. "No. That's what our family nanny called him when we were kids. It spread from our house to his school friends. But, Esme, truly I had no idea Barry hadn't told you. He loves *you,* though. You're getting married."

Dian inspected her nails. "Everything about us is ancient history."

"When did you break up?" Esme demanded.

"Years ago, wasn't it?" Susanne stretched the truth as far as it would go. It wasn't a lie. The first engagement had ended more than a decade before.

Dian looked Esme in the eye. "Long enough that I don't remember the specifics. Esme, I'm sorry this has made you uncomfortable. I'm happy for Barry. And for you."

"How can you be? You're alone."

Susanne read the rage in Dian's body language, but her voice was smooth and sweet as Karo syrup when she answered. "By choice. And that has nothing to do with wanting the best for my friends, old and new." She tilted her coffee cup and looked in it. "Empty. Shall we get on the road now?"

"Now is good. I need to check on things with Trish before dinner," Susanne said.

Esme tucked her purse under her arm and stood. "I think I'd like to have an evening in. You all can go to dinner without me."

The three women left without another word said. Not in the mall, not in the Suburban, and not in the hotel walking to their room. Susanne reached the door first. Her whole body ached with the need to see Trish with her own eyes, to hug her daughter if the girl would accept it, and to try to make things better for her. She hated bringing Esme's tension in the room with her. Maybe Trish wouldn't pick up on it.

Entering, she called, "Trish, we're back." Then she felt silly. *That's obvious.*

Dian followed up with, "You're going to love the things I bought for you with your dad's money!"

Esme closed the door.

Trish didn't answer.

Susanne walked all the way into the room and turned in a circle. Trish wasn't there. She checked the bathroom. The door was wide open. No Trish in there, either. Susanne frowned.

"Where is she?" Esme asked.

Susanne couldn't hold back the snap in her voice. "How would I know?"

"Excuse me," Esme snapped back. "I thought maybe she'd told you when you called her from the mall."

Susanne pressed her knuckles to her lips. "She didn't."

Dian ran her hand across the desktop. A half-eaten burger and fries sat there, dry and sad on a plate. "Is there a note? Maybe she went for a walk."

A thorough room search didn't yield a note. Or her coat. Or her purse. Only her suitcase.

Trish is gone. Susanne trembled. She was frightened and had no idea what to do next.

Esme's voice was small, but the anger had left it. "She probably didn't realize we'd be back before dinner. Maybe she went to get something else to eat. This hamburger looks like it was from lunch. She'll be back soon."

She was probably right. *But what if someone took her?* There was no sign of a struggle, though. "I'm going to kill her for scaring me like this. She knows better."

The phone rang. Susanne lunged for it, tripping over Trish's suitcase and catching herself on the edge of the desk. "Hello?"

"I only have a minute, Mom. I—"

"Patricia Flint, where are you?" Susanne's voice cracked.

"Getting on a bus."

Susanne screeched like a parrot. "What?"

"Mrs. Sibley called me. Ben is out of jail, but he left a note that he had to leave. He's disappeared." Trish's voice sounded sad but determined. "I'm sorry. I love you, Mom, but I have to go. I'll see you at home."

"Go where?" Susanne asked.

A dial tone was her only answer.

CHAPTER THIRTY: EXAMINE

North of Clear Creek Resort, Bighorn Mountains,
Wyoming
Friday, December 30, 1977, 5:00 p.m.

Patrick

Patrick cut off the engine to his snowmobile. He and Dr. John parked beside Jenelle and Mandy, who were riding double, since Jenelle's machine had broken down. Patrick's ribs were grateful for the respite. He was a staunch believer in pain building character. After today, he was going to have enough to last his lifetime.

"This is where they were." Jenelle looked to her friend for confirmation. "But where did they go? It would help a lot if we had some light." The sun had set, and the light was growing dim on the mountain.

"You're the expert on the area, but weren't we further into the park?" Mandy said, pointing. "Near that hump of snow? I think I see yellow."

Jenelle nodded. "And there are some tracks. Follow me." She lowered her face guard and gunned the engine on her machine.

Patrick and Dr. John fell in behind them. Less than a minute later, they stopped at a mound of snow. The yellow was a Ski-Doo snowmobile, flipped and partially buried in snow stained with something dark. Patrick's stomach clenched. Barry had been riding a Ski-Doo. Wes, too. But so had everyone else the lodge rented to that day, in addition to anyone who might own one of the popular machines and be riding one in the area.

Mandy said, "I don't get it. If this is their machine—and I think it looks the same, plus, it seems like that's blood from the injured guy—then the other one and the men are gone. Maybe someone else already gave them a ride?"

Jenelle shook her head. "We would have seen them. That was the only way back to the resort."

Patrick smacked one fist into the other palm. "Where the heck are they?"

He couldn't believe how long it had taken the four of them to get there from the lodge. Between the poor visibility, people getting stuck, and Jenelle's snowmobile breaking down, their progress had been agonizing. At least they hadn't wasted time on the crippled machine. Jenelle had just squeezed on with Mandy and forged ahead.

Dr. John put a hand on his shoulder. "We'll find them, Patrick."

Patrick felt his lips moving. He didn't want to look like he was talking to himself in front of the others, but his stress was so high, he was powerless to stop. *Don't let it be Barry. Or Wes. Or George.* He wouldn't wish a wilderness injury on anyone, but he couldn't help being most concerned about his family and friends.

A gust of wind so strong that it knocked him back a step ripped across the park. He leaned into it. When it died down, he thought he saw smoke rising over a rock outcropping.

He pointed, energy infusing his voice. "Is that smoke over there? Or is it just a snow devil?"

Three heads swiveled.

Dr. John frowned. "My distance vision isn't what it used to be."

Jenelle nodded. "Could be. Definitely could be."

Patrick hopped back on his snowmobile. Was the smoke from a wrecked machine? Or a man-made fire? He eyed the park, trying to get a fix on what he thought he saw between them and the possible smoke. Soft-edged depressions seemed to cross the expanse—parallel lines filled with the last dump of snow. They headed toward the smoke. Or at least he thought they did. It was hard to tell. "Those could be snowmobile tracks leading over to it."

Dr. John tapped his shoulder. "Let me break trail for you. We'll go see together."

"All right."

"Give me some room in case I get stuck. Don't let your speed drop once you get going, though, or you'll founder."

Patrick nodded.

"We're going, too," Jenelle said.

"I'll bring up the rear, then." Patrick dropped his face shield and pulled the starter.

Within seconds, two of the three snowmobiles were growling and roaring into the face of the blizzard. Patrick took a deep breath. He was a neophyte, but he'd had most of the day to build his skills, especially in the last hour over deep powder. Now it was time to test himself, broken ribs or not.

No fear. Don't blink.

He depressed the throttle and steered his snowmobile into the deep tracks left by the others.

His machine all but levitated across the snow. The sensation was like floating, but somehow lighter. It was close to the one flying his plane gave him. *This is what the land speeder in Star Wars must have felt like.* The experience would have been an almost perfect peace, despite the storm, if not for the whine of the machine's belt as it struggled and the disquietude he felt about what might be waiting for them on the other side of the park.

Halfway there, darkness fell like a cloak. With the heavy clouds, there was no sun, no moon, and no stars. By the time Patrick's group had reached the rocks, it wasn't just a whiteout, it was a blackout. Patrick couldn't see the tracks in the snow, the machines or the rocks in front of him, the buttons on his dash, or even tell where the land ended and the sky began. He hadn't asked how to turn on his headlamps before. *A critical error.* A button? A switch? Where? It wasn't something he could figure out while he was fighting powder. With the roar of the machine added to the darkness, the sensation was simultaneously isolation and claustrophobia. He'd experienced something similar when he'd turned off the lights to his plane while flying at night once. But he'd known all he had to do was flip them back on then. He had no such reassurance now. He could plow into or over one of his friends without advance warning. Or the rocks.

How far ahead of me are they? For a moment, he thought about stopping, but, just as he was about to let off the gas, he saw bouncing light illuminating rock faces. *The others turned on their lights.* The relief made him feel giddy, especially since he now saw that the trail cut to the left of the rocks. Without the lights, he might have plowed right into them. He barked out a laugh that was swallowed by snowmobile noise.

The snow wasn't as deep close in to the rocks, and a loud scraping noise and jolt scared the bejeebers out of him. Rocks under the snow, he realized. They jerked his handlebars to the left, toward the enormous boulders. He was face to face with towering rock, only inches away, before he regained control and swung the machine's nose back to the right. His sled veered away from the base of the cliff.

In front of him, one set of lights disappeared. Then the second set was gone, too, leaving him in darkness once again. *They've rounded a corner.* He slowed, searching for an end to the rocks, a fold, a cave, anything, and unable to see their tracks anymore.

He shouted, "Hello?"

There was no answer. Of course. He eased the machine forward at the lowest speed he dared. If he got stuck, how long would it be before the others realized they'd lost him and turned back for him?

As he was worrying through his options, a figure hidden against the stone face leapt out at him. Upright. Huge. Looming.

Bear!

He pulled hard to the right, away from it. But then he realized the upright form was wearing a brown jacket. One he recognized, too. Wes. Patrick had never been so glad to see his friend and co-worker. *Please let the others be with him. Barry. George. Abraham.*

Wes waved Patrick in toward the rock. Now Patrick saw snowmobiles parked in an alcove of sorts, with tall rock walls sheltering them on three sides. Dr. John's, with the light still on, and four other machines. One red, one blue, the others yellow. He matched colors to riders. Red. Abraham had been on a red one. George had ridden the fancy blue one. Jenelle and Mandy were on a yellow Ski-Doo, as were Wes and Dr. John.

Whose machine was out in the park—Barry?

He pulled up beside the last snowmobiles in line and turned his off. The silence rang louder in his ears than the noise had, it seemed, and it felt like his whole body was vibrating.

He lifted his shield, ripped off his helmet, and hurried over to Wes. "Can't tell you how glad I am to see you."

Wes pulled him into an excruciating hug. "Not as glad as I am to see you and Dr. John, Sawbones. When I heard those snowmobiles coming, I don't mind telling you I cried. Like a damn baby, Doc." Wes released him. Patrick could see the redness around his eyes. His friend wasn't kidding.

"We heard someone is injured."

"Yes, and I'm sorry to say it's your brother-in-law."

"How bad is he?"

"Come see for yourself. He's in the cave back there."

Cave? Patrick grabbed the medical kit from the snowmobile, then followed Wes. They walked past the other sleds toward the rock wall. As Wes neared it, he rounded a standing rock that shielded the mouth of a recessed area. A rock overhang covered it from above, high enough that an adult male could stand up under it. Patrick wouldn't have called it a cave, but it was close enough to one to provide protection from the elements. George and the two women were huddled around a fire. From their body language, Patrick guessed George and Jenelle were friends, or at least knew each other previously. Mandy was listening to their conversation.

Dr. John and Abraham were crouched close to the fire. A pot was wedged in the coals, heating water. Patrick saw the booted feet of a prone figure on the dirt-packed ground between the men. The feet were elevated and resting on rocks.

Barry.

Patrick joined them, his heart jammed so high in his throat he couldn't swallow. "How is he?"

He stared at the pale face of his brother-in-law. Patrick had been friends with Barry most of their lives. Since they were boys. Before he'd starting dating Barry's cute little sister. To see him like this was a blow to the solar plexus. But then the doctor in him asserted authority, pushing him into a steely-eyed medical response. There would be time for emotion later.

Barry's closed eyes popped open. "Not dead but wish I were."

"You're awake."

"Not by choice. Hurts like the dickens." His voice was reedy.

Dr. John's usually sparkling eyes were grave. He motioned Patrick away from Barry. "Wes has done a fine job of slowing the bleeding, taping up the wound, and stabilizing him, but he was impaled in the side by a metal spike. The volume of bleeding is troubling."

Wes stepped closer. He crossed his arms. "It wasn't me who helped him, Dr. John. It was Abraham."

Patrick ignored the extraneous information. A metal spike to the side. Profuse bleeding. There were so many possibilities for internal injuries, not to mention the impact of blood loss and shock, and any secondary injuries that were being overlooked elsewhere. Broken bones, concussion, dislocations, other soft tissue damage. "He looks to be in shock. Any fever?"

Dr. John said, "He is in shock, I think. But he doesn't feel feverish."

"Any vital organs pierced?"

"I think we'd have already lost him if so, but we need to check. And we need to stop that bleeding."

Surgery in the wilderness. It was tricky. Patrick kept thinking about that metal spike. So many things it could have damaged. Intestines, spleen, and the list went on. "Are you thinking about operating on him here? I've got about everything we'd need in my bag."

"Do I get a vote in this?" Barry said.

"No," Patrick answered.

Dr. John sighed. His eyes were warm and empathetic. "I think we need to get that bleeding stopped sooner rather than later. Transporting in this storm would be risky, even if we could figure out how to move him. We could end up losing a lot of time he doesn't have. Or worse, getting stuck somewhere that makes this place seem like a state-of-the-art operating theater."

Wes said, "I don't see how we could move him. I don't even see how we could navigate ourselves."

Jenelle had been listening. "I can't help on how to move him, but I know the way back blindfolded. Is there something I can do?" The way she swallowed the vowel in "back" gave her away as a lifelong Wyoming resident.

Patrick rubbed his palm back and forth across his forehead. "Are you sure?"

"Positive."

"Okay, then. A real stretcher. Something we could belt him into that would shelter him from the weather and absorb the bumps."

Barry groaned. "No bumps. Please no bumps. So much pain."

Dr. John rolled his neck. "Better yet, a helicopter, but I don't see that happening in time."

Jenelle nodded. "I'll radio Buffalo. You never know. George, would you ride back with Mandy and me? We're down to one snow-mobile. It's not smart to ride alone at the best of times in daylight. This is anything but that."

"Escort two beautiful women or stay in a cave with a bunch of smelly guys? Easy choice." He grinned. "Seriously, it's going to be tricky going out there. If we get lost or stuck, we'll need to huddle for body heat. I just want you to know I'm willing to make that sacrifice for you."

Jenelle smiled at him. "I've got a pup tent and a feather weight sleeping bag. We'll be fine. You, on the other hand, might freeze to death."

Patrick now felt sure they knew each other, and that they wanted to know each other better.

"I believe I can be of most assistance here, George, if you agree." It was Abraham, who hadn't spoken since Patrick arrived. His upper lip was beaded in sweat and his voice was shaky. "If someone were to have to try to get him back to the resort tonight, I would be best suited, because of my snowmobile skills."

George gave Abraham a pointed look. "I'm counting on that."

Patrick caught George's eyes and mouthed *what is that about?* George shrugged, then mouthed back *nothing.* Patrick wasn't so sure, but he assumed the two guides had argued about Abraham and Barry getting separated from the group. Which made Patrick wonder why they had. But they had bigger problems for him to worry about now.

Jenelle spoke to Patrick and Dr. John, dividing her eye contact between them. "If we can't get anyone up the mountain with a real stretcher, we'll build you one. And when I return with it, I'll have food and hot drinks."

"If the weather doesn't clear, wait for daylight," Dr. John said. "We don't need anyone else hurt or lost."

"See you for breakfast, then."

The emotion Patrick had tamped down welled up again, and his voice wobbled. "Thank you. All of you."

Mandy, George, and Jenelle picked up their helmets and disappeared into the night.

Patrick heard the snowmobiles fire up and depart. He laid his jacket on the ground, inside up, and arrayed supplies from the kit on it. Scissors, stitching line, a needle, betadine, alcohol, gauze and bandages, antibiotics, lidocaine, morphine, syringes, a stethoscope, a thermometer, and more.

Barry rolled his head, trying to get a look. "I know I call you a quack, Patrick. But right now, I'm really praying you're not one. Are you sure we need to do this? I can survive the pain."

"He's not. And we're sure." Dr. John looked over the selections. "You're so well-equipped, it's like we're in the operating room back in Buffalo."

Patrick half-smiled in acknowledgement of the compliment. "How about I'll prep and assist, and you operate?" God had blessed Dr. John with the hands of a surgeon, and then he'd put them to good use as a Navy surgeon in the Korean War. It was a time he wouldn't talk about, other than to say his skills were battle tested. The volume of surgeries was lower in Buffalo, and he kept his fingers limber by building grandfather clocks. He'd invited Patrick over once to watch him at work. The small parts, the intricate ways in which they meshed—Patrick had been amazed that Dr. John could fit his hands into the tiny spaces and operate his tools there. He was unflinching and had no tremor. Patrick wished he was half the surgeon Dr. John was. "You've got the magic hands."

Dr. John smiled. Patrick's offer had been only confirmation of the division of labor that he would have insisted on. Not only was he the better surgeon, but he was the better physician to care for Barry. Barry was Patrick's friend and family member. Patrick could have attended to him—would help attend to him—but best practice was to eliminate even the possibility of emotion getting in the way.

Wes said, "I'll keep the fire fed and water boiling. In fact, I'm going to start gathering more firewood now. Gotta brush it off and get it in here to dry, so we'll have it ready when we need it."

"I can assist with the procedure in any way you need," Abraham said.

Patrick almost protested. Abraham could gather the wood. But Wes had said Abraham was good with Barry earlier. They could always call Wes back if they needed him. He washed his hands in the snow beside Dr. John, who was doing the same thing. Then each man rubbed their hands with a small amount of alcohol.

Patrick squatted beside Barry and put a hand on his shoulder. "If I were in your shoes, there's no one in the world I'd rather have operate on me than Dr. John."

"Let me know how to help you best," Abraham said. "I see you have painkillers." He gestured at the supplies.

Patrick settled back on his heels, scrutinizing Abraham. He was knowledgeable about medicine. More than simply a snowmobile tour guide and racer. Then again, he should have expected Abraham to have a "day job." George guided tours, and he was a fine electrician.

"Are you a nurse?" Patrick asked.

Abraham said, "I have had medical training."

"Hmmm." *Intriguing.* Patrick had poor needle skills. "How are you with giving shots?"

Dr. John said, "Neither of us usually operates the needle."

"Great," Barry muttered.

"I am good with a syringe. Would you like me to administer five milligrams of morphine? And I can inject lidocaine. Possibly twenty cc's? Or thirty?"

Patrick did a calculation in his head and found to his surprise that Abraham was spot on. "That sounds right on the morphine. Let's go with thirty on the lidocaine. And he'll need some of the ampicillin."

"Two hundred and fifty milligrams?"

Patrick was no longer surprised. "Yes. Thank you. I'll start prepping him."

Abraham knelt to wash his hands at the mouth of the cave.

Patrick began rolling up the edges of Barry's upper layers of garments, while Dr. John took his vitals. In the cold temperatures,

Patrick couldn't afford to cut the fabric, but neither could he run the risk of dirty fabric getting in the wound. He decided to stitch it loosely out of the way, then cut the stitching when the surgery was over.

"No temperature," Dr. John said. "That's a good sign."

Patrick tied off his stitching and returned the needle to Dr. John. Dr. John moved on to sterilizing the scissors, needle, and line, and Patrick could tell he was taking care to minimize the waste of alcohol as he did so. In the hospital operating room, the alcohol would have been used much more liberally. Even wastefully. But their supply was limited out in the wilderness.

Abraham returned. He prepared the morphine and inserted the syringe into its rubber top. Patrick watched him out of the side of his eye. The man seemed to know what he was doing. "May we use the betadine to clean the injection sites?" he asked.

"I've got it." Dr. John grunted. "Show me where."

"His uninjured side for the morphine and antibiotic." Abraham touched Barry's exposed injury site. "Here for the lidocaine?"

Dr. John rubbed the areas clean with a small amount of betadine on a gauze pad.

"Thank you." Abraham injected the needle and depressed the plunger. "Morphine."

"Will that knock me out? Please tell me it will," Barry said.

Patrick responded, "Sorry, buddy. You're going to be awake for this. Sleepy, maybe."

Barry moaned. "This pain is worse than anything I went through in Vietnam. When are you giving me the shot?"

"I have already administered the first one," Abraham said.

"Huh." Barry pursed his lips. "I didn't even feel it."

He's skilled, Patrick realized. "I only have the one syringe."

Abraham was already cleaning it. "I understand. I will take care."

Patrick was sure now that the needle work was in good hands. He began trimming Barry's hair away from the area around where the metal shaft had entered his side. When that task was completed, he washed it gently with gauze and alcohol, then rubbed betadine over the entire area.

"In case you were wondering, I still feel that. And by feel I mean you're killing me," Barry said.ß

Abraham pushed the syringe needle into Barry, delivering the lidocaine. "You won't after this one." To the doctors, he said, "I packed the wound with fabric before I taped it closed. I apologize. I did not have sterile materials, but I did the best I could."

"I understand more than you could guess. In the wilderness, you make do with what's available," Patrick said.

Outside, a coyote howled. "That wasn't as far away as I would have liked," Dr. John said.

Abraham nodded, his face creased with worry. "Antibiotic." He gave Barry the third shot. After he had cleaned the syringe again, he said, "I'll be prepared to help staunch blood flow when you have removed the tape." He held gauze in both hands.

"Thanks. The lidocaine should have kicked in by now. Let's do it." Patrick held Barry's skin down as he peeled back the tape, moving slowly toward the wound. He didn't want to rip up skin or tear the opening further.

"I feel pressure," Barry said.

"That's not a problem. Tell us if you feel pain."

Blood gushed around the edges of the tape and what looked like part of a fleecy sweatshirt. When Patrick had the tape off, he lifted the fleece as carefully as if he was clipping wires on a bomb. Abraham pressed against the bleed with his gauze. It didn't do much to stop it.

Dr. John grunted. "There's a lot more blood than I'd like to see."

Me either. Moving as fast as he could, Patrick cut the remaining hair away, cleaned it with alcohol, and irrigated the entire area with betadine. Abraham kept pressure on the wound. The gauze was soaked through.

"All yours, Dr. John," Patrick said.

Dr. John wiggled his fingers like he was warming up to play the piano, a pre-surgery ritual Patrick had seen him perform countless times over the last few years. In reality, the man didn't play the instrument, but he did play the banjo like a member of the Grand Ole Opry. Surgeon, clock maker, banjo player. A true Renaissance man.

Dr. John puckered his lips to the side. "The light's not great. Lucky for you, Barry, I'm not having to stitch your face." He looked up at Abraham and Patrick. "I guess it doesn't do any good for me to say 'suction,' but I'd appreciate it if the two of you could keep things as dry as you can, so I stand a chance of poking him in the right spots."

"Not making me feel any better about this," Barry mumbled. He sounded softened, like the morphine was taking the edge off.

Patrick smiled. Dr. John had a jovial way of defusing tension. Another gift from his maker.

"No problem, Dr. John," Abraham said.

"Let's see what we see." With two fingers, Dr. John probed in the wound. He frowned and moved his fingers first one way, then the other. "If you had to guess, Patrick, what would be your diagnosis?"

"Based on the bleeding and shock, I'd say you'll need to tie off at least one bleeding vessel," Patrick said. "And I'd pray that's it." Beside him, Abraham nodded.

"I concur. And I think I've found the main bleeder. I'll look around while I'm in there and see if anything else was damaged, but tying off this vessel will be my first task."

Patrick couldn't argue with that.

Dr. John picked up the scalpel. "All right, then, gentlemen, let's get down to business."

Patrick and Abraham shared a glance. Patrick hoped his eyes didn't look as worried as Abraham's, but he had a feeling they did.

CHAPTER THIRTY-ONE: SWITCH

Patrick

Patrick leaned over the hole in Barry's side, nearly bumping heads with Abraham and Dr. John. He had two pieces of gauze at the ready, and he and Abraham were taking turns absorbing the fluid that could otherwise make it impossible for Dr. John to do his work.

A splash of blood landed in an abstract splatter pattern on Barry's intact skin. On it. Not dripping from it. Patrick looked up, first at Abraham. He'd seen it, too, and made wide eyes of acknowledgement at Patrick. It didn't look like it had come from him. Abraham shook his head, and Patrick took that to mean it hadn't come from Patrick, either. Patrick glanced up at the ceiling of the cave. He didn't know what he thought he'd find, maybe an owl or bat with its dinner.

There was nothing.

His eyes moved to Dr. John. Blood was trickling from one nostril, around his mouth, and down his chin, where another drop was poised at the precipice, ready to torpedo Barry's open wound. "Dr. John, your nose," Patrick said.

Dr. John grunted. "What about it?"

"It's bleeding. Profusely. And falling onto Barry near the incision site."

"Wha-at?" Barry said. He sounded woozy now. Patrick was glad the morphine was doing its job.

Dr. John froze. He couldn't wipe his face with his hands mid-surgery. "Can one of you wipe it before I contaminate the surgical site?"

Abraham swiped at Dr. John's chin, then up the blood trail, smearing it. He pulled the gauze away. For a few seconds, they all held their breath. Maybe it had stopped. Then the flow gushed anew.

"Didn't work," Patrick said.

"The dryness out here. Been needing to get this cauterized. Of all the bad timing, when I've got Barry open. But all I had left to do was the stitching. Unfortunately, there's going to be a whole lot of stitching." His eyes met Patrick's. "I'm going to need you to take over for me."

Patrick's throat tightened. Operate in the wilderness on his brother-in-law? But Dr. John was right. Of course he was. "Let me wash my hands again."

"Move fast. I want to get this over with quickly."

Patrick fumbled over to the snow at the cave mouth and scrubbed his hands, trying to calm his overactive nerves. *It's going to be all right. You're not going to kill Barry. Go in, find your bleeder, tie it off. Then approximate the muscles and tissues as anatomically as possible and align the skin as best you can. Even though right now it looks like the broken teeth of a saw blade. Keep it clean, close it up. No problem.* Then he returned to the line of supplies. Abraham had the alcohol ready and poured a small amount into Patrick's palms. Patrick rubbed his hands briskly together.

"This reminds me of medical school. They taught us to tie off sutures by having us do it with our hands inside a jar and the lights out," he said.

Dr. John was pinching the bridge of his nose, his head leaned back and chin tilted up. "Some things never change. That's why I took up working with clocks."

"I've heard other doctors tie flies for the same reason."

"Or so they say. Any excuse to fish."

Patrick smiled. He realized the knot in his stomach had eased. He'd be fine. He'd done harder surgeries than this hundreds of times.

"Wait. You guys are letting the quack operate on me?" Barry said.

"Where's a gas mask when you need one?" Patrick said. He picked up the line, threaded it through the needle, and leaned in. "All right. It's time to put Humpty Dumpty together again."

CHAPTER THIRTY-TWO: HUNKER

Ben

No lights were on at Piney Bottoms when Ben arrived. The ranch's lone hand lived by the axiom of "early to bed, early to rise." Ben figured he'd probably finished up and tucked into his cabin an hour before.

Just as Ben had been counting on.

He didn't want to be disturbed. He was tired into his bone marrow and had nearly driven off the road multiple times in the last hour, which wouldn't have been good—he was driving much too fast for the weather and bad roads. Now all he was looking for was a decent night's sleep after he'd packed up his things. In the morning, he would evade the watchful eyes of the hand and start the next leg of his journey.

He parked behind the house. When he turned off his truck, he dropped his forehead on the steering wheel. He'd been partly relieved and partly disappointed that Trish hadn't been home when he'd dropped by her house on the way through Buffalo. As much as he loved her, it would have been a hard conversation, one he'd rehearsed in his mind for hours. *Yes, I just gave you a promise ring, but I'm leaving, I'm not one hundred percent sure where I'm going or what I'll be doing, and I have no idea when I'm coming back, if ever.* He wouldn't have been surprised if she'd have picked up a baseball bat and chased him back to his truck. He tried to imagine how he would feel if she were dumping him and running away.

He'd be devastated and want to understand why.

But he didn't know how to explain something to her that didn't make complete sense to himself. He just knew that he had to do this. No matter how badly it hurt to walk away from her and the Sibleys, he needed a fresh start in a place where he wouldn't disappoint or hurt anyone. Where his past wouldn't follow him. A beautiful, remote, rugged place. Under a new name. Not the one his criminal father had hung around his neck like an iron collar. He'd forge a new path. His own path. Not college. He wasn't going to waste his or the Sibleys' money. He belonged outside, doing something physical.

He jerked and his forehead bounced on the steering wheel. His chin felt wet, and he wiped it with his hand. Drool, all the way down to his neck. He'd fallen asleep.

He forced himself to sit up and stretch. Time to go inside. Crawl into his comfortable bed in the nicest house he'd ever lived in. He opened the door and hopped down, almost falling in the process. He looked back at his bags. There was nothing he needed in them. He shut the door softly and walked through the snow to the back door. It was dark out, but he didn't have to worry about a key. It was always left unlocked.

He opened the door, which creaked on hinges he had forgotten to oil the week before. He stumbled over Henry's work boots in the vestibule, even though he knew they were always there, sitting below the hook where his cowboy hats hung, straw for summer, felt for spring and fall. The vestibule emptied into the kitchen. It smelled sweet, of the old bananas Vangie saved up to make her famous banana bread. He walked past the big refrigerator. It was always well stocked. Ranching was hungry work, and Ben raided it for snacks several times a day. Tonight, he was just too tired to eat. He passed it, moving on through the dining area where only a few weeks before there had been a huge Christmas dinner with more food than he'd ever seen at one time in his life, then into the living room and the hallway to the bedrooms.

His footsteps echoed on the wood floors. The house seemed empty, like him. *Funny to feel alone now when I've been by myself so much of my life.* His mom had disappeared before he was old enough to remember much about her, even what she'd looked like. He tried to bring up a picture of her in his mind's eye, but it was fuzzy. She'd been on the tall side. Or maybe that was just how a toddler saw the world. She was pretty. He'd been told he got his dark eyes and hair from her. She'd smelled good, like cinnamon and sugar and butter. She'd sung him to sleep at night—he couldn't recall the song, only her voice. It was one of the few things he remembered for sure about her, other than her bruises and black eyes, and that he'd loved her. He was sure he had.

But she hadn't stuck around. She hadn't kept him safe.

He stopped in the bathroom with the lasso wallpaper that he'd used since he moved in, staring at himself in the mirror as he splashed warm water on his face. A week after his mom had left his life, his father, worthless piece of horse manure that Chester Jones was, had taken after Ben with an empty whiskey bottle to the head for the first time. Not hard enough to break the bottle, but hard enough to drop Ben to the floor. The first few times, Ben had thought his dad was just sad because his mom was gone. But it kept happening, and it was even worse when his dad's half-brother, Ben's Uncle Billy Kemecke, showed up to drink with Chester. The brothers were big men, and Ben was just a little boy. Once, they'd gotten tired of playing cornhole and had forced Ben to stand against the wall in the Jones' foul-smelling little house while they took turns knocking beer bottles off his head with the beanbags. When Ben had started crying, his dad told his Uncle Billy to give Ben something to cry about. But Ben hadn't cried any more, because he'd passed out when Uncle Billy had jerked him across the room and dislocated his shoulder.

It hadn't taken many episodes like those for Ben to learn to speak softly and become invisible. He became so good at hiding that most of the time his dad couldn't find him when he was wasted and looking for something to wallop. By the time Ben reached his teens, he'd even forgiven his mother for her disappearing act. Maybe she'd believed her husband wouldn't hurt their son. Ben had certainly become adept enough at disappearing, but, unlike her, he always had to come back.

Deep down, Ben couldn't shake his growing certainty that she hadn't left. That Chester had killed her and hidden her body. He'd never know for sure. His father was dead. There would be no confession, no trip to a grave where Ben could weep for her and tell her goodbye.

Trish used to worry that Ben would hate her someday because Dr. Flint had killed Chester during her rescue. Ben had tried to convince her that he would never feel that way, but he'd been too afraid to tell her the truth—that he was glad his father was dead, and about *why*, and what his father had done to him.

Ben opened the closet in the hall. He kept a box in it from his old life. This is what he'd come to Piney Bottoms for. Part of him wanted to burn the pictures, his birth certificate, and the family Bible his mom had recorded his birth in. The hateful fact of his paternal parentage was memorialized in all of it. The only time Ben let himself think about his dad now was when he was reminding himself of the kind of man he didn't want to be.

The truth was he was grateful to Dr. Flint for setting him free. He probably would have killed his father someday himself if Dr. Flint hadn't beaten him to it. His dad's death had been the beginning of the process, for Ben, of moving away from fear. Not that he hadn't been scared in juvie. He'd been almost as scared there as he'd been at home in Cody.

But when he'd been released from custody, he'd gotten a second chance with the Sibleys. Ben hadn't felt safe from the time his mother disappeared until he moved in with Henry, Vangie, and baby Hank. Here, in this empty, echoing house, he'd been able to breathe and relax and stop looking over his shoulder, for the first time in years. Maybe ever. He'd felt like part of a normal family in this house.

The house he was going to leave behind in the morning.

He pulled the box off the shelf and set it against the baseboard in the hallway. Wherever he was going, it would have to come with him. He would bury his past when he had a handle on his future.

After a quick detour to oil the creaky hinges, he entered his bedroom without turning on the lights, diving headfirst onto his bed, and was asleep almost before his face landed on the pillow.

CHAPTER THIRTY-THREE:
INTERROGATE

North of Clear Creek Resort, Bighorn Mountains,
Wyoming
Friday, December 30, 1977, 9:00 p.m.

Patrick

Patrick watched the rise and fall of Barry's chest as he slept, alert for the slightest change. A tapering, a shallowing, the sound of distress. *So far, so good.* His brother-in-law's pale greenish gray skin color wasn't great, but he'd just endured a traumatic injury and wilderness surgery, the operation performed by firelight in the middle of a blizzard. Patrick couldn't expect him to be in the pink of health. He'd done well during the surgery, though. Patrick had worried the painkillers wouldn't be sufficient to keep the pain at bay, but they'd done the trick. *A blessing.* The fact that he'd survived the accident was a miracle, much less the surgery, and Patrick thanked God for that grace repeatedly, each time asking Him to keep Barry alive a little longer and a little longer still. Occasionally he threw in a bit about how glad he was there had been no damage to internal organs, especially the GI tract. A bowel perforation wouldn't have been something even Dr. John could have saved Barry from, given their lack of the types and quantities of antibiotics that would have warded off a peritoneal infection and sepsis. He touched Barry's forehead. The skin was warm, but warm from the fire, not from fever.

Patrick stood and stretched. Smoke swirled up from the fire and hovered against the roof of the cave. It felt like he'd put his head right into a cloud of it. The smoke got into his nose and his throat. He coughed and sat back down quickly. Wes was kneeling by the fire, feeding the flames. Abraham was standing in the mouth of the cave watching the weather.

Snow was piling up like a wall outside. The firelight danced on the rock like a puppet show. Demons, jumping and ducking, chased smaller monsters off the wall, where they disappeared before being replaced by others of their ilk. It wasn't a settling interpretation. Patrick wished he could relax. If he'd had his book, maybe he could have distracted himself in Michener's fictional account of Colorado from prehistory until the present, but *Centennial* was in his room back at the lodge. He doubted he could have read well by firelight or focused on it under these circumstances, though.

Dr. John was leaning against the wall. His nosebleed had stopped. "Try not to worry, Patrick. His pulse is strong and steady. It's a good sign." He shaved a curl of wood from the stick in his hands with his pocketknife. *He can whittle, too. Of course.* It was already recognizably a stag after just a few minutes. The man had gifted hands. That was all there was to it.

Wes stood and walked toward the cave mouth. "I'm going for more wood. Back soon."

His departure roused Abraham from his storm watch. He nodded when he caught Patrick looking at him.

"I don't suppose it looks any better out there?" Patrick asked. Not that it would make a difference at this point. They weren't going to drive back to the resort in the dark. Still, part of Patrick felt like he would do anything to get Barry back to civilization. An equal part wouldn't dare to move him when he was so vulnerable, no matter the light or the weather.

"If anything, it has worsened." Abraham took a seat near Dr. John.

The older doctor didn't stop whittling. "The snow will have covered the trail back to the resort by now."

"Not good for us tomorrow, if no one shows up to help us," Patrick said.

Wes returned, his head and body coated in fresh flakes. He dropped an armful of dead branches, then picked one back up and beat it against the wall to knock off excess snow. He snapped it into two sections of two feet each, set them close to the fire, then grabbed another length.

Patrick touched Barry's forehead with the back of his hand. *No change.* "Wes, you look like the abominable snowman."

"I feel like him, too. But I'm trying to stay ahead of the fire." *I like a man who takes his job seriously.* "We're going to need to sleep before long, and none of us will want to gather wood then."

"Let's talk about that. We do need sleep. I'd like one of us to stay awake at all times, to monitor Barry and feed the fire."

Wes nodded. "Two-hour shifts, maybe?"

Dr. John frowned in concentration. His knife was making small cuts now. An antler had formed out of a fork in the stick, so fast it was as if he were conjuring. "It's a little after nine now. Sunrise is seven-thirty or so. We can't leave before then, even if the storm breaks. That's ten hours to cover, between the four of us. Two and a half hours each sound right to you, gentlemen?"

Patrick rubbed his forehead. "I'll take the first one, if that's okay with everyone. I'm too wired to fall asleep yet."

Dr. John blew debris from his stag. "And I'll take the second. Hopefully five hours from now we'll have a good sense of how Barry's recovering."

"Why don't I take third shift?" Wes dropped more cleaned logs onto the warming pile. "It will probably be the wood gathering shift.

That leaves you with four-thirty to seven, Abraham, if that's okay with you."

Abraham closed his eyes and dipped his head. "This is a schedule that works well for everyone and that I agree with."

Dr. John snapped his knife shut and slipped the stag into his pocket. Out came a pocket watch in its place. "I've set an alarm for the first shift change." He placed the watch on a rock. "I'm not wasting a minute of my shut-eye, though. See you at eleven-thirty, Patrick. Good night, all."

He crawled on hands and knees to the far side of Barry, but still close to him. He put his backpack against the wall and set his head on it. Less than a minute later, soft, rhythmic snores filled the cave.

Wes returned his last cleaned piece of firewood to the pile. "Dr. John must have learned that sleeping trick in the Navy. I'm going to turn in, too. Wake me if you need anything, Sawbones." He placed his backpack near Dr. John's feet, then curled up facing the rock.

Abraham remained where he'd been sitting, hands in his lap, eyes downcast.

Patrick lowered his voice. "Aren't you going to grab some sleep, too?"

Abraham didn't look up. "I've been working as a ranch hand for many months. I don't require much rest."

"A ranch hand?"

Abraham shifted. "It is honest work."

"I just assumed you worked in a hospital." When Abraham didn't respond, Patrick continued. "With snowmobile guiding as a weekend hobby, like with George."

"Yes. Guiding is not my occupation."

Probably a good thing, given that he'd been the one with Barry when they got lost and Barry was hurt. "So, what happened earlier?"

"What do you mean?"

"How did you and Barry get separated from the rest of us?"

Abraham's jaw bulged. After a long pause, he said, "It was my fault. Barry strayed from the group, and I didn't realize it until too late. I am responsible for his injury. For all of it. I will never forgive myself."

The man's humility in owning up to the blame impressed Patrick. "Seems like you made up for it by saving his life."

Abraham rolled his lips inward but didn't reply.

Wes's snores joined with Dr. John's in a syncopated duet. Patrick glanced at Barry's chest. *Still breathing.* When he looked back at Abraham, the other man was watching Barry, too. "Where'd you do your residency?"

"San Francis—" Abraham stopped mid-sentence. He shrank back against the wall.

"So, you *are* a doctor. I thought so. What's your specialty?"

"I didn't—"

Patrick held up a hand. "Listen. I don't know what happened that you don't want to talk about, but it's clear you're skilled and knowledgeable. I'm just glad you were here to keep Barry alive. Thank you, Abraham."

Abraham finally met Patrick's eyes. His own were wary, but he took a deep breath and said, "You're welcome."

"You're a California native then?"

"I am."

"I've been trying to place your accent. I wouldn't have pegged you as a Californian."

"I—one of my parents was born overseas."

"Oh. Do they still live abroad?"

"My father passed away some years ago. I lost my mother recently."

"I'm sorry."

Abraham nodded.

Patrick felt like he was hunting a deer. He concentrated on staying motionless and not making a sound so as not to spook Abraham, which grew harder as the seconds ticked by.

The strategy worked, though. Abraham started talking, his lips moving quickly, like he was trying to keep the words from escaping his mouth. "I studied internal medicine. At Stanford University. I was at San Francisco General for residency."

The silence following his confession made the cave feel stuffy and crowded. The man had opened up, even though admitting he had left the practice of medicine to work as a ranch hand raised more questions than it answered. *Burn out? Personal crisis? A patient death he couldn't get over? A malpractice suit or censure?* None of them would be things a physician would easily discuss, more than likely.

Patrick decided not to press him on it. "Well, I will rest easier tonight knowing you're taking a shift with Barry."

Abraham dropped his eyes back to a patch of rocky dirt by his feet and didn't say another word.

CHAPTER THIRTY-FOUR: RECONCILE

Trish

Trish grasped the edge of the bus door as she descended the steps in Buffalo. She couldn't wait to get off. The terminal in Denver had been one of the smelliest, scariest places ever. The stench of urine was stronger than when Ferdinand had been relegated to the garage as a puppy before he was potty trained. Did people there actually go into the bathrooms to relieve themselves, or did they just squat in the ticket line? The people were the saddest and most desperate she could imagine. Most of them looked tired, hungry, and dirty. Crusty, oily, dirty.

A few didn't. She'd never seen prostitutes and pimps in real life before, although she'd seen a few in movies her parents didn't know she'd watched. Until tonight at the bus station. Women wearing tight clothes in gaudy colors and prints, exposing too much skin for the cold Colorado air, strutting in high-heeled boots made from fake animal skin. Two men in suits with big lapels and silky shirts opened down their chests showing off more gold chains than Trish and her mom owned, put together. One of the men had asked her if she was alone and where she was going. He'd offered her a chance to stay in Denver and "make some dough," then promised to show her a good time, flashing a handful of pills. She'd turned him down without answering his questions and avoided eye contact with him until she'd been able to board the bus.

The bus was no better. The driver had leered at her as she climbed on, and he kept using his rearview mirror to stare at her. His Adam's apple bulged every time he swallowed, and he swallowed every time she noticed him looking at her. She'd buttoned her coat all the way to her throat and pulled it as far down her thighs as it would go. The seat was ripped, with springs sticking out, and so sticky that she'd worn her gloves and leaned a little bit forward so her hair wouldn't touch it. The bus had smelled worse than the terminal—like week-old hamburgers, cigarettes, body odor, and dirty diapers.

Between worrying about the driver and gagging over the odors and the nasty seat, she hadn't slept. And boy did she ever wish she had, because they'd driven through a major storm, barely crawling along the interstate. She'd been terrified they'd have to pull to the side of the road for the night. What would she do about the driver, then? Would anybody on this nasty bus even help her if he attacked her?

As it was, the storm had them running hours late. She wouldn't be taking a bus again soon, if ever.

"You can ride the dirty dog with me any time, little mama," a smoker's voice said from behind her, raising the hair on her neck.

She glanced back involuntarily. *The driver.* He licked his lips, and she ran a few steps on the sidewalk to put distance between herself and him, stumbling in the pre-dawn light and deep snow. Laughter rang out from inside the bus. Not just his.

She kept pushing forward. Away, away, away. When she'd put

twenty yards between herself and the bus, she stopped and took a deep breath. Fresh, clean-smelling air filled her lungs. It was a huge relief, even if it was absolutely freezing inside her chest. She coughed.

Hugging herself and shivering, she looked around. The town was sleepy and still. *No drug dealing pimps or prostitutes or perverted drivers.* The buildings were frosted in several inches of fresh snow. There were no people exiting the bus except her. One old man in winter coveralls boarded and the door shut behind him. She suddenly appreciated normal and quiet.

She turned in a circle. There were no vehicles driving by. But there was one parked at the curb. Marcy Peterson, her signature brown braids hanging from each side of her head, was waving to Trish from the driver's seat of her mom's baby blue station wagon.

"Thank you, God," Trish said aloud.

She had sucked up her courage and called Marcy from Casper a few hours before. It had already been really late. Or really early. Luckily, Marcy had her own phone line in her room, and she'd picked up on the first ring. She hadn't even made it awkward when Trish had asked for a ride home at dawn, just promised to set her alarm, sneak the car out, and be there.

Trish trotted to the wagon and opened the passenger door. The radio was turned up to max volume, blaring "More Than a Feeling." Marcy was obsessed with the band Boston. The heater was cranking at max, too, and it felt wonderful.

"You're the best. I can't believe you came to get me," Trish said.

"Of course. You're my friend, Trish Flint," Marcy said, flashing a freckle-faced grin.

"How long did you have to wait out here?"

"Um, like an hour or so. I fell asleep. It wasn't that bad."

"Thank you. Thank you, thank you, thank you."

"I've missed you."

The girls leaned to the center of the bench seat and threw their arms around each other. Trish held on tight for several seconds.

Marcy was familiar and welcoming. Tears threatened again. She'd needed a hug. She'd needed a friend.

"I've missed you, too, Marcy. I'm sorry I've been so preoccupied with Ben and stuff."

When they'd released each other, Marcy put the car in reverse. "That's okay. If I had a fox boyfriend like Ben, I'd ditch you, too, you know. Your house, right?"

"Right."

"The roads are bad. This won't be fast. The DJ said it's like the worst storm in years, you know? They've shut down the interstate north of Sheridan, and you can't cross the mountains up there, either. They've got it way worse than us."

Trish had already noticed there were barely any cars on the road. *Thank God the bus made it to Buffalo.* A snowplow passed them going the opposite direction on Main Street. She wondered if her dad and Perry were snowed in at their lodge. If her mom, Dian, and Esme would be able to drive home. *If Ben is here and if he'll be able to leave.* "Be careful. Your mom will kill you if you wreck her baby."

"We're going to take real good care of the Mamamobile." Marcy turned on Fort Street, heading west. "But speaking of a mom who's gonna kill you—how much trouble are you going to be in for this? It's almost like you've run away. But kinda in reverse."

Trish groaned. "So, so much trouble. I don't have a choice, though."

"It's time for you to spill, girl. What's going on?" Marcy looked over just as Trish pushed her hair off her face. "Oh, my God! Is that a ring on your hand? What? Are you engaged?"

Heat flooded Trish's face. The ring. Ben had given it to her and then bailed. *How humiliating.* "Not engaged. It's my birthstone."

"On your ring finger? It's from Ben, isn't it?"

"Um . . . yes."

"I knew it! Are you promised?"

"I don't know anymore." Trish closed her eyes. She didn't want to tell Marcy about Ben leaving. She wanted to pretend none of it had happened. Was happening. But she owed Marcy a little of the truth, and if she trusted her friend, it would go a long way to repairing their bruised relationship. "This has to stay between me and you, all right?"

"Are you pregnant?"

"What? No! We haven't done *that*—no, no. It's not about me. It's about Ben. He, uh, he got arrested."

"Again?"

"He wasn't, I mean, he was never really arrested before, he just kind of went to juvie. But, whatever. He got arrested in Laramie." She sighed. "That's not the problem, though."

"It sounds like a pretty big problem to me."

"It is, but he's innocent. It would have been okay, I think, but he left."

Marcy shot her a glance, then cut her eyes back to the treacherous road. Trish was impressed. Her friend was driving really well in the snow. "What do you mean *he left?*"

Trish stared straight ahead, unseeing. *Good question.* "Took off. Without a word to me. Just a note to Henry and Vangie."

"Where did he go?"

An even better question. "He didn't say. But I think I might know. And I've got to stop him."

Marcy turned onto the road to the Flints' house. The snow was even deeper there. "Whoa."

The back end of the station wagon fish tailed. Marcy bit her lip as the car struggled to get through.

"Don't let your speed fall." Trish had gotten stuck on this same road in her truck before.

"Yeah." Marcy's knuckles were white on the steering wheel. She looked tiny stretching as tall as she could for better visibility. The drifts were shoving the station wagon toward the side of the road.

Trish decided not to bring up the deep drainage ditch buried under the snow.

When they reached the Flints' driveway, Marcy stopped by

letting off the gas. "If I turn in there, I'll never get out. If I continue straight here, it reconnects to the road back to my place."

"You're probably right." Trish hugged her again. "But are you sure you don't want to come in and brave your mom's wrath? I don't want you to get stuck out there somewhere by yourself."

"I won't. I'll be careful."

"You'd better. Thank you, Marcy. For everything."

"Call me. Call me the second you know anything."

"I will. And you call me when you make it home. Promise?"

"I promise," Marcy said.

Trish got out. The snow was halfway to her knees. She trudged toward her house, turning once to wave to her friend. Man, was she ever glad she'd worn her moon boots on the bus. Hurrying, she dug out her key ring, careful not to drop it. Finding it in the deep snow wouldn't be fun or easy. Just as she felt like she was about to turn into an icicle, she reached the door. Extended her key ring to unlock it. Saw a paper fluttering where it was tucked into the jamb.

Her heart caught in her throat, and she pressed against it with three fingers.

She pulled the paper out. It was a receipt from Big Horn Tire. She frowned, staring at it. Why was a receipt stuck in the door? The wind blew it from her fingers. She leaped after it, snatching it out of midair as it tumbled. The back of the receipt was face up this time.

Ben's familiar handwriting was scribbled across it, tiny, and filling every speck of white space. *Ben was here!* Greedily, she read:

Trish, I'm not good enough for you or anyone else. I never will be. Bad things follow me around. You have such a great future ahead of you. I won't be the thing that drags you down. I'm stopping at my old house to get some stuff and make some cash for my trip. I'm going where I can make money, and no one knows about me. I'm sorry. I will always love you, more than anything. Please keep the ring and remember me. Ben

Trish's jaw clenched and unclenched. Tears flowed. *This makes no sense. What is he thinking?!* She read it again and could barely see the words through her tears. It didn't make any more sense to her the second time. She started to read it a third time, then stopped. Standing, motionless, she tried to get her brain and heart under control. *Something is wrong with him. This isn't the Ben I know.*

She hesitated only a second more before she wheeled around and ran for her truck.

CHAPTER THIRTY-FIVE: LEAP

Buffalo, Wyoming
Saturday, December 31, 1977, 7:30 a.m.

Susanne

Susanne scrubbed at her eyes with a fist. Only a few miles to go until Buffalo. The Suburban veered as the foot of snow in a drift won its battle with the groaning wheels. It shocked her back into a state of high alert. *Careless. I can't be so careless.* With both hands on the steering wheel, she fought her way back into the tracks of the eighteen-wheeler in front of her on the interstate.

She was just so tired. Unearthly, unbelievably, unbearably tired. After talking to Trish, she'd been in a panic. What had that call even meant? Ben was missing. Trish had to go. She hadn't known what to do. Call Patrick at the lodge? She'd tried, but the phones were down. Call Vangie? She didn't know how to get hold of her in Laramie. Call the police? Trish would never forgive her if Susanne had her pulled off a public bus. *At least she's not hitch-hiking. But is the bus that much better?* Besides, she wasn't even sure what police to call if she did. Denver? Buffalo? The state police?

For better or worse, and she really hoped it wasn't for worse, she'd decided to trust her daughter until morning.

So, she'd managed to hold herself together, and she'd herded an unrepentant Dian and a taciturn Esme into the Suburban and headed north. Trish hadn't told Susanne where she was going, but she had said, "see you at home," so that's where they were heading, as fast as Susanne could get them there. Even if Trish was running away with Ben, Susanne believed she'd go there first. She'd left her suitcase with all her clothes and toiletries at the hotel. She'd need her truck. Her things. And if Trish wasn't there when they arrived, Susanne would call Ronnie. Ronnie would know who to contact and what to do.

The atmosphere was as chilly in the vehicle as outside it. No one spoke a word for the first four hours. Susanne didn't care. If they didn't have anything positive or helpful to say, she'd just as soon they stayed quiet. And there was plenty of noise in her own head, a buzzing that she knew wouldn't go away until she could pull her daughter into her arms. At least she hadn't had a migraine. Thank goodness for her medicine. She'd taken two back in Denver. One in the morning, and one—dry—when she got in the Suburban.

But just south of Casper, they'd run into a major storm. A blizzard really, that made her glad Patrick had insisted on snow tires for her vehicle. It was coming down so hard and thick that it was like a stream of powdered sugar pouring from a heavenly cannister, except there was nothing heavenly about it. She turned on her low beams and strained to stay on the right side of the reflective poles on the side of the road. How come she'd never noticed how far apart they were?

It had been a struggle just to get to the outskirts of town. There, she saw neon signs proclaiming NO VACANCY at three consecutive hotels. Then she found the C'MON INN. The name had not been enticing. *Beggars can't be choosers.* But she would have paid any price and stayed in any flea bag she had to at that point.

The hotel had been surprisingly okay, what she'd seen of it before she threw herself into bed with Dian. A cavernous log cabin interior. Hot tubs on individual patios. Greenery—fake—hanging off balconies. All Susanne cared about was how it smelled, the odor being the surest indicator of ongoing cleanliness, and the hotel and the room had smelled antiseptically fresh and the whole place slightly of chlorine. She couldn't fall asleep, though, and spent most of the short night counting the minutes until they could get going toward her daughter again. Fortunately, when she went to the front desk at four a.m. to check the roads and weather, the worst of the storm had passed, and the plows were out. She'd rousted her unhappy companions and had them back in the car by four-thirty with hot coffee the desk clerk had made specially for them.

From Casper to Buffalo, the roads had been slow, but not slick. Susanne would rather drive on snow than ice any time. And now, they were only half a mile from the exit into Buffalo. Only three miles from the Flints' home. Where Trish might. . . or might not . . . be. *Dear God, let Trish be there. Where I can kill her with my bare hands for using the worst judgment ever.*

Susanne's brain started buzzing again, this time with irritation at her daughter. Had it even occurred to Trish that her choices had ended the weekend for Dian and Esme—not that it mattered, since neither of them wanted to be within a hundred miles of each other anymore, but Trish hadn't known that—and forced the women to drive after her at night, putting everyone at risk? Had she thought of the dangers to a sixteen-year-old girl traveling by bus, from a big city terminal like Denver? Susanne had heard stories about bus terminals. Diseases. Thieves. Drug dealers. Sexual predators. About pimps looking for young runaways to hook into drugs and prostitution. Even serial killers. She shivered.

A crunching sound and blow to the front of her vehicle tore her attention away from her daughter.

She'd hit something.

In the backseat, Esme let out a series of piercing shrieks. Beside Susanne, Dian gasped once.

The hood of the Suburban folded on Susanne's side like an accordion blind. Yet, whatever they'd collided with hadn't been big enough to stop the Suburban, because it was still doing thirty miles an hour, albeit swerving in and out of the snow tracks she'd been following. She let off the gas and scanned for the other party to their accident, as she fought to keep the Suburban under control.

She didn't want to hit it again, whatever it was.

But something about the way the vehicle was pulling to the left and a movement on the front driver's side drew her eyes back to the front end of the Suburban.

Dian said, "Susanne . . ." and pointed where Susanne was already looking.

A huge buck mule deer's rack of antlers was caught under the hood. All four of its hooves were scrambling for purchase. It had survived the collision, and it wanted away from the spinning wheel near its head.

"What is it?" Esme said, her voice a squeal.

Dian said, "Deer. Its antlers are stuck in our car."

Esme started moaning.

Susanne's first instinct was to stomp on the brakes. But that might send the car into an out-of-control spin. Her next thought was to steer right, away from it. Susanne didn't want to run the Suburban off the road, but if she steered a little to the right, the deer might be able to break free.

"Buckle your seat belts," she said.

"Already done!" Dian shouted.

Esme whimpered. "Got it."

"Now hold on." Susanne eyed the roadside. The terrain looked flat. The Suburban had slowed to ten miles per hour. It was now or never. If she was going to do this, it was going to require some muscle. She gritted her teeth and jerked the wheel to the right.

The Suburban lumbered off the shoulder.

"He's loose," Esme screamed.

Susanne's heart leapt. She wished she could see the animal running away to safety. She hoped it would survive. But right now, she had to focus on getting the Suburban back on the road.

She steered to the left. Nothing happened. She pressed the brake. The Suburban didn't respond, just kept heading to the right. It started to buck and bounce over ground that, underneath a foot or more of snow, apparently wasn't as smooth or flat as it seemed.

And then the front end dipped.

"Oh, no," Susanne whispered.

With a sickening tilt, the vehicle slid nose down into a ditch, where it landed with a jolt.

"Oomph." Susanne's upper body smashed into the steering wheel, diaphragm first. It knocked the wind out of her, and she couldn't draw a breath. Dazed, she clutched her chest. *Please don't let my ribs be broken.* She'd lose the high ground with Patrick if she hurt herself doing something as dumb as him. All she could hear was Esme's muffled sobs in the back seat. Dian reached over and put her hand on Susanne's knee.

When Susanne recovered enough to speak, she unbuckled her seat belt and said, "Is everyone all right?" The pain in her chest eased. But a stabbing sensation behind her eye got her attention.

"I'm okay," Dian said. "It was barely a bump to me."

"F-f-f-ine," Esme said.

"Good." Susanne turned up the heater. "I'm so sorry."

"It's okay," Dian said. "And I think the deer made it."

"I have to go take a look outside."

"Do you need me to help you?"

"No. I'll just be a minute."

Susanne was already wearing her coat. She'd learned during her first year in Wyoming to always be prepared for the worst, which meant never shucking winter wear in a car. She donned her hat and gloves, then opened the door and hopped out. Her body sunk all the way up to the waist in powdery snow. *Spit in a well bucket.* She wasn't walking the perimeter of the car unless she had to. If she fell over, she'd have a heck of a time getting herself up and out.

Once, when she, Patrick, and the kids were up in the Bighorn National Forest cutting down their Christmas tree, she'd separated from the group to find a place to answer the call of nature. Never mind that she'd asked to stop at Clear Creek Resort to borrow a real bathroom. Or that she only had one small scrap of Kleenex. Or that it was only ten degrees outside. She'd been irritated and wasn't paying enough attention to where she put her feet. Down she'd gone into a snow-covered depression. It had probably been about three feet deep, but from a prone position it felt like a bottomless pit. She'd floundered for the better part of five minutes until Perry found her and sent his dad to pull her out. Her feckless husband and children had laughed at her for days. She was just glad she hadn't pulled her britches down before she fell. But, honestly—she'd been scared nearly to death down in that hole. If she'd been truly alone, she didn't know how she would have gotten out of it. With snow, things underneath weren't always what they seemed, and it didn't take an extraordinary amount to cause a heap of problems.

She braced herself on the edge of the Suburban's door and peered around the back end. Amazingly, there was no snow up on the side of the ditch. She had a clear view of the path of their slide. And of the rear end of the vehicle. One of the back wheels was off the ground, by almost a foot. *Not good.*

She climbed back in, bringing a yard of snow with her. Her head pain intensified. "There's no way I'll be able to drive us out of here. We're close to a gas station, though. A quarter of a mile. I'll walk there and get help." She reached for her purse, dug for her migraine pills, and fumbled with the bottle.

"Should we come with you?" Dian asked.

"If you're up to it—and your footwear is."

Esme yowled like a drowning cat. "I can't. But I don't want to stay here by myself."

Susanne was sure Esme didn't want to be stuck in the car with

Dian, either. The woman was running out of options. While Susanne hated that she'd put them all in this position, she found she couldn't squeeze out a drop of sympathy for Esme. Susanne needed to get moving. This predicament was costing her precious time searching for Trish. If she missed her at home, that would be the biggest tragedy of this situation, not whether Esme got her feet wet or had to sit by herself for half an hour.

A sharp rapping sounded on the window by her ear. Susanne startled and jumped halfway across the seat toward Dian, dropping the open bottle of pills. Esme screamed. Only Dian remained calm.

"It's a woman," she said. "In a uniform."

Susanne turned to find herself gazing at a welcome sight. Her friend, Ronnie.

Susanne cranked her window down. "Are you clairvoyant or something? I was about to walk to a gas station and call you."

Ronnie shook her head. "I was heading in the other direction and saw your car before you hit that buck. Geez, Susanne, you took ten years off my life. You know better than to steer away from an animal. It's your life or theirs."

"I don't know what got into me. Too much *Bambi*, I guess."

"I'm just glad you're all right. How about your passengers?" Ronnie leaned in and looked at Dian and Esme. "Hello, ladies. I'm Johnson County Deputy Ronnie Harcourt. Former next-door neighbor of the Flints." Gorgeous and nearly six feet tall, Ronnie exuded the confidence and competence of a ranch-raised Wyoming woman, and that was a whole lot of both.

"I'm good." Dian reached over and shook Ronnie's hand, introducing herself.

Esme lifted a limp hand in greeting. *What does Barry see in her?*

Susanne said, "We're all good. Except that I'm mortified and embarrassed. And there's one other problem that I need to talk to you about in a minute."

"My truck is warm, and I can give you a ride home while I call for a tow. The snow's deep here, though. You might do better crawling out the back end."

"I can attest to that."

Susanne picked up all the pills she could find in the floorboard and returned all but one to the bottle. She dry swallowed and put the container back in her purse. Three pills in twenty-four hours. That probably exceeded the recommended dosage. It wasn't something she was going to confess to her husband, but she'd lay off them now. The women climbed over the seats to the way back and disembarked, bags and all. Five minutes later, Dian and Susanne had loaded their things and climbed into Ronnie's truck.

Ronnie boosted Esme up. She got in herself and pulled slowly onto the roadway. "You're headed home, right?"

"Yes. I can't thank you enough."

Ronnie lifted her radio mic and clicked the button. She arranged for a tow, then returned the mic to its holster. "I've been trying to reach Patrick about the O Bar M case for two days. Is he at home?"

"No. He and Perry are up at Clear Creek Resort. Dr. John put a group together to go play in the snow."

Ronnie smiled. "I knew that but forgot. Dr. John's annual guys' trip. That's a much sought-after invitation. Well, if you talk to him, tell him I need him."

You and me both. Patrick had no idea his daughter had left Denver on a bus to find her runaway boyfriend. Susanne had decided to hold off talking to Ronnie about Trish until they got to their house, just in case Trish was there. She already felt like enough of a failure as it was. "Is there progress on the case?"

"A little. We can't locate the ranch hand we're looking for, but we did find evidence that there'd been an unidentified vehicle on the ranch. There was a knife near where it was parked, and it had finger-prints on it. We're analyzing them now. I'm starting to think there was at least one more player, maybe driving a getaway car." She pulled into the driveway.

Half-tuned out, Susanne said, "Patrick will want to hear that. I hope I can get hold of him." She scanned the property for Trish's truck. It wasn't there. Susanne knew her daughter was well, but it was no solace. Trish had come to Buffalo, all right. Come and gone. She put her face in her hands.

"Susanne, is something the matter?" Ronnie sounded worried.

Susanne drew in a shuddering breath and lifted her head. "We're having trouble of our own."

"Oh?"

"Trish. We were in Denver for a girls' weekend, and she took a bus out of town."

"What? That's not like her!"

Esme muttered, "That's not my experience with her."

"Any idea why?"

Susanne shot Esme a look, then turned back to Ronnie. "What reason do teenage girls ever have for doing really dumb things?"

"Ben?"

"Yes," Susanne said.

Dian reached for Susanne's hand and squeezed it.

Ronnie sighed. "I heard he was arrested. Vangie and Henry dropped off Hank to stay with Jeff, Will, and me on their way to Laramie. Tell me what happened."

"After Ben was bailed out, he skipped town."

Ronnie's jaw dropped. "What? Poor Vangie. And—oh my gosh— where did he go?"

"We don't know."

"And Trish?"

"I don't know where she is, either." Susanne pointed. "But her truck is gone. She's been here this morning."

"How do you know that?"

"She took a bus from Denver last night. Her truck was here when we left and now it's not. I think she's going after Ben."

"That bus usually gets in around five, but with this weather, it was probably later. It's only eight now."

"She doesn't have too much of a head start, then." Dian patted Susanne's leg.

Ronnie nodded. "Do you have her license plate number?"

Sometimes being married to Patrick paid off. He had insisted everyone in the family memorize the license plate and vehicle info for each of the cars they owned. Susanne gave Ronnie the make, model, color, and plate number for Trish's truck.

"I'm going in the house," Esme announced.

Don't let the door hit you on the behind on your way in. "Fine," Susanne said.

"Do I need a key?"

Susanne had left her keys in the ignition for the tow truck. "Under the mat."

Esme's reply was inaudible, which was probably a good thing. She got out, but Dian stayed in the truck.

"That one's unfriendly," Ronnie said.

Susanne said, "You have no idea."

Ronnie radioed Trish's information to dispatch and asked for a BOLO. After she hung up her mic, she said, "Don't worry, Susanne. We'll catch up to her. I'll go after her myself."

"I'm coming with you."

Ronnie shook her head. "I wish I could let you do that, but I need you by the phone in case she calls."

Susanne drew in a deep breath. She hadn't thought of that. "I hate it, but you're right."

"Of course I am. I'll call you the second we have her."

Susanne nodded, fighting tears as she got out of the truck with Dian, and headed into her big, empty house.

CHAPTER THIRTY-SIX: RESENT

Perry

The first thing Perry did when he woke up was look over at his dad's side of the bed in their room at the lodge.

Empty.

Perry balled the covers in his hands. He knew his dad was smart and had a way of getting out of scrapes, but he was still worried. The wind had howled all night. He sat up. The windows were covered in frost and snow. It wasn't the kind of night to spend outside, even with shelter. George had come back around dinner time with the two girls Perry had seen when they were putting up the sled dogs. He'd tried to convince Perry that the cave and fire were warm enough. That his dad was safe.

But Perry still had a heavy ball in his gut.

He knew he should be more worried about Uncle Barry. George hadn't said so, but Perry knew Uncle Barry would make it, even though Dr. John was going to operate on him. His dad always said Dr. John had magic hands. But it was still scary. In the wilderness. In a blizzard. Much better to be in a hospital. A warm, dry hospital with nurses and medicine and everything else a doctor would need.

Perry had a sudden thought. What if his dad was back, but he'd stayed with Uncle Barry, to take care of him? Or maybe he just hadn't wanted to wake Perry up. He could be eating breakfast in front of the fire right that second.

Perry threw the covers off. The room was cold—cold as a bear with no hair—and his teeth chattered as he hopped on one foot and stuck the other in the leg of his jeans. When he had them on, he added yesterday's sweater with no shirt underneath. He glanced at his toothbrush and toothpaste but decided bad breath wasn't going to matter today. He'd slept in his wool socks, so he jammed his feet into boots that he didn't bother tying, grabbed his coat, and dashed from the room.

Perry's and his dad's room was on the first floor. He sprinted down the shallow hall to the central room with its enormous rock fireplace and a breakfast buffet that ran along the entire length of one wall. He was in a hurry to see if his dad was there. His stomach rumbled. But he was also hungry. Eggs, sausages made locally in Sheridan, pancakes, oatmeal, and fruit. It was terrible to be thinking about food when he should be worried about his dad. He could be both at the same time, though. He ran faster.

He came to a quick stop at the entrance and searched the room. He didn't see his dad, and his heart sank like a bucket of cement. But George and the two women were there, eating. Their plates were nearly empty, though.

George waved him over. "Good morning, young Mr. Flint."

Perry didn't have time to yip yap with George. "Have you seen my dad yet?"

"No, but we didn't expect to. It wasn't safe for them to travel at night in the storm. I was hoping Search and Rescue would be here by now, but they haven't been able to get through. That's okay, though.

We made a warm stretcher on a sled for your uncle. The storm has stopped, and the sun is up. We're going to get them ourselves." He clapped Perry on the shoulder. "It's going to be okay, Perry. You'll see."

One of the women said, "My mom made them thermoses of coffee and hot food. We'll be on our way in five minutes."

Perry nodded. "I'll go get ready." He turned to run back to his room.

"Whoa, whoa, whoa." George grabbed him by the elbow. "That's not happening, buckaroo."

Perry's face flamed and he shook George off. "I'm old enough. And it's my dad and uncle."

George's lips pressed together. He shook his head slowly. "No can do. I'm sorry." He stood. "That storm laid down a ton of new powder. It's going to be difficult for even the most experienced riders. We can't afford to slow down for anyone getting stuck. You understand, right?"

The women stood, too.

Perry nodded, his neck jerky, but he didn't say a word. He watched them walk away, his anger simmering, and a plan forming in his mind.

CHAPTER THIRTY-SEVEN: SLEUTH

Piney Bottoms Ranch, Story, Wyoming
Saturday, December 31, 1977, 8:00 a.m.

Trish

Trish shivered. Her old truck took forever to warm up, and it was like an ice box inside it, even after she'd been driving for fifteen minutes. The reflection of the sun off the snow was blinding, and despite her sunglasses, Trish still had to squint. Nothing looked cleaner, prettier, and brighter than Wyoming after a blizzard. As beautiful as it was, it didn't cheer her up. She was searching for the boyfriend she had thought loved her, but who had left her to run off who knew where, after he put a ring on her finger. She looked at her hand. A pretty little amethyst ring. A promise that they would be together.

Her eyes burned from crying, but she was out of tears. That was a good thing. Tears meant she wouldn't be able to see where she was going. If she got stuck or ran off the road, she wouldn't be able to catch up with Ben.

But catch up with him where? She knew he'd gone through

Buffalo, but that was it. She had no idea how far ahead of her he was, and only a guess that he'd headed to Piney Bottoms. She mulled it over for the thousandth time. If he'd driven out of Laramie yesterday afternoon, he'd probably left the note for her on his way to the ranch the night before. *Probably*. He might have done it after he left Piney Bottoms. She didn't think so, though. It made sense that he'd stop on his way.

So, would he have spent the night at the ranch or grabbed his things and kept driving? That was a harder question. Was he more worried about falling asleep on the road or about being intercepted at Piney Bottoms? He couldn't have slept much in the jail. Driving after two nights in a row without sleep would be dangerous. Foolish. He knew that Henry and Vangie were in Laramie. But if they'd left to return to the ranch immediately after reading his note, they might make it back before he got away. And what about Trish and her family? It was a short drive from Buffalo to Story. For all Ben knew, the Sibleys could have sent the Flints after him. Would that bother him? It wasn't like anyone could stop him. Not really, short of holding him at gunpoint. He was an adult. He could do what he wanted.

Including breaking up with her. Ugh, the possibilities. At least the heater had started to make a difference in the cab. She was exhausted from cycling through the possibilities. Her brain wanted to collapse in a heap.

Talk about stuck. Mentally, at least. She decided that none of it made a difference. Not really. Because no matter where Ben had spent the night, her search for him had to start at the ranch. Had to.

Luckily, getting her truck stuck didn't seem likely. The snow-plows had been out in force on the interstate, and she drove slowly and didn't have any trouble. Until she turned off pavement, that is, and onto the four miles of dirt road leading to Piney Bottoms Ranch. Only one strip had been plowed, right down the center of the road. A very narrow strip. Not even the width of the blade of a commercial snowplow. More like the blade on the front of a pickup of someone who needed to get to work.

She eyed the road, the plowed strip, and the snow on either side of it. Did she have any other options? If she drove to Story and approached Piney Bottoms from the opposite direction, she'd still be on the same gravel road, with four miles to cover either way. Piney Bottoms was smack in the middle of it. And there was no guarantee anyone had plowed at all from that direction. Her choice was simple. Go, and risk getting stuck on a road with almost zero traffic, which meant she'd be alone and without help. Or not go, and risk missing Ben or at least clues about where he was headed.

I'm dressed okay for the weather, and I'm not going to starve to death. Didn't her parents always tell her, "nothing ventured, nothing gained?" Usually that had to do with trying out for a new sport or applying for college scholarships. They wouldn't be pleased to know she was applying their logic to driving down a drifted road after Ben.

"Come on, Trish. You can do this." She pounded her mittened hand on the steering wheel, then gently pressed the gas.

Her pickup seemed to float. She concentrated on driving a straight line, barely breathing at first. Her truck crept up a hill. Was she going too slow? She could bog down. But if she sped up, she might lose traction. Would the road be worse or better if it wasn't so cold out? Winter weather fluctuated wildly in their area, as did the properties of snow and strategies for driving in each type. It would morph from deep and drifted and smooth as frosting to cottony and lumpy, then to oozy, and on to dense and icy, all before it thawed. None of them were easy to drive in. *Ice is the worst. But drifts are second worst.*

Her head started to hurt, and she realized her shoulders were nearly up to her ears. *Relax. Be calm.* She took several long, slow breaths. *You've got this.* She relaxed her death grip on the steering wheel and allowed herself to take in a little of the landscape. A deer pawed down to the grass in the pasture next to Fort Phil Kearney, but other than that, the snowscape was smooth and unbroken. It made her feel alone. And she was alone, not just because right this minute she was in the only vehicle she could see—the only person around for who knew how far. Her family wasn't anywhere she could reach them. Her mom was in Denver. Her dad and Perry were in the mountains. Marcy had come to Trish's rescue when she called, but the two of them weren't close anymore.

And Ben was gone. Or maybe not. Maybe he'd be at Piney Bottoms, snowed in, with the power out like happened so often in a blizzard, wrapped in a blanket in front of a roaring fire. Happy to see her. She could talk him into staying while they waited for the power to come back on. Probably not, but it could happen.

She approached a stream crossing. The water was still running but with ice at the edges of the creek. A few horses were sunning on its banks, their backs covered in solid blankets of snow and their empty turn-out shed behind them. She slowed to cross the earthen bridge, then gradually increased her speed up a hill on the other side of the creek. A family was sledding beside the road, taking turns on long plastic toboggans. Across the road from them, a man was hitching two horses to a sleigh. It looked like they were all having fun.

Sadness twisted her insides. She wanted fun. To be in front of that fire she imagined at Piney Bottoms, with Ben. In Denver buying clothes and makeup with her mom would be okay, too. She'd even be happy up at Clear Creek Resort with her dad and brother.

She just wanted to feel good. Ben had always made her feel good. This—leaving her—was the exact opposite.

She rounded a bend. The gate to Piney Bottoms was in sight. *Finally.* The plowed strip had continued all the way there. That had been a stroke of good luck. But it didn't turn into the gate. She stopped, evaluating and looking. There was a single set of tire tracks over the cattle guard leading to the house and ranch buildings. A drumroll started in her chest. *Ben. Maybe.* But coming or going? She had no way of knowing anything, other than they'd been left after the snow.

She positioned her truck in the tracks and drove carefully toward the house. It wasn't as easy as following the plowed strip, but it was only a few inches deep since the north wind tended to blow most of the snow away there. She tried to keep her eyes on the road, but it was impossible not to search for Ben's truck. She didn't see it anywhere. Henry's either. The twisting feeling in her midsection started up again. When she reached the main house, she jumped out and ran to the front door. She knocked but didn't wait to see if anyone answered. They never locked the place. She opened the door.

"Ben! Ben, where are you? It's me. Ben!"

The inside of the house was quiet. Quiet as her school had been one time when she and Marcy had sneaked in after hours to get a book Trish had forgotten in her locker. She sniffed, hoping to detect the scent of breakfast or Ben—his wonderful mix of soap, sunshine, dirt, and clean sweat.

Nothing.

She ran into the kitchen.

Empty.

Back through the great room.

No Ben.

Down the hall to his bedroom.

No one was there.

And into the bathroom.

The lights were out, and the door was open.

She slumped against the wall in the hallway. Ben wasn't there. Might not have come there at all. She thought about the tracks. They were most likely his, but she couldn't be sure. Not about who left them or when.

But she would assume they were Ben's. It was her best option.

Which direction had the tracks gone—back the way she had come or towards Story? She hadn't noticed. She fought an urge to run back to her truck and follow them. She could do that. Would do that. But she was already in the house. She had to see if he'd left a note while she was still there. Look for any clues he might have left accidentally.

She walked into his bedroom. His absence was palpable, but so was the fact that he had been there the night before. Now she knew something for sure. His bed was made, but sloppy, with the lumpy covers pulled over but not tucked around the pillow. Like he'd done it instead of Mrs. Sibley, because Mrs. Sibley liked things to be *just so*. Trish leaned over the bed and caught a whiff—just a trace—of Ben. It made her feel a weird pressure in her chest. She ignored it. Now wasn't the time to get emotional.

Trish opened each drawer in his dresser. They were empty. Of course. He'd taken most of his clothes to Laramie. She'd sat in his desk chair and watched him pack. She looked around the room. It was like he'd never lived here. No pictures. No mementos. The rocks he'd collected last summer were gone. The lucky horseshoe he'd found his first day at the ranch—not there.

Ben didn't plan on coming back.

Alaska, a voice inside her whispered. She knew in her heart of hearts that he was making a break for Alaska. She didn't know how she knew it. Ben had only mentioned Alaska a few times. She just did, because she knew him. *Inside and out.*

But it would take a lot of money for gas all the way to Alaska. To buy food. To pay for places to stay, whenever the weather wasn't nice enough to camp or stay in his truck. That would be a lot of the time. It was the dead of winter. Ben didn't have enough money to get to Alaska.

Yet he'd been here and was gone. For a split second, she wondered if he'd stolen money from Vangie and Henry. She dismissed that thought as fast as it had come. Ben wouldn't do that. Never in a million years. Not just because he was a good person, but because he was determined to prove he was nothing like the criminals in his family.

So, what would he do to get the money?

She stared out the window. It looked out on rugged pastureland and up the mountains. The view. There was nothing like the view from Piney Bottoms. In the distance, a herd of black Angus cattle were huddled with their butts to the wind. They'd stand like that for hours, waiting for someone to come throw them hay. To take care of them.

Ben wasn't like that. Ben took care of himself.

And that's when it hit her. In his note, Ben had told her *exactly* where he was going and what he was going to do. She pulled it out of her jeans pocket and re-read it. "I'm stopping at my old house to get some stuff and make some cash for my trip. I'm going where I can make money, and no one knows about me." He wasn't talking about Piney Bottoms. He meant his old house, where he'd lived with his mom, before she disappeared, and then with only his dad.

Ben was on his way to Alaska, with a stop in Cody first.

Trish sprinted back to her truck, tripping in the deep snow in the yard. She tumbled to her hands and knees, then all the way onto her chest, getting a face full of cold and wet. She scrambled back to her feet and ran again, not slowing down. She threw herself into her truck. It was freezing in there again. She restarted it.

"Come on heater. Do something. Please." It made noises and spit out air. Cold air. She pumped the gas to help it along.

Then she dug through her glove box. Her dad had given her a bunch of maps when she bought the pickup. The Wyoming map was on the bottom. Everything piled on top of it spilled to the floor. A box of tissues. A Chapstick. A hairbrush with ponytail holders in different colors wrapped around its handle. A box of raisins. She ignored the mess and spread the map out on the seat. Cody was on the other side of the Bighorn Mountains, somewhere in the middle of the state. She drew a line with her finger from Buffalo west across the mountains. Scanned the area. Found Cody.

"Yes!"

She studied the map. It looked shorter to cross the mountains north of Sheridan, but Marcy had said those roads were closed. Trish would have to go back through Buffalo and connect with Highway 16. But did she have enough fuel? Her tank was close to full. She added up the mileage along the route. She'd probably make it. If not, she had a few bucks left of the Christmas money from her grand-parents.

And if she ran out of gas and money, she'd figure out what to do about it then.

She looked at the amethyst ring on her finger. She was going to Cody. To find Ben, and to convince him to come home.

CHAPTER THIRTY-EIGHT: FOLLOW

Patrick

Patrick batted his eyes open, then shook his head gently to clear the cobwebs. Sun was streaming in the mouth of the cave. Had he overslept? His ribs seemed like they'd kept him up half the short night. He sat up and looked around. Snow was piled three feet high just past the cave's mouth, where the overhang shed onto the ground. Inside, everyone else still slept. Except for Abraham, who Patrick didn't see.

He crawled over to Barry. Despite his goal to rest and rely on the others to care for Barry during their shifts, Patrick had woken repeatedly, worried about his friend and brother-in-law. He hadn't managed to sustain solid sleep until the wee hours of the morning.

Barry's color looked better, and his skin was dry. Those were good signs. Patrick touched his face. It felt on the warm side of good.

Not a full-blown fever. Not yet. But something to keep an eye on. He'd feel much better when they could admit Barry to the hospital and give him a full course of antibiotics.

Barry's eyes fluttered to slits. He groaned. His eyes widened and dilated then flitted around, taking in the rock walls of the cave. When he spoke, his lips clung together, and his voice was weak and raspy. "I hurt like a son of a gun." He tried to raise his head. His skin paled and he winced.

"That's your body telling you to be still."

"I knew you were a quack." Barry fanned his eyes shut.

"Rest while I wake the others."

Barry didn't bother to reply.

Wes and Dr. John had both begun to stir. Patrick glanced at his watch. It was eight a.m. He whipped his head around, looking for Abraham again. The man was supposed to wake them all by seven, so they could prepare to leave and be ready when help arrived. Where was he? Why hadn't he woken them?

He jostled Wes's shoulder. "Time to get up. It's eight. Have you seen Abraham?"

"Uh uh." Wes rubbed his eyes and sat up.

"Abraham's gone?" Dr. John said, without opening his eyes or moving a muscle.

"Yes. And we all overslept. I'm worried about him," Patrick said.

If Abraham had gone out to relieve himself or gather wood, could something have happened to him—a predator or moose attack, the weather, falling rocks, a heart attack? But he thought back to Abraham's odd behaviors and reticence in conversation the night before. Something was off about the man. If Patrick had to guess, Abraham was hiding something.

Or from something.

"Barry's a little warm." But he was in good hands with Wes and Dr. John. "I'm turning him over to you guys and going to see where Abraham is."

Dr. John grunted. He rolled up onto his side. "We need to stay in twos."

Patrick began pulling on his boots. "You and Wes will make two. Abraham will be my second when I find him. I won't go far."

"You're armed?"

Patrick snorted. "Have been since I moved here." He had slept in his jacket, but now he zipped it up over the holster he'd never removed.

Wes's face was puckered in a frown of consternation. "I don't like it, Doc. Fire a shot if you need us, okay?"

Patrick saluted with a gloved hand, then put on the other one and his helmet. "When the cavalry arrives, you do the same, so I'll know to come back."

"Will do."

Patrick trudged out toward the snowmobiles. *When the going gets tough, the tough get going,* he reminded himself. He swam through the deep snow pile, knocking as much out of the way as he could. Someone had left evidence that they'd fought through there earlier—tracks, of a sort—but to Patrick's eyes the holes looked partially snowed in, with feathery powder softening the edges. Not completely fresh. Abraham had taken shift around four thirty. When Patrick had woken to check on Barry at about that time, the snow had still been falling. And Abraham had been there, just stirring to start his shift.

That meant Abraham had left the cave after four thirty and before eight. It wasn't much to go on and left out the essential fact of *why.*

The snow depth lessened away from the mouth of the cave. Patrick's breaths were already ragged and sweat trickled down his back. Amazing how much effort it took to fight through snow, and how taxing it was at this altitude. He stepped out from the shade of the enormous rock face. Painful sunlight blinded him, and he held a hand over his eyes then pulled down the face shield on his helmet. It helped some. He gave his eyes a few more seconds to adjust. Finally able to see through a tight squint, he scanned the park.

Nothing but white. On the ground. On the trees. Over rocks. Even the sky looked white. He blinked and tried again, moving his eyes in wide sweeps. Were there shapes, color, movement, or disruptions that didn't belong?

Still unsuccessful, he turned back to the line of snowmobiles, trying to decide whether he should take one to look for Abraham. That's when he noticed the red Ruff wasn't there. Tracks from the sled wound off through the trees. *Son of a buck.* Patrick should have looked there first. But who would have expected Abraham to ride away? And a snowmobile was loud. Patrick couldn't believe he'd slept through one starting up, even though they were parked away from the entrance to the cave and blocked some by boulders. The storm noise must have muffled the engine noise.

He tried to ignore the sick feeling rising in him. He needed to diagnose the situation. To use logic. There might be a legitimate reason Abraham would be out on a snow machine, and he didn't want to rush to judgment before he considered all the possibilities. What if Abraham had needed help? Easy answer. There were three able bodied men in the cave. He should have woken one of them. Try as he might, Patrick couldn't come up with anything else. Nothing that made sense.

Abraham had left for his own reasons, whatever they were. *Running from something,* Patrick thought again.

Snippets of their conversation the night before replayed in his mind, almost as if he was hearing Abraham's words for the first time. In a way, he was. He'd been so exhausted and worried about Barry. He hadn't given Abraham his complete attention.

"I've been working as a ranch hand for many months. I don't require much rest."

Why would a doctor be working as a ranch hand?

"One of my parents was born overseas"

There was nothing sinister in that statement, but it niggled at Patrick's brain. And it wasn't just what Abraham had said or the words he had used. It was his demeanor. In retrospect, his secrecy seemed furtive. Maybe fearful? Patrick cycled back through the facts troubling him. A ranch hand. With dark hair and eyes, olive skin, an accent that didn't sound Californian, strange diction, and a parent born overseas.

While overseas included many places, it could mean an Arab country. Like the O Bar M ranch hand from the middle east who had disappeared when his co-workers had been killed. Muhammed, the one wanted for questioning in connection with the murders.

Patrick grabbed the handlebar of the nearest snowmobile. *Could Abraham be Muhammed?*

If so, that might provide a clue about what he was running *from* and why he was so secretive. He could have been the one who wielded the knife that killed the other two O Bar M hands. The bloody, gruesome scene replayed in Patrick's mind. Abraham hadn't seemed like a murderer. That didn't mean he wasn't one though. Most people had it in them to kill. Their reasons might vary, but if they had to, they would. Patrick had, to save his daughter. Maybe this Muhammed had been defending himself.

Or maybe he wasn't the killer but had witnessed the murders.

Yet he had somehow ended up with George at Clear Creek Resort. The fact of that connection seemed to shoot a hole in Patrick's Muhammed theory.

Except that everything else seemed to fit.

A cold chill ran up his spine. He might have just spent the night sleeping beside a murderer in a cave deep in the wilderness.

But he was the man who saved your brother-in-law's life and stayed with him even after help came.

He brushed the snow off the seat of his snowmobile. Maybe he should go look for him. But then he stopped, thinking better of it. He shouldn't endanger himself going after a man on the run. A man who didn't want to be found, most likely. He had a brother-in-law to get off the mountain. A wife and children to return to.

But Abraham stayed to save Barry.

The quiet was suddenly shattered by a loud buzzing. Engines.

Snowmobiles. Moving fast. Patrick whirled around. Had help arrived? But the noise was coming from the wrong direction. Away from the lodge. And the snowmobile that appeared in the park was a familiar red one.

Abraham was back.

Or was he? Instead of turning in to rejoin Patrick and the others at the cave, the red snowmobile raced by. Two yellow snowmobiles flew out of the trees after him, their belts screaming with strain. Like the Ski-Doos from the fleet at the resort. Maybe this was a different group and not Abraham at all. But in these conditions and this far away from the resort, it was unlikely.

Running from something.

A sadness flickered inside him. The yellow sleds could be law enforcement out here to bring Abraham in, borrowing the Clear Creek Resort machines. From this distance, there was no way for Patrick to tell.

Then one of the Ski-Doo riders pulled out a handgun and started firing at the red snowmobile. BOOM. BOOM. BOOM. The shots ripped off so quickly, Patrick recognized it as a semi-automatic. The other Ski-Doo rider followed suit. BOOM. BOOM.

It felt wrong, and he only had to think about it for a second to identify the reason. Abraham—if it was him—hadn't fired first. Law enforcement wouldn't fire into the back of a fleeing suspect. These couldn't be deputies. Not good ones anyway.

"Are you okay? I heard gunfire," Wes shouted from the mouth of the cave.

"It's not me. Two riders are chasing Abraham by snowmobile. They fired on him."

"What in tarnation? Who would do that?"

"I have no idea." Patrick didn't take the time to explain his suspicion about Abraham. Or that despite his suspicion, his instincts pointed in the opposite direction, to the man's essential goodness, and that he felt an obligation to help him now. It wouldn't make sense to Wes. He wasn't sure it made sense to himself. All he knew was that it felt like the truth, and that he couldn't live with himself if he stood here and watched these two men hunt Abraham down and kill him.

He unzipped his coat, removed his revolver from its holster, and spun the cylinder. It was loaded. He returned it to its holster. Then he ran back to his snowmobile and attempted to start it. The engine was cold. *Come on, come on.* He braced his foot and pulled over and over. It coughed and spit and finally sputtered on with a smelly belch. Patrick gently depressed the throttle. The engine answered with a snarl then a roar.

Wes appeared right in his face, shouting to be heard over the noise of the machine. "What are you doing?"

"They were trying to kill him. I have to do something."

"Yeah, and if you go after them, they might try to kill you, too."

Patrick knew his friend was right. He mounted the snowmobile anyway.

Wes spat out a few choice words. He shook his head. "If you're going, Sawbones, I am, too."

Patrick nodded. "They're getting away. Make it fast." He gunned the sled, and it shot across the powder, defying gravity.

CHAPTER THIRTY-NINE: FIRE

Clear Creek Resort, Bighorn Mountains, Wyoming
Saturday, December 31, 1977, 8:15 a.m.

George

Inside the shed, George poured fuel into snowmobiles. He needed three: his and one each for Jenelle and Mandy. The selection was limited to four machines now. On their way back from the cave the night before, they'd been unable to get Jenelle's disabled machine to start. They'd left it out on the trail. George planned to repair it or haul it in, but that was a task for later, after Barry was safely on his way to the hospital and all the guests and other sleds were back at the resort.

"Which ones do you and Mandy want to take?" he asked Jenelle, trying not to look at her. It was impossible, though. His eyes were drawn to her like a hummingbird to sugar water. He let himself sneak a glance. *Jeez—when it rains, it pours.* Just when he found a nice girl like Lisa, he met the cute cashier at the gas station, and then he became reacquainted with Jenelle of the curves and killer dimples.

His father always teased him that good-looking women seemed to come into his life in threes. And they left the same way, each unhappy about him and the other two.

"Mandy's going to sit this one out. We're a little short on machines, anyway. Mom rented some to the day guests early this morning." She leaned over to adjust the thermoses and bags of food that she'd bungie corded onto the stretcher they'd rigged up from an extra-long toboggan before breakfast.

Maybe he could pick one girl this time and not end up alone. It would make his mother happy. Sunday dinner would be more relaxing without her asking him about when he'd settle down and give her grandkids, every single time. It was a shame Jenelle lived two hours away in Gillette.

BOOM. BOOM. BOOM.

Jenelle stood up with a hand to her ear. "Gunfire. In the direction of the cave, it sounded like."

George wondered if it was elk hunters. But it hadn't been the crack of a rifle. The shots were fast, like a semi-auto. And those weren't hunting guns. "Not hunters."

BOOM. BOOM.

Jenelle nodded. "Definitely not."

"Target shooters?"

She frowned. "That's way too much trouble to do in the dead of winter out there."

"Agree."

"Someone in trouble?"

"Maybe. Hopefully not someone from our group." George knew it wasn't safe for him to ride out alone to figure out what was going on, but he didn't want to drag Jenelle into the middle of a problem involving gunfire. "We should call it in, to be on the safe side."

"Good idea."

Together, they jogged back to the lodge, where they quickly toed snow off their boots at the door. Inside, Jenelle ducked behind the check-in counter. She stuffed her gloves in her pocket and picked up the phone receiver. She listened, then shook her head. "Still down. But Mom and Dad use a radio to communicate directly with emergency services in Buffalo. It's in their office. Follow me."

She turned down a short corridor behind check-in and led him into a cozy room at the end of the hall. There was a radio on a table behind a desk. George stopped in the doorway.

Jenelle picked up the mic and keyed it. "This is Clear Creek Resort calling for Johnson County. Come in Johnson County."

After she paused, a dispatcher radioed back. It was impossible for George to tell if the gruff voice was male or female, only that it was from someone closer to his grandmother's age than his own. "This is Johnson County Dispatch, Clear Creek Resort. What's your emergency?"

"Multiple shots fired, possibly from more than one gun, in the vicinity of a stranded party. Please send law enforcement."

"Confirming shots fired from multiple weapons near Clear Creek Resort. Requesting law enforcement."

"As soon as possible."

In a softer voice, the dispatcher said, "You know season is still open for elk?"

"These aren't hunters. The guns were semi-automatic. They weren't from rifles."

"Gotcha. A distress call?"

"Possibly. We don't know."

"We'll get someone up there as fast as we can, roads permitting."

"Can you check on the status of medical help for Barry?" George whispered.

Jenelle nodded. "Also, I need to make sure you're aware we're waiting on help with a resort guest who is in serious medical condition and was stuck out in the wilderness overnight. That emergency is ongoing."

The dispatcher said, "Yes. Search and Rescue is on standby for safe roads."

"We're about to leave to try to bring him back to the lodge

ourselves. We're going to need help getting him down the mountain as fast as possible."

"Understood. Medical transport is also on standby."

George and Jenelle exchanged a worried glance. He understood the danger of bad roads and didn't advocate putting lives at risk unnecessarily, but he sure hoped the plows were working on Highway 16.

Jenelle's eyes widened. "Oh, and I almost forgot. Our phones are down."

"Will someone be manning the radio?"

"No. We're over extended. But we'll check in when we can."

"10-4, Clear Creek Resort. Johnson County Dispatch, over and out."

"Over and out." Jenelle looked up at George as she replaced the receiver in the holster. "I don't mind telling you, the gunfire near our group is making me nervous."

"Me, too." The dimples were in hiding, but her clear gray eyes were just as enticing to George. "I don't suppose I can talk you into staying here at the lodge?"

"Not a chance."

They hurried out together. When they reached the reception area, they found Mrs. Murray, Ari, and Cyrus.

Mrs. Murray was standing with her fists on her hips, an apron over her sweater. "We heard semi-automatic gun fire. What's going on?"

Jenelle answered her mother. "We don't know, but I radioed it in."

George said, "Jenelle and I have to get going. We've got the stretcher to bring Barry in."

Cyrus said, "I'm ready. I'll come with you."

Ari didn't look eager, but his voice was firm. "Me, too."

Mrs. Murray shook her head.

"What?" Cyrus asked.

She held up one finger, then dashed down the hallway. She came back with a rifle in each hand. "I know George and Jenelle are armed. But you're not going without these, city slickers. Do you know how to use them?"

Cyrus smiled, but it was grim. "Ari is former Israeli military. I grew up hunting in Maine. And let's just say I've had a lot more field training for my past jobs than I'd like."

Strength in numbers. George had faith in himself and Jenelle, but he wasn't going to argue with adding a few to their rescue party.

CHAPTER FORTY: SUMMON

Buffalo, Wyoming
Saturday, December 31, 1977, 8:30 a.m.

Ronnie

Ronnie eased her county truck up to thirty-five miles per hour—only five miles over the Main Street speed limit. She folded a stick of Juicy Fruit in her mouth and chewed as if she could chomp her frustrations away. She'd intended to head straight for Piney Bottoms to intercept Trish. Assuming that was where the girl had gone, and it seemed like a safe bet. Ronnie had been a teenage girl herself once, and knew how their brains worked—or didn't.

That seemed ages ago. She and her husband Jeff had adopted their son Will right after her thirty-fifth birthday. She loved Will more than anything, but he made her feel old and tired like the modern Wyoming Methuselah, female version. It had been even harder on her *before* she'd returned to work, when Jeff had taken over nighttime baby duty. At least now Ronnie was getting some sleep. A few of Jeff's friends had given him the side eye for taking on so much of the parenting, but it didn't faze him. He delivered propane. The job had flexible hours, and Will could ride with him in the truck. Ronnie's own father had been distant and uninvolved. Jeff was a great dad. She and Will were lucky.

See? There I go again. Brain off the rails. Mommy brain was what she was calling it. When she wasn't thinking about Will's bowel movement schedule, his red corkscrew curls, or his infectious laugh, she was still distracted. Not herself.

Anyway, the sheriff himself had called her before she left for Piney Bottoms, instructing her to return to the office to give him a debrief on the O Bar M murders. Ronnie had laid out the case for him at light speed, but he was no dummy, and he'd asked questions. Lots and lots of questions. Answering them had consumed a quarter of an hour. When she'd finally satisfied his burning need to know everything, she'd bolted out. First thing she'd done in her truck was light up the radio, seeking an update. Hoping to hear someone had found Trish.

No such luck.

She sighed, activating her left blinker and pulling her braid out from between her back and the seat, then turned onto the interstate's access road. She had a good idea where to look for Trish, but not how to handle her when she found her. If Trish had been a young horse, Ronnie would have known better what to do. Growing up a rancher's daughter might have been short on affection, but it was long on horse sense. When a horse would run off, she'd work the animal until it realized how much worse running was than just being agreeable and getting down to business in the first place. Something that would backfire with Trish, or any human female teenager, she was sure. *Thank goodness Jeff and I have a boy.*

Her radio crackled to life. The familiar voice of Pat from dispatch said, "Deputy Harcourt, are you still in town?"

She wanted to pretend she hadn't heard the call. If she answered it, she'd be yanked away from chasing after Trish. Again. And would be letting Susanne down. But if she didn't pick it up, she'd be ignoring her duty, and she could never do that.

She stuck her gum on the wrapper she'd saved in the ash tray. Then she keyed her mic. "Harcourt. Near enough. What's up?"

"Semi-auto shots fired near Clear Creek Resort. Not hunters. Suspicious circumstances. The Murrays have requested law enforcement assistance. You're closest. Can you respond?"

Clear Creek Resort was in the opposite direction, all the way up in the mountains. Ronnie was only fifteen minutes from Piney Bottoms and, maybe, Trish, but driving to the ranch first would put her another half hour away from responding at the resort. She wrestled with herself. She had a job to do. Every law enforcement officer in the state had Trish's information. A missing teenage girl in this weather would be something they all took seriously. And the Flint family was well known and appreciated for their support of law enforcement. That couldn't hurt.

Who knew—maybe she'd get lucky and could talk to Patrick about O Bar M while she was up there? He'd appreciate an update. Plus, there was a detail about the case that was bothering her. Everyone in her office seemed convinced that Herman, the O Bar M hand, had identified Muhammed as the killer shortly before his death. She remembered Patrick's story differently; that Herman hadn't specifically ID'ed anyone. If she was right, it was telling. Herman would have just said it was Muhammed if his co-worker had been the killer, wouldn't he? And Patrick was the only witness to what Herman said.

She wanted to hear Patrick's story in his own words again herself.

"Turning around and heading their way now. ETA—" she paused. That would be completely dependent on the roads. "Unknown, pending firsthand inspection of Highway 16 into the mountains. But I'd be half an hour away on clear roads."

"Thanks. The plows are working in that direction. At worst, you should be able to follow them up."

"10-4."

"You should be aware they've also got a guest stuck out in the wilderness with a serious injury. They're trying to bring him in to the lodge on their own, since Search and Rescue hasn't been able to get out there yet. I'm trying to find a medical unit to dispatch for transport."

Ronnie was momentarily speechless. Patrick. Perry. Dr. John. They were all guests at the resort. She keyed the mic on, off, and back on again. "Who is the patient?"

"I don't know. But I'm told Dr. John was going to operate. Out in the wilderness in a blizzard, no less."

Ronnie took a deep breath. Well, it wasn't Dr. John. But she wouldn't know if it was Patrick or Perry until she got there. There had to be other guests at the resort. Dr. John brought people in from all over the world for his annual trip. But it was a small lodge. The odds for the Flints weren't good. God, how she didn't want to be the one to tell Susanne more bad news. The woman was stronger than she gave herself credit for, but she loved her husband and kids more than anything. A woman could only take so much.

"10-4." She paused. "I have a hunch about Trish Flint. Is there anyone close enough to Piney Bottoms Ranch to see if she's there? Ben Jones, too."

"Ben Jones is missing?"

"Ran off. But he's of age. Still . . ."

"I'll see what I can do."

"Thanks. Anything else?"

"That's it. Dispatch, over and out."

"Harcourt, over and out."

Ronnie settled the mic back in its holster, resigned about her mission but filled with unease. The miles had flown by while she talked with Pat. She was already west of town cruising up the highway past the veteran's home on the grounds of old Fort McKinney. A plow was just ahead of her, starting its ascent into the mountains. Beyond it, the road was covered with snow.

It was going to be slow going. She smacked the steering wheel with her palm. Clear Creek Resort was less than ten miles away, but the plow would average thirty miles per hour. Maybe less. *Another half an hour to get there. Then an hour or two evaluating the shots fired. Another half hour back down.* It was going to eat up most of her day. She wouldn't be the one to find Trish and take her back to Susanne. Someone would, though.

Ahead of her, a motorist was standing on the side of the road by a pickup. Stranded, most likely. Ronnie was torn. Something had rattled the Murrays and good for them to call in law enforcement over shots fired. They'd lived in the mountains for decades. They weren't ones to overreact or cry wolf. Ronnie had to assume theirs was a serious situation. An emergency. Whereas a car stuck on the side of a well-traveled road on a bright, sunny day wasn't life-threatening.

But as a deputy she couldn't just drive by, either.

Ronnie decided to stop and let the traveler know that she was radioing for assistance. This being Wyoming, someone would dig and tow the person out long before the sheriff's office could dispatch a unit. The driver would be miffed at her and inconvenienced, at worst.

She let off the accelerator and coasted to a stop in the middle of the road, ending up beside the truck with her passenger door even with its driver's door. After putting her vehicle in park, she leaned over and rolled down her passenger side window. The glass on the truck's window was frosted over. It started to descend. A blonde head came into view.

Trish Flint turned to face Ronnie, and she didn't look happy to see her.

CHAPTER FORTY-ONE: DISPATCH

Susanne

Susanne paced the kitchen with a coffee mug in her hand, mumbling to herself a la Patrick. *They say married couples become more alike over time.* Like him, she couldn't care less if she seemed crazy to Dian or Esme. The only difference between her and Patrick, really, was that Susanne was one hundred percent aware she was doing it. She couldn't hold it in. Her feelings were leaking out all over the place. Her daughter was missing. Had possibly run away.

The phone rang. *Ronnie!* Susanne dashed to the phone and snatched up the receiver. "Did you find her?"

A woman's voice—vaguely familiar, but not Ronnie's—said, "Find her? I'm sorry. I must not be who you were expecting. Is this Susanne?"

"Yes, it is."

"This is Wendy Nelson, from the JoCo Women's Club. I was calling to see if you'd considered our request to chair our fundraiser?"

The call was so out of left field that Susanne couldn't find the words to answer. *Trish,* she wanted to scream. *The only thing that matters right now is my daughter.* The silence stretched on. Susanne lost track of it. Lost track of the telephone in her hand. The receiver dropped to her shoulder.

"Susanne? Are you there?" Wendy sounded put out.

Susanne lifted the receiver to her ear. Her voice wooden, she said, "I'm sorry. Now isn't a good time for me to talk."

Wendy responded in a no-nonsense manner. "When would be, then? We need to get the ball rolling, don't we?"

Pushy. Insensitive. Rude. "I'll call you." Susanne hung up the phone and resumed pacing.

Dian walked over from the great room, where she'd been pretending to watch the TV, without any volume. She grasped both of Susanne's upper arms, holding her in place. "It's going to be okay."

What if Trish has a wreck? What if she gets kidnapped . . . assaulted . . . raped . . . worse? What if she doesn't find Ben and it breaks her heart? What if she does and it's the same result? But what if it isn't? What if she elopes with him? What if she gets pregnant? What if she throws her bright future and her family away and never, ever comes back?

Susanne didn't say any of what she was thinking aloud. She nodded.

Dian ran her hands down to Susanne's elbows, then released her. "Is there anything I can do for you?"

Susanne set her mug on the table. "No. Nothing. There's not even anything *I* can do for me. I'm completely sidelined and helpless without a vehicle." Then she had a thought. "Maybe I could rent a car and go after her."

"If that would solve it, I'd let you take mine. But it won't." Dian went for a mug of coffee, shaking her head. "Go after her where? Your deputy friend has already done that, and other law enforcement are looking for Trish. They'll find her. She'll be home soon. And you've got to be here when she arrives, because that girl is going to need her mama."

Dian's words pierced the armor around Susanne's heart. Susanne had been operating under the belief that what she felt was fear for her daughter and anger at her for putting her mother and everyone else in a horrible position. But a new emotion burst to the surface. A pure pain, empathetic and maternal, took her breath away. Her daughter was hurting. Ben had hurt her daughter. Maybe not on purpose, but that didn't change the facts. *The price of love.* But a mother never wanted her children to have to pay that price.

All the energy in her body leaked out, dissipating into nothing. She sagged into a chair at the table, bowed like an old woman. "My baby girl," was all she could say.

Dian set her coffee down. She sat in the chair next to her and held her hand.

Esme appeared and stopped in the space between the eating area and the great room. "Have you heard from Barry or Patrick?"

Dian stiffened.

Susanne straightened. "No. I tried to call the resort, but the phone lines appear to be down from the storm." *Patrick doesn't even know his daughter has run away.* How was she going to tell him? She needed him to know. They were partners. Their shared fear made things less scary. Shared grief, less crushing.

"What are we going to do about it?" Esme said.

Dian stood, backing away. "It was wonderful seeing you all and your home, Susanne. Going to Denver with you. But I need to get on the road to Billings. Could you give Trish the things I bought her when she gets back?"

If she gets back. "Of course." Part of Susanne wanted to beg Dian to stay. A larger part of her was relieved she was going. The tension between Esme and Dian added to the stress of Trish leaving was too much. It was all too much. "Let me walk you out when you're ready to go."

"I turned on the car to let the heater and defrost work their magic, oh, maybe ten minutes ago, when I put my bag in it. I'm all set."

The phone rang again. Susanne glanced at it, then back at Dian.

Dian pointed at the telephone. "You should get that. I know you love me. I'll see you at the reunion in June, okay?"

Susanne nodded and mouthed, "Thank you." She snatched up the phone receiver. "Susanne Flint speaking." She wasn't making the same mistaken assumption twice. But if it was Wendy, she was going to hang up on her.

A gravelly voice said, "Mrs. Flint, this is Pat. I'm the dispatcher with Johnson County. Ronnie asked me to relay some good news to you. Are you ready?"

A tingly lightness came over Susanne. *Trish.* She put her hand over the receiver. "I think they've found her!"

Dian blew her a kiss as she backed away. "See? I told you so."

Esme pouted, looking unhappy at her earlier question being ignored.

"I'm ready," Susanne said into the receiver.

"Ronnie picked Trish up at the base of the mountains on Highway 16, where she'd gotten her pickup stuck."

Thank God. "That's great news! Is she bringing her home or should I come in to get her?"

"No, ma'am. It's going to be a while before you can see her, I'm afraid."

That made no sense. Ronnie wouldn't torture Susanne like that. Pressure that had only just lessened built back up in Susanne's chest. "Why? Is Trish in trouble?"

"Nothing like that. Ronnie was on her way to Clear Creek Resort when she ran into Trish. Trish is riding up the mountain with her." Susanne drew in a deep breath. *It's okay.* "Clear Creek has a few emergencies up there, and—"

Just like that, Susanne's world heaved and spun again. "What? What kind of emergency at Clear Creek?"

The dispatcher's voice dropped. "I probably shouldn't be telling you this, but, since your daughter's going up there . . . there's been some unexplained shooting, and—"

"Were guests involved?"

"They're not sure. But the shooting is making it harder to rescue the injured guest."

"Injured . . . what? Who?"

"Someone was stranded in the wilderness overnight. Dr. John apparently performed surgery in the blizzard. Or that's what we were told."

"What?" Susanne shrieked.

Esme put a hand to her chest. "Are you okay, Mrs. Flint?"

"My husband, my son." She looked up at Esme. "My brother. Who is the patient?"

"Are Dr. Flint and your son up there?"

"Yes, with Dr. John."

"Oh, I'm so sorry to hear that. I'm sure everything will be all right. They didn't say who the patient is, but Ronnie's on her way. And Dr. John is the best. Well, I'm sure Dr. Flint is wonderful, too. Shoot. You know what I mean. And our ambulance is getting ready to head up there now."

"Tell it to wait."

"What?"

"I'll be there in five minutes. I'm riding up with them."

She dropped the phone and yelled, "Dian, stop!"

"Where are you going?" Esme said.

But Susanne didn't answer her. She was sprinting out the door.

CHAPTER FORTY-TWO: COMBAT

Patrick

Patrick gripped the throttle and held it tight with numb fingers and thumb. His toes were ice blocks. He'd lost feeling in one of his cheeks, in the marathon of excavating snowmobiles out of snow drifts and searching for, chasing after, and losing Abraham and the shooters, over and over on repeat. Patrick knew Abraham had been a snowmobile racer, so it made sense he was skilled at staying unstuck, but who were these men that equaled him in skill?

More than once while digging, Patrick and Wes had discussed whether to give up and return to the cave. Not because of Barry—even though Patrick worried about whether he was spiking a fever that was the start of a dangerous infection. Dr. John was with him, and Barry couldn't be moved until help arrived. But because their plan—or mostly their lack of one—seemed futile. Their goal had been to rattle the shooters, so they'd give up the chase. Or just create a distraction long enough that the men ran out of ammunition. Neither had happened yet. Patrick was driven onward by a dogged loyalty to Abraham that wasn't one hundred percent rational. Wes was concerned that Abraham would accidentally lead the shooters back to the cave.

So far, they had soldiered on, weapons loaded and accessible, although the last thing they wanted was to involve themselves in a firefight. Patrick had put in extra time at the gun range the previous summer, including working on ambidextrous shooting. He was glad he'd practiced, but he still wasn't as accurate shooting with his left hand, which is what he would have to do if the snowmobile was in motion. The chase couldn't go on forever, though. It had already dragged on far longer than Patrick could have expected. One of them could have a wreck or break down. Eventually, they'd run out of fuel. The shooters might even turn on them. Patrick didn't like any of those scenarios. He hated, too, that Dr. John would be worrying about them, not knowing what was going on. He didn't want to be the reason the party splintered further or that care for Barry was delayed.

It was feeling like time to call off whatever this was they were doing.

He stopped on a rise over-looking Circle Park. His ribs were throbbing. It was hard to draw a breath, and his shoulders ached from holding himself rigid to minimize the jarring to his mid-section. He shut down the engine and climbed off the snowmobile. The inside of his face shield had fogged up. Glad to finally have a chance to see, he lifted it. The mountains rippled with snow, completely white except for rocky spires and frosted forests. The cirque of peaks, with Cloud Peak holding its white head just a fraction higher than the others, looked down on him, as if passing judgment on his and Wes's efforts. He was sure the judgment was negative.

"Think George and Jenelle have made it to the cave?" Patrick asked.

Wes had parked and was standing beside him, helmet off, hair standing up in sweaty, spikey clumps. "Hopefully, and with Search and Rescue, too."

"Strength in numbers would be good. I want these shooters to leave our group alone. And, with enough people, they probably will."

"I expect you're right, Doc. And I'd like to be part of those numbers."

"Me, too." Patrick shook his head. "We're not doing Abraham any good that I can tell."

"We can call the sheriff's department to help him when we get back to the lodge."

Patrick nodded. He liked that he could count on Wes. He liked even more that the man was sensible. Or at least that he usually agreed with Patrick. "Good plan. I'll follow you."

Wes grinned. "Sure. Make me break the trail."

"It's just deference to your greater experience and skill." Patrick wiggled his numb fingers inside his gloves and rolled his shoulders, which pulled on his ribs. Everything protested. Everything hurt. *Okay, yeah, I'd love for Wes to spare me the harder job on the way back.*

"Try to keep it out of the ditch."

Patrick fully intended to. If he never dug another snowmobile out of a drift, it would be too soon.

The ever-present whine of engines intensified in the distance. Patrick was used to it now. Because of the way sound carried in the mountains, the machines weren't always as near as they seemed. The effect was like an auditory mirage. But this time, they were very close. Three snowmobiles flew into view above a roll in the terrain, popping over one after another like red and yellow fireballs out of a Roman candle. They were heading straight for Patrick and Wes at a speed that had the two of them scrambling for the cover of their sleds.

Abraham's snowmobile zipped past, headed back in the direction of the cave.

Patrick leapt onto his machine. The other two snowmobiles were bearing down on him. He pulled the starter. The engine sputtered.

He tried again. Another sputter. *Every single time. Can't it just for once start quickly when I need it?* He pulled again, feeling desperate. Wes's engine roared to life, and he blew past Patrick, headed toward the oncoming Ski-Doos. *Toward them? What is he doing?*

A shot rang out, and Patrick heard a PFFT as a bullet whizzed past. Another bullet buzzed by on the other side.

He pulled the starter, his heart pounding sickly fast. Then a shot like a sonic boom went off, so close it felt like the vibrations had come from his own gun.

BOOM.

Ahead of him, he saw Wes, with his weapon up.

BOOM.

Wes was firing back!

BOOM. BOOM.

A metallic ricochet. He'd hit something. Fifty feet away, one of the yellow snowmobiles made a horrible noise. The lucky shot had hit pay dirt. Patrick knew Wes was a good shooter, but a moving snowmobile? It was impressive.

"Yeah!" Patrick shouted.

Smoke rose from the machine's engine, and it whined to a stop, but the other one bore down on them without slowing. The rider raised his pistol. Wes gunned his engine, cutting to the left and out of the way. Patrick dove to the ground behind his machine for cover.

Bullets peppered the snow around Patrick's snowmobile, sounding muffled like they were being fired into a homemade pillow silencer. One made impact with the Ski-Doo.

The shooter barreled past in a wake of exhaust.

Patrick scrambled up. He leapt onto his machine and pulled the starter—the engine caught, finally—as he scanned the area. One of the shooters was still chasing Abraham. Clearly, Wes and Patrick were only secondary targets. They were after Abraham and just trying to get the men out of the way.

In the other direction, the disabled snow machine was smoking. Its rider had vanished. Nearer to Patrick, another yellow snowmobile stood out from the white landscape, nose down in a drift and tail up, with Wes still clinging to the seat and handlebars. The belt was rotating against air.

Wes rolled off. He stood and waved at Patrick.

Patrick zoomed over to him. "I've got to head them off from Dr. John and Barry."

"Do you have your gun?" Wes yelled.

"Yes. You?"

"Lost it." Wes made a "go, go" motion with his arm and hand. "I'll follow as fast as I can."

Patrick nodded. He pushed the throttle partway in, bracing himself for the rib pain. He stood on the runners for a better view over the windshield and made a wide turn, keeping his speed up and aiming for the highest terrain. When he was pointed in the right direction, he took a deep breath and depressed the throttle all the way. He couldn't believe the situation he was in. He was conservative by nature. Had never aspired to race on anything faster than his own two feet. Rocketing across uneven ground in and out of trees chasing an armed man, gritting his teeth so hard his jaw bulged, straining to see through a frosted face shield and flying snow, holding onto the hand grips as if it would be the death of everyone he loved if he eased up. All of it would have seemed unthinkable the day before, yet here he was.

A rise in the trail took him by surprise, and his sled went airborne. Another thing he hadn't aspired to do—jump snow machines, especially at top speed. The belt squealed. His balance was slightly off, and he felt the whole machine tilting to the side. *No. No. No.* He was afraid to overcorrect, but he straightened his upper body. The runners made contact with the snow, first the left, then the right. The landing was so painful that for a moment he thought he would black out.

Time hung, suspended. The world spun on its axis. The machine screeched its way forward. Ahead of him, the shooter seemed to dip from side to side.

Then Patrick's view of the trail in front of him went to zero as one of Perry's snownados spun from the ground to the sky. *Come on, come on. Move.* He was driving blind. After long seconds that felt like hours, it vanished into the sky. The path was revealed. Dead ahead of him, the straightaway ended at a standing boulder.

Patrick released the throttle and mashed the brake. Every bit of speed he could rob from the snowmobile counted toward preventing a rollover or a head-on collision with the rock. He had only fractions of a second until he had to start the turn. He didn't think he could make it but knew he had to try.

Now.

He stood on the runners, using all his strength and the leverage of his body weight, turning the handlebars inch by inch and leaning to the left. If his ribs hurt, he was too terrified to notice. The skis resisted. The machine propelled itself like a torpedo at the rock. He leaned further, all but lying sideways on the ground.

Should I ditch? If he gave up, the sled would crash into the rock. He'd be stranded. Abraham and the shooter would be headed unimpeded for Barry and Dr. John. *No.* He pulled harder. Bounced on the runners. Looked away from the unforgiving granite. Willed the snowmobile to turn. Whispered a prayer. *Dear God, take care of my family.*

And somehow, by fractions of an inch, with his right ski scraping, scraping, scraping, he kept the sled off the rock.

There was no time to celebrate. The trail plunged downward, dipping and rising, dipping and rising. No time to recover. To congratulate himself. He stayed on his feet, knees flexed, fighting the weight of the machine as it resisted the winding forest path. Tree branches whipped across his shield. Puffs of snow exploded from under the skis up and into his line of vision.

But he could still hear the other machine in front of him, and he didn't give up. He was drawing closer to it. He gave his sled more gas. His muscles were screaming in protest. He could feel his long underwear top clinging to his sweaty back. His arms and shoulders quivered with strain.

Then he broke from the trees, back into an open park. Snow pellets wacked his face shield. There, only one hundred feet ahead of him, was the other rider.

"Yes!" he shouted, the sound trapped inside his helmet and shield.

Far on the other side of the park, ahead of the shooter, Patrick caught a glimpse of red. Abraham's snowmobile. Abraham was still heading roughly toward the cave. He turned left down a slope toward a forested area. But when the shooter reached the spot where Abraham had turned, he veered *right*.

Had he lost sight of Abraham in his efforts to ditch Patrick? Patrick didn't care what had happened. He was just grateful. *It worked. I did it.*

BOOM.

A bullet went wide of Patrick. He hadn't seen the man raise his arm before. But he saw it now.

Patrick weaved to the left and then swooped back to the right. *Don't get stuck.* He kept his thumb firmly on the throttle.

BOOM.

The man turned forward again, lowering his gun. The path he was taking had been steadily rising. A tall, steep slope loomed in front of him. Patrick expected him to steer away from the pitch, but instead he pointed the snowmobile straight up it.

Patrick just thought the earlier terrain had made him nervous. This horrified him, and he wasn't afraid to admit it to himself. Did he dare follow? Did he even need to? He'd herded the man away from his friends. But if Patrick quit harassing him, the shooter might double back and re-engage with Abraham. He could be down to the cave in minutes. In dangerous situations past, when Patrick had been threatened, he'd known the reasons why. This time, with these men, he had zero idea of their motivation. What did they stand to gain? Or lose? How far were they willing to go to get Abraham?

At a minimum, they'd showed they were willing to kill Wes and Patrick if they got in their way. Patrick couldn't give up the chase.

He steered his sled uphill, full throttle. He blocked every thought out of his mind, except getting his machine safely to the top.

The whine of the other snowmobile's engine grew shriller as it neared the summit. Higher. Higher. And higher still. Patrick leaned his weight all the way forward, feeling the force of gravity pulling him backward. His hand began to slide from his glove, and he dug his nails into the lining.

The other Ski-Doo was nearly to the top. From Patrick's vantage point, it looked like the shooter's skis had lost contact with the ground. His stomach lurched, knowing he and his machine were next. The shooter's Ski-Doo shot into the air above the ridge, flying at a crazy angle, nearly vertical. Then it landed. Patrick couldn't hear it over the whine of his own engine, but he didn't need to. He saw it disappear on the other side of the hill. Not crest and descend along a ridgetop but *disappear*.

Terror closed his throat. He released his throttle, and his machine stopped immediately. Then it started to slide backward. He jumped off, rolling to the side, and watching as it started its downhill journey without him, gaining speed.

When it had come to a stop where the slope flattened out, he drew in a few ragged breaths, which reacquainted him with the pain in his side. He tried to get up. Emphasis on tried. The snow was too deep. The effort winded him again. After a few moments to recover, he pointed himself uphill and crawled on his hands and knees the last twenty feet to the summit. His breathing was so raw and labored when he reached it that it felt like his lungs were bleeding. He had snow inside his face shield. Agonizing pain made him wonder if he'd broken more ribs.

But he made it. He paused until he was able to rise to his feet for a view over the top.

What he saw made him sink back to his knees. He pushed his hands into the snow, searching until he found solid ground. The earth seemed to tip, and he felt a tug on the center of his body that was almost impossible to resist, pulling him toward . . . nothing. A void. Empty space.

Because the top of the hill was nothing more than the edge of a cliff.

He rocked backward, panting, his vision blurry. "Calm down. Calm down. You're fine." He counted to ten, timing his breaths, looking upward. Did it again. And again. And again. Until he'd mastered the physical symptoms of his panic and could trust himself.

He peered back over the edge. At the foot of the rocks far below was a snow-covered pond, with water lapping against the rocks at its edges.

And in the center was a mostly submerged snowmobile, nothing visible of its rider but his feet sticking out of the water.

CHAPTER FORTY-THREE: CONVERGE

Trish

Trish chewed what was left of her thumbnail, staring out the window at nothing. Well, snow, and trees of course, but, other than that, nothing. She'd been stuck in this lodge for over an hour, waiting, waiting, waiting. Coming out of her skin with worry.

When Ronnie had dragged her up to the resort, the lodge owner —a woman named Mrs. Murray who looked as frazzled as Trish felt —had given them a quick rundown of everything that had happened. All of it was bad. Uncle Barry, seriously injured in a wreck, had overnighted in a cave during the blizzard. Her dad had stayed with him, to try to keep him alive. Who knew whether he'd succeeded, because no one had talked to them since.

There had been gun shots all over the place in the last hour. Trish had heard them herself, each one making her jump and steel herself to the possibility that someone was shooting at her dad. Loud, whining snowmobile engines sounded far away, then close, then far off again. George and Mrs. Murray's daughter had taken a stretcher for Uncle Barry, and they were out in the thick of the gunfire. And now Mrs. Murray suspected Perry had snuck out after George, who'd told Perry he couldn't go with them on the rescue mission. Trish could confirm Perry was nowhere to be found, because she'd searched for him herself, in the room he'd slept in, the lodge, outside, in the outbuildings, everywhere.

Perry was gone. And she couldn't do anything about it.

That was the story of her life. Not able to do anything about Ben, who was driving away from her, maybe forever. Not able to do anything about her uncle who might be dying or her dad who might be on the wrong side of a gunfight or just freezing to death. It sucked. She hated it. She was tired of the drama, tired of being scared, and tired of crying. Tired of not being able to *do* anything.

And she was mad at her mother for siccing Ronnie on her. She hadn't broken any laws. She wasn't running away forever. What right did they have to kidnap her? Meanwhile, Ben was driving west, then north, further away every minute.

So, Ronnie had ridden off on a snowmobile, loaded up with weapons and ammo, ready to save the day, and ordered Trish to stay put, cooling her heels in the lodge. Out of sheer boredom and frustration, Trish had scavenged from the breakfast buffet until Mrs. Murray came in to clear it away.

The woman was wiping down the buffet tables with a cleaning spray that smelled like bleach. She stopped and spoke to Trish. "You look worried. I'm sure your brother will be just fine."

Trish turned toward the lodge owner, a little confused, but then she realized Mrs. Murray thought she was upset that Perry had run off. Maybe she was. A little. She knew Perry would be fine. He was always getting himself into scrapes and then back out of them. But mostly whatever was written across her face was about Ben. Some about her dad and Uncle Barry, too. She decided not to explain it all to the woman. It wasn't like she was heartless and didn't care about her brother. She just had a lot on her mind.

Trish said, "Perry is pretty tough. But he doesn't know his way around here, and the snow is bad. So being out there by himself isn't great."

Mrs. Murray repacked her cleaning materials in a bucket. "He's definitely resourceful. I was in our equipment shed a minute ago. It appears he borrowed a pair of cross-country skis. Does he know how to use them?"

"Um, I don't know. But he's good at regular skiing. Downhill, I mean."

Mrs. Murray shook her head. "Not the same thing. He's going to have a fair amount of trouble mastering them. I have an idea, though."

Trish cocked her head, listening.

"We can go out and get him in my big Sno-Cat. I think he'll appreciate a ride back after trying to teach himself to cross country ski in deep powder."

"Do you know where he is?"

"Oh, I'm sure he just followed everyone's snowmobile tracks. Would you like to come with me?"

Trish felt some of the knot of tension loosen in her stomach. It would be good to do something. Anything. Bringing Perry in off the trail would be a distraction from thinking about Ben, too. Five more minutes alone with her thoughts in this lodge, and she was going to go out of her mind. And she did want to make sure the little squirt was okay. He was annoying, but he also made her laugh like crazy.

And the fact that Ronnie wouldn't like Trish leaving the lodge made it even better.

"Cool. Thanks."

"I'll pick you up near the back door in five minutes. In the meantime, why don't you gear up? My daughter is about your size, and her outerwear is in a closet down the hallway." Mrs. Murray pointed.

Trish hadn't thought about gear, but she was grateful. The trick to avoiding winter misery was never getting cold in the first place, and, wearing only what she had with her, she'd be freezing her tushy off from the get-go. "Thank you."

Mrs. Murray walked out toward the kitchen with her bucket. Trish wandered down a hallway jam-packed with pictures. She slowed down to take them in. Hunters with giant elk and moose, and one with a black bear. People in vests and hats holding up trout and fishing poles. Horses lined up, their riders smiling, mountain peaks in the background. And what must be the Sno-Cat, orange and boxy, in more snow than Trish had ever seen. Walking on, she found the closet and picked out a pair of winter overalls, heavy snow boots, an enormous jacket, a wool hat, and some good thick gloves.

It took her five minutes just to get dressed, and by the time she made it outside, she was sweating. Mrs. Murray rumbled to a stop beside Trish in the Sno-Cat. Trish hauled herself up into the funny looking cab. The vehicle had four tracks instead of wheels. And it was loud. Hurt-your-ears loud. Trish pulled her cap down further and lifted the hood of the jacket up. It muffled the noise some. *Better.*

She felt a pang in her chest. Ben would have loved this thing.

Mrs. Murray held up a thumb, her face asking the question *Are you good?*

"Far out," Trish yelled.

Mrs. Murray smiled. She yelled back. "It's a beast. But living up here in the winter, we've really needed it." She set it in motion, and they began chugging forward.

"How fast can it go?"

"Five miles per hour is about its max."

"You can't sneak up on anyone."

"No, you can't. But at least we know where Perry was going. I checked, and his tracks follow the trail the snowmobiles made. We'll catch up to him out there."

They rode in silence—except for the roar of the Cat—for half an hour. It was so beautiful out there that Trish almost forgot to worry about things. The branches of the trees were drooping like weeping willows under the weight of the snow. A coyote streaked across a park chasing a snowshoe hare, little puffs of snow mushrooming behind them with every leap and step. Snowmobile tracks carved a line ahead of them, barely leaving a mark. The world was so pristine, so clean, so white, so peaceful that it was hard to believe her uncle was lying out there hurt somewhere.

Movement in front of the Sno-Cat caught her attention. Something dark blue or black against the snow. It was Perry, crawling on his hands and knees out of a snow drift, pausing every few feet to push his skis and throw his poles ahead of him.

"There he is!" Trish pointed at her brother.

"Doesn't look like he and the skis are getting along," Mrs. Murray said, amusement in her voice.

"You were right."

When Perry reached level ground, he rolled over on his back with his arms spread. He sunk and was almost hidden in the snow. Then he lifted a hand in the air. It was either a wave or a gesture of surrender. Mrs. Murray stopped the Sno-Cat beside him.

Trish opened the door. "Need a ride, shrimp?"

Perry sat up. "What are you doing here?"

They didn't have time for that long story. "I came with Ronnie. Did you see her?"

"Yeah. But she didn't see me. Are you going to get Dad and Uncle Barry?"

Mrs. Murray said, "George and Jenelle already went after them. Ronnie, too. They'll bring them back.

He stood but didn't make a move to climb into the cab. "There's been a lot of shooting."

Trish reached a hand toward her brother. "It'll be okay. Get in here and get warm."

Mrs. Murray motioned him in. "Climb on in, young man. Everyone is meeting back at the lodge. We'll be safer there."

Perry made a surprised face, then turned to look in front of the Sno-Cat. Had he heard something?

"What is it, squirt?" Trish asked. Maybe he saw a moose or something.

Perry's mouth fell open. His eyes went wide, and he raised his hands over his head. A man stepped into view, pointing a gun at Perry's head. He motioned for Trish and Mrs. Murray to get out of the Sno-Cat. Trish was so surprised that she barely had time to feel scared. She and Mrs. Murray looked at each other. They couldn't make a run for it. Not with Perry out there, and not with the Sno-Cat's top speed not much faster than a man could run in this snow. An armed man. And bullets were definitely faster than the machine.

Mrs. Murray bit her lip, then nodded at the door. Trish stepped out, sinking to her knees in powder. She shut the door behind her. The man hadn't said a word. The Sno-Cat's engine stopped. The only sound was Perry's heavy breathing. Trish locked eyes with him. *Hold still. Don't freak out.* If they cooperated, maybe the guy would tell them what he wanted and let them go. She snuck a glance at him. A black balaclava covered his face, except for the eyes and mouth. He was wearing snow pants that looked brand new. In fact, all his clothes seemed fresh off the rack from the Sports Lure, the place where everyone in town bought their outdoor gear. His eyes were cutting from the back to the front of the Sno-Cat, but Mrs. Murray didn't appear.

"Why are you doing this?" Trish blurted out.

The man turned dead eyes on her. "I must secure a vehicle."

Something about his voice was weird. The words he used. The accent. Maybe both. "Why? What are you doing out here without one?"

"You ask too many questions. I had a snow machine. It got . . . it is broken."

Definitely a foreign accent. One she didn't recognize. But him needing a vehicle was good news. They could give him the Sno-Cat. He didn't need to hurt them. "Fine. Take ours. You don't have to point a gun at us."

His voice became a snarl. "You talk too much even when you aren't asking questions. Shut your mouth, girl."

Trish heard the sound of heavy breathing and a commotion behind the Sno-Cat. Her own breath froze in her chest. Mrs. Murray! What was she doing? The man growled and shoved Perry to the ground. He bounded through the snow to the back of the Sno-Cat.

Trish watched in horror as he lifted his gun and fired.

CHAPTER FORTY-FOUR: SURPRISE

North of Clear Creek Resort, Bighorn Mountains,
Wyoming
Saturday, December 31, 1977, 10:45 a.m.

Patrick

Patrick scooched on his rear away from the drop-off until he felt the
decline on the safe side. He wanted to throw himself backward, away
from the cliff, but he tamped down the urge. There was nothing he
could do for the man who had flown over, except let the authorities
know where his body was.

He turned and saw Wes waving whole-armed to him from below.
Patrick raised his hand. Then he worked his way over to the descent
trail left by his snowmobile. It wasn't much of a pack, but better than
virgin snow. He gave walking a brief try, but, when he fell on his rear
and started sliding, he discovered it was an effective way down. Using
his hands to guide him, he sledded on his back until he glided to a
stop near Wes and the snowmobiles. There, he stood, shakily, using
his own snowmobile for support.

"What in hell's half acre happened up there?" Wes asked.

"He went over." Patrick unbuckled his helmet and yanked it off. He needed air. Lots and lots of fresh air.

Wes gaped. "Like drove away on the other side of the mountain?"

"There is no other side."

"Whoa," Wes said with a whistly exhale. "Did he make it?"

Patrick shook his head. "He did not." He told Wes what he'd seen. The glare from the snow was painful, and he held a hand over his brow. "Did you go after the other guy?"

"No. He's on foot. Less of a threat. I followed you."

Patrick gave Wes a weak smile. "I'm glad you did."

"Want to go meet up with our crew?"

"Very much so." He winced. "I hope my machine isn't mangled."

"I think it's all right. I turned it around for you. But how are you, Sawbones?" Wes reached toward him, then pulled his hand back as if he was afraid of insulting Patrick.

"No pain, no gain, right?" In truth, Patrick would have been vomiting if he'd had anything to eat since noon the day before. He wanted to go home and sleep the soreness off. Crawl into his warm bed, sipping broth while his beautiful wife fussed over him. Except that Susanne wasn't a fusser. Make that while she scolded him for getting himself in his present condition. With love, of course.

"That's what some crazy doctor always says anyway."

Patrick reached for the starter on his snowmobile and thought better of it. As much as he hated admitting weakness, he was done. "Would you mind starting this for me? Broken ribs." He patted them.

"No problem." Wes got the engine going in two pulls. Then he yelled, "Follow me. I'll take it slow.'"

The men rode out, and Patrick was able to keep up with Wes as he tested his machine for damage. The skis were straight, the handlebars intact. He couldn't believe it had survived its slow-motion crash so well, but it was in better shape than him.

Wes took the trail Abraham had cut when he'd separated himself from his pursuer. Soon, they were cruising through a stand of trees.

When they emerged on the other side, Patrick saw a big orange Sno-Cat parked smack in the middle of a park. Two people were standing on one side of it. Patrick frowned. They were familiar. He squinted to get a better look.

It was his kids. Both of them.

There was movement at the back of the Sno-Cat. A man. A man on foot. A man with a gun, which he raised, pointing it at something or someone out of Patrick's line of sight.

BOOM.

Ahead of him, Patrick saw Wes's snowmobile hurdle forward. Patrick gunned his own and went to the opposite side of the man. They converged on him in seconds. He turned, gun still up. Patrick killed his ignition and vaulted from his sled, ripping off his right-hand glove, unzipping his coat, and reaching for his .357 Magnum in a fluid series of motions. He managed to draw the gun from his holster, but his cold hands felt stiff and awkward. He took a step forward, gun in hand, and nearly fell over a pair of skis. He didn't have time to wonder why they were there. He stopped five feet from the man. The man's weapon was pointing from him to Wes, then back at him, back at Wes. His eyes were flat.

"He shot Mrs. Murray, Dad," Trish yelled.

"Do it, Sawbones," Wes said.

Patrick pulled the trigger. Instead of drawing it back, his numb finger jerked and knocked the gun off balance. The revolver tumbled into the snow and sunk. Just before Patrick dove into the snow after it, another man ran out of the trees, stumbling in the snow and clutching one arm to his stomach with his other hand.

This man Patrick knew. Abraham.

Abraham screamed something at the shooter, but Patrick couldn't understand what he was saying. The man holding the gun turned toward Abraham and answered him. Their words and accents sounded similar—like people Patrick had only heard on international news. News about the oil embargo. OPEC. Unrest.

Middle Eastern. They're speaking a Middle Eastern language to each other.

The shooter's eyes cut back and forth between Wes and Patrick again. Abraham shouted even more frantically, walking forward and waving his arms over his head like he was trying to get the man to look at him. As Abraham drew closer, Patrick saw blood dripping from the cradled arm, landing in crimson splotches that sunk and disappeared in the snow. Abraham had been shot.

Then, in English, Abraham said to Patrick, "I instructed him not to kill anyone. That I offer myself in exchange for your lives."

"What's going on here, Abraham?" Patrick eyed the snow where his gun had disappeared, wondering if he could find it before he got shot, if he moved fast.

"I am afraid I know something I should not. This man works for the secret police in another country. They were hunting me, and I hid here in Wyoming. My knowledge, and my flight—they led to the assassination of my mother. To the execution of my friends and coworkers at the O Bar M. I can't cause the death of anyone else. My death will end it all." It was a start, but it didn't exactly clear everything up for Patrick. Abraham continued. "If you kill him, they will just deploy someone else like him. It must stop now."

"His buddy is dead." Patrick didn't bother to explain the circumstances.

Abraham bobbled his head. "They will not desist until I am dead also."

The shooter started shouting at Abraham in the Middle Eastern language again, gesturing with his gun at Wes and Patrick. Patrick doubted this man would be satisfied with just killing Abraham. The rest of them were witnesses to whatever this was. Wes, Patrick, and the children of Patrick's blood. Patrick understood what Abraham was trying to do and he respected him for it, but that didn't mean he agreed with it.

And if he didn't agree, then he needed to act.

The shooter turned back toward Abraham. Patrick gave up on his gun. He crouched and picked up the ski, took two steps, and swung it as hard as he could at the back of the man's head.

THWACK.

The man grunted and crumpled to the ground.

Patrick and Wes leapt on him.

"You hold him. I'll get his gun and search him for other weapons," Patrick said.

"Got it." Wes kneeled on the man's back and restrained his arms by the wrists.

Patrick confiscated the shooter's gun—which had landed beside him—a backup pistol, and a knife. He stood. "There's rope in those emergency kits under your snowmobile seat, Wes."

Abraham looked stricken. "I will get the rope. I have caused so much trouble."

"Dad!" Perry flew into Patrick.

Patrick returned his son's hug, even though it hurt.

"Are you okay?" Trish was next in line. "Who is that guy who came out of the trees?"

"I'll tell you all about it later," he whispered, squeezing his daughter and kissing her head. In a normal voice, he said, "I'm fine. But what about Mrs. Murray? You said she was shot?"

Another voice called, "He shot a hole in my best jacket, and I played dead when I heard Patrick and Wes arrive. I didn't want to cause a distraction that messed things up. Is it safe to come out now?"

"Mrs. Murray, you're all right!" Trish shouted. "Yes, it's safe. Dad saved the day."

Patrick would have smiled if he wasn't in so much pain.

Abraham gave the rope to Wes, then returned to stand beside Patrick. Loud engines approached, and a brigade of snowmobiles burst into the park. When they pulled to a stop and removed their helmets, Patrick saw that it had been Ronnie leading the way, with George behind her pulling a bundled-up Barry in a stretcher, and Jenelle, Ari, Cyrus, and Dr. John bringing up the rear.

Ronnie stood on her runners. "What the heck happened here?"

Abraham dipped his head. "My problems followed me across the ocean and all the way to Wyoming. Many people have died, to my shame, and today it almost cost the life of my new friends. But because of their heroism, we are all alive."

Ronnie looked confused. "Who is this guy?"

George answered. "My co-guide in the snowmobiling adventures this weekend." Then, to the others, "I promise, I didn't know any of this when I hired him."

Patrick held up a hand, "Let's get Barry back to the lodge and off the mountain, and then maybe Abraham can help us figure more of this out."

Barry's voice wasn't loud, but it was clear. "Yeah, let's get Barry out of here. Please."

But Cyrus stepped forward. In his no nonsense New England accent, he said, "A word please?" He gestured for Patrick and Abraham to join him away from the others.

Patrick had an ominous feeling about the conversation Cyrus was initiating. He wished he'd paid more attention to what Cyrus did for the Carter administration. And he hoped that his request to talk to him and Abraham had nothing to do with it. "How about the rest of the group gets going. Abraham, where's your machine"

"I parked it back in the trees so as not to be heard," Abraham said. "Good."

Ronnie said, "What about that one?" She pointed at the trussed and unconscious shooter.

Cyrus walked over to her and whispered in her ear. Whatever he was saying, it widened her eyes and went on for almost a minute. Then, loud enough for everyone to hear, he said, "Leave him here, please."

A funny look crossed Ronnie's face, but she didn't argue. She circled her hand in the air. "The rest of you. Load 'em up and move 'em out."

Dr. John walked over to Patrick. In a low voice, he said, "You're in good hands with Cyrus. The best. Don't worry."

Patrick glanced at Abraham. The man looked anxious. Patrick hoped Dr. John was right.

CHAPTER FORTY-FIVE: DEAL

Patrick

The line of snowmobiles and the Sno-Cat exited the park toward the lodge five minutes later. Patrick was relieved his kids were leaving the danger zone and that Barry was one step closer to getting the medical care he needed. He'd done a more-than-competent surgery on his brother-in-law, but he'd feel much better when Barry was in a hospital and could be monitored until he was out of the woods, no pun intended. He didn't like how warm he'd been that morning, and he had a feeling a major course of antibiotics was warranted. As for himself, Patrick wanted to conclude whatever this business was as soon as possible. Food and a handful of Tylenol sounded like heaven.

But Cyrus seemed in no hurry to get on with things. Something about the man was more imposing than it had been earlier. He stood taller. His eyes were steely as he studied Abraham unapologetically.

His demeanor, commanding. Patrick was beginning to feel as anxious as Abraham looked.

The engine noises faded, and Patrick was alone with Abraham, Cyrus, and the unconscious shooter. Suddenly, he felt exposed and isolated. How could they be sure only two men had been hunting Abraham?

Patrick ticked through the facts as he understood them. Two men in the mountains, after Abraham—who had previously gone by the name Muhammed at the O Bar M—because of something that had happened overseas. Rosa Mendoza's revelation that Muhammed was Middle Eastern. The dying declaration of the ranch hand Herman that he'd been killed by an Arab. Abraham's anguished confession that the hands had been murdered by men who were after him.

And then Patrick's mind latched onto pieces he wasn't sure fit the puzzle but looked an awful lot like they did. A green sedan at a gas station. Two foreign men with strange accents who had asked about Clear Creek Resort. A green sedan pulling up to the lodge. And suddenly and clearly, he remembered a green sedan driving away from the O Bar M when he and his kids had been on their way there to see the horse, two men in the car who could have been Middle Eastern, now that he thought about it. And a deer running across the field at the O Bar M in his mind's eye, which, he realized with a start, had been a man—something he'd forgotten so completely that he'd never told law enforcement about it.

If all of this was connected, then it was likely there were only two shooters, but it wasn't guaranteed. And even though Abraham *had* been running away, he wasn't a murderer. He was a target. Patrick's instincts to protect and trust him had been correct. It restored some of Patrick's faith in his own judgment and in humanity.

Cyrus dropped his voice. Patrick moved half a step closer so he could hear him. Abraham did, too. "Young man, are you Iranian?"

The look on Abraham's face was stricken. "Why do you ask?"

"You've been speaking Farsi."

So that was what Abraham and the other man had been speaking.

"My mother was Iranian. My father was American. I have dual citizenship, and I grew up in California."

Patrick almost nodded. It made sense. And was a lot more than Cyrus had asked for. Patrick noticed Cyrus hadn't used Abraham's name. Had used his voice to draw him closer. Had established a hierarchy between himself and Abraham. Whatever Cyrus was up to, Patrick knew they were dealing with a pro. But a pro at what?

"Am I correct in assuming that man," Cyrus gestured at the shooter, "is Iranian as well?"

"As was his partner, who I am told by Patrick is deceased."

Cyrus's bushy brows shot up his forehead. "A partner? How did he die?"

Patrick raised his hand. "He was chasing Abraham. I was trying to head him off, and he went over a cliff. It was an accidental death. Either from impact or drowning when he went through the ice in the water he landed in."

Cyrus's face was impassive. "Assassins, then."

Abraham swallowed and nodded.

"SAVAK?" He turned to Patrick. "That's the Iranian intelligence and secret police."

Abraham said, "Yes, sir."

"Here?" Patrick's head swiveled as he searched the meadow. *He'd been chasing someone from the Iranian secret police?* It seemed so peaceful and serene. Not somewhere Iranian secret police would be running around. *Or hiding.* If there were more assassins out there, Patrick, Cyrus, and Abraham were sitting ducks in the middle of the park.

"I take a vacation, and work follows me into the Wyoming wilderness." Cyrus sighed.

Patrick frowned. Something had been bothering him. "What I don't get, Abraham, is why you kept circling this area for so long and didn't break away from it?"

Abraham said, "I thought I could get them stuck in the deep snow. Or possibly, like you ultimately did, incapacitate them more fully. What I did not want was to inadvertently lead them to women and children at the resort, where innocents might be harmed. But the SAVAK are well trained. I should not have underestimated their abilities, even at snowmobiling."

Cyrus shot a finger at Abraham, taking the conversation back over in a blink. "We've heard about you."

Abraham took a step back. In the deep snow, he lost his balance and almost sat down. The movement jarred his gunshot arm, and he grimaced. It was still bleeding, but the drops in the snow were fewer and farther between. From the looks of it, Patrick figured it was a meaty mess that was going to require surgery. "Who is *we?*"

Cyrus waved his hand to banish the question. His face was expressionless.

"What have you heard about me?" There was terror in Abraham's voice now.

Cyrus didn't try to settle Abraham. He seemed comfortable with Abraham's discomfort. "There's a rumor you have certain information about the Shah."

If the ground had opened and swallowed them whole, Patrick would have been less surprised than to be standing in the Bighorn Mountains having this conversation. The Shah? As in the *Shah of Iran?* One of the most controversial men in the world?

Abraham's voice shook. "My mother is—was—Caspian, a cousin of the Shah's wife. After my father died in California, she moved to Iran. Even though I was grown, I was an only child. All she had. I went with her and became one of the Shah's physicians."

Cyrus nodded with satisfaction, like the answer was confirmation of facts he already knew. "You're Farhad Ali."

Abraham's face paled. There was a sheen to it. Sweat. "How do you know this?"

Muhammed. Abraham. Farhad. Who was this man, really? It was a lot to keep straight, but Patrick was hanging on every word.

"It's my job to know this," Cyrus said.

"You work with the government of the U.S.?"

"I do." *That's an understatement,* based on what Patrick knew. "If you let me help you, I can save your life and avoid an international incident."

Abraham fell to his knees, still holding his arm. "The SAVAK will never stop until they kill me. The Shah . . . the Shah thinks I will tell the world what I know. He believes I am an American spy, because of the identity of my college roommate."

Across the park, a tall, thick mule deer strode out of the trees and down the packed path left by the train of snow machines. His coat looked bushy, and his antlers towered over his head. He was close enough that Patrick was able to count his points. Five on the left. Six on the right. A magnificent stag. An alpha who had survived multiple rutting and hunting seasons, besting other bucks and rifle-toting humans alike.

Cyrus spoke casually, confidently. "You're speaking of Jerry Durham."

Patrick almost asked who that was, but he didn't dare interrupt again. Cyrus had the situation in hand, and he seemed to be leading Abraham to something a lot more important than the identity of Jerry Durham.

"Yes," Abraham whispered.

"Whose father was in the U.S. State Department."

Durham. Durham. John Paul Durham, former Secretary of State? Of course. Abraham's association with the son of a U.S. Secretary of State could be problematic for him in Iran.

Abraham's voice was raw. "How do you know all of this about me?"

"We'd been told to be looking for you, Farhad. By mutual friends."

"Please don't call me that. I have left that name and that life behind. After the assassination of my mother, Farhad Ali has nothing left."

A former physician, now a ranch hand on the run from Iranian secret police in Wyoming, whose mother had been assassinated.

Patrick felt sick for Abraham. Cyrus seemed to suspect him of some-thing. Or at least want something from him. But to Patrick, Abraham was a fellow human. A man with a good heart in a bad situation. Still, Patrick was a patriot. He clenched his jaw and let Cyrus make his play.

Cyrus turned and gazed into the forest. "I'll make you a deal. If you'll tell me what you know about the Shah, I will make sure that Farhad and any other identity you've been using are buried so deep, SAVAK will never look for you again."

Abraham looked at Patrick, then at Cyrus. Patrick kept his eyes on the ground. "But how?"

Cyrus smiled, turning back to Abraham. "Farhad will die in the mountains of Wyoming, in a tragic snowmobile accident that took his life and that of one other Iranian tourist."

"But he is alive. That one." Abraham pointed with his head. The shooter groaned and twitched.

"He will be our witness to the Iranians about your death, which we will stage very convincingly. But we need to move fast. Before he wakes up."

Abraham gaped. Patrick didn't like the look of his skin tone. The man seemed to be weakening. His jacket was soaked with blood. "But then what will become of me?"

Patrick interjected, directly to Cyrus. "Whatever happens next, we've got to get him to the hospital before he collapses."

Cyrus ignored Patrick. "If you tell me what you know, Abraham, I will help you establish a new life," Cyrus said.

An idea formed in Patrick's mind. A beautiful, perfect solution. If all went well, he'd pitch it to Cyrus as soon as they were off this mountain.

Tears leaked from the corners of Abraham's eyes. With difficulty, he stood. Straightened his shoulders. Took a deep breath. "The Shah of Iran has cancer and is refusing to seek treatment. He is weakening. He is fearful of his enemies learning of his condition. It is affecting his judgment." He dropped his eyes and his shoulders sagged.

Patrick felt the skin of his forehead stretch as his eyebrows shot up. The stag, who had been pawing the snow, lifted his head, ears perked, eyes on Abraham. He leaned forward, regal, powerful. Then he bounded into the trees, disappearing in a blink.

Cyrus's smile was grim. "Thank you. You made a good choice. The SAVAK agent is stirring. Abraham, how good are you at playing dead?"

Suddenly, everything about the last few days made a lot more sense to Patrick, in a most horrible way.

CHAPTER FORTY-SIX: RESOLVE

Patrick

Patrick pulled two mugs from the cabinet. "Susanne makes wonderful coffee. Would you like a cup?"

"I would appreciate one, but I do not want to impose." His guest tried to stand, but the repaired arm strapped to his chest combined with a stitched and bandaged leg made it difficult, and he gave up, smiling apologetically. It turned out that Abraham had been shot twice. In the arm and in the leg, although his black waterproof pants had hidden the latter injury. He'd tried to refuse medical attention after they'd finished staging the snowmobile wreck against a nearby cliff face, the wreck Patrick and Cyrus had "chanced upon" when taking their SAVAK witness back to the lodge, supposedly to hand him off to the authorities. Patrick deserved an Academy Award for his anguished pronouncement that Abraham was deceased. It had been enough to convince their SAVAK witness that his quarry was dead, and when the man had managed to escape soon after, he had no idea that it had been because Cyrus had let him go, intending that he take the information about Farhad's death back to Iran with him.

While Patrick could admire and identify with the kind of toughness that led a man to fight through injuries in the worst of conditions when he had to, Patrick hadn't taken no for an answer. Abraham had undergone surgery to repair the damaged muscle in his arm. Then he'd tried to check himself out as soon as he awoke. Patrick had put a stop to that, too.

He knew the man was terrified. Abraham was living on the edge of a scimitar's blade. Patrick hoped they hadn't made the wrong choice letting the assassin live. But there comes a time when a man has had enough of killing other men, especially when that man is a doctor whose mission it is to save lives, not take them. Patrick wasn't going to be the one to end that man's life, no matter who he was. So, the assassin had been sent back to Iran programmed with the narrative about Farhad Ali's death created by Cyrus, to be fed to the Shah and his regime. If the Iranians found out Abraham hadn't died, at least as long as the Shah was alive, there was a chance they'd deploy SAVAK officers after him again. Especially if the Shah discovered that Abraham had leaked word of his cancer to the U.S.

Cyrus had promised to be discreet, but life—and politics—came with no guarantees. It was a risk Abraham had no choice but to take.

So, Abraham was hiding and recuperating at the Flint residence, with Susanne's blessing. She'd been waiting with the ambulance at the lodge when Barry and the rest of the group had arrived there, where she'd learned about the efforts of Abraham, Wes, Dr. John, and Patrick to save her brother. That made Abraham A-OK with her, no matter his confusing and unsettling past . . . and present. And with Dian gone and Barry in the hospital for several more days, they had the room at their house. Just barely.

"Sit. Doctor's orders," Patrick said. "How do you take your coffee?"

"Black, please. And thank you very much," Abraham said, lowering himself back into his chair.

Patrick poured both mugs to the rim and carried them to the table. He set the coffee beside their plates. Susanne had made French toast, which Patrick had cut into strips so Abraham could use his good hand to dunk the pieces in a pool of syrup on the plate.

Abraham bowed his head. His lips moved. When he'd finished his prayer, he lifted his head and fastened his intense, dark eyes on Patrick. "It troubles me that knowledge of my past may put you in danger."

"Far less than you are in, my new friend."

"You must forget you know the Shah's secret. And me. Do not talk of me or knowing anyone like me. It could draw the wrong kind of attention. The world is much smaller than most people believe and getting smaller every day." Abraham's expression was grave and his voice chillingly serious.

Patrick nodded, but he didn't agree. "I can't do that. I mean, I can forget about the Shah. But not about you. In fact, I've been talking to Cyrus, and I have a proposal for you. A place where you can go and hide in plain sight, making a difference by using your medical skills."

Abraham looked interested, if wary. "What is that?"

"The Wind River Reservation here in central Wyoming. The Eastern Shoshone and Northern Arapaho who live there are in desperate need of good medical care."

"But without my name, I don't have my physician's license."

"Cyrus took care of that." Cyrus, it turned out, could make almost anything happen that he wanted. It was one of the perks of being the Secretary of State of the most powerful country in the world, which, it turned out, was his role in the U.S. government. *I really need to start paying more attention to politics.* "If you want to do it, that is. I think with your coloring, you would blend in well there. Not to the locals. You don't look Shoshone or Arapaho. But to outsiders, you'd be close enough not to attract attention, with your dark coloring."

Abraham took a small bite and chewed slowly, his eyes in a faraway place. When they came back, they were eager. "I would like it very much."

"I was hoping you'd say that. Most of the arrangements have already been made. I can get you there whenever you say the word. But I'll warn you—you won't make much money."

"Money has never brought me happiness. But caring for the health of others has." Patrick couldn't agree more. "And, someday, I might be able to return to my mother's country and the family I have left. Time is ticking for the Shah if he doesn't seek treatment. Probably even if he does."

"Good. It's settled then. I'll make the final arrangements with Cyrus." Patrick waved at Abraham's plate. "Your food is getting cold. Don't let me slow down your breakfast."

Abraham took a bite. But soon he was talking again, like a man who'd been starved of the conversation of a likeminded friend for too long, which Patrick supposed he had. "Have you received an update on Barry's condition this morning?"

"I called about an hour ago. The second surgery was a complete success, and the IV antibiotics did the trick. No fever. He's cranky and asking to go home."

Abraham smiled. "That is what Dr. John would call a good sign."

"Yes, it is."

"And your ribs? Are they any better?"

Patrick touched them. Truth be told, they hurt like a son of a gun. "No worse. Another good sign."

He'd broken down the night before and told Susanne the bucking bronc he'd taken flight from was a horse he'd been considering for her, and that he'd climbed aboard it in a storm and even after it was acting flighty. She'd looked him in the eye and said, "There's not one good decision anywhere in that story, is there?" He wouldn't be receiving any sympathy from his wife. Nor would he be buying her another horse anytime soon.

Abraham said, "I hope George will forgive me some day. And Mrs. Debbie Murray."

Neither George nor Debbie would be privy to Abraham's real story. Patrick doubted they'd ever look fondly on their memories of him. He chuckled. "George will survive. And Debbie has insurance on the snowmobiles."

"Good morning." Susanne breezed into the kitchen. She looked even prettier than usual, and Patrick had an urge to sweep her into his lap, but he'd hold off until their full household dispersed.

Abraham said, "Good morning, Mrs. Flint. My thanks for the delicious breakfast."

"You're welcome. And please, call me Susanne."

"Then you must call me Abraham." Cyrus had agreed that since the SAVAK had been looking for Farhad Ali and found Muhammed, Abraham could keep his most recent assumed name.

"Abraham it is, then." She smiled at him and went to refill her own coffee cup. Patrick made a note of the one she was using. A white mug with purple lupine painted on it. He'd be the one to put it in the sink later when he found it behind the television or on a closet shelf or on the hood of a car. "Patrick, did I overhear you saying my brother is cranky?"

He swallowed a slug of coffee. "That you did." He cut off a healthy chunk of French toast and put it in his mouth. It was so good he wanted to let it dissolve instead of chewing and swallowing it.

She waggled her eyebrows. "He's going to be even more cranky after Esme's through with him."

"Oh?"

"She's at the hospital now breaking off their engagement."

Patrick gawked. "But he nearly died."

"She didn't like hearing about his ex-fiancée from the woman herself, while on a girls' trip and stuck together in a hotel room. Honestly, I wouldn't have been happy with him if I were her, either. But it's not like he cheated on her."

Dian had left for Billings before Patrick had gotten home. He could only imagine how tense things had been between the women. "I did wonder why I saw her suitcases by the door this morning."

"That would be it. She's catching a Greyhound to Denver after she tells him. Which, according to Trish, is going to be a little less refined mode of transportation than Esme is used to."

Patrick harrumphed. "And not even a goodbye to the rest of us?"

"I think we've all been tarred and feathered with the same brush as Barry. And after I'd committed to do all this women's club volunteer work that she talked me into."

"You said yes?"

She nodded. "But I limited it to five hours a month, no chairing any committees at this stage. I should be able to work that in."

"It might even be fun."

Abraham stood. "I hope to relieve you of the burden of hosting me soon, too."

Susanne smiled at him. "You're welcome here, Abraham. No need to rush."

Patrick knew Abraham would be in a hurry now, running *to* something instead of *from* it. "I'll make that call. With any luck, we can have you on your way whenever you are ready, although I second my wife and urge you to give yourself time to heal before you throw yourself into work. You're welcome here, for as long as you need."

Abraham bowed. "Thank you. I am forever in your debt."

He turned on his heel. Patrick heard his footsteps climbing the stairs. Susanne shot Patrick a questioning look—he couldn't tell her as much about Abraham as she'd like, but she hadn't given up asking yet. The phone rang. She reached over the counter and lifted the receiver.

"Hello?" Her eyes went round. "Kelsey Jones? For Perry?" After a pause, she said, "He's asleep. Does he have your number to call you back?" She picked up a pen and notepad and scribbled something down. "All right. I'll tell him. Goodbye." When she had hung up the phone, she shook her head. "Girls calling boys. What is the world coming to?"

Patrick laughed. His son was growing up. Of course, the boy still wanted a snowmobile more than a girlfriend. Or at least, that had been the lay of the land the day before. "You did ask me out first, you know, back in the dark ages." It had been a Sadie Hawkins dance. Not that Susanne had needed an excuse to go for what she wanted. The woman had enough moxie for two.

"Details." She winked at him, and his heart skipped a beat. How did she still do that to him after seventeen years of marriage? "I was hoping that would be the other Jones in our lives. Ben instead of Kelsey."

"He still hasn't called Trish?"

"Not a word. Vangie and Henry haven't heard from him, either. Meanwhile, their attorney in Laramie confirmed that Ben's finger-prints weren't on the bag of drugs the cop confiscated from his pocket. Or the bags in the glove box. Not only that, but the awful roommate had multiple drug arrests. Laramie PD is dropping all charges against Ben."

Patrick stood and walked over to her. "There's no way for the Sibleys to even give Ben the news."

"None. No one knows where he is. Trish swears he's in Cody, gearing up to go to Alaska to work on a fishing boat. But that's just a guess. Vangie and Henry searched for him in Cody, but they didn't have any luck. So, Ronnie had them file a missing person report. I think they're going to hire a private detective, too." Susanne leaned her head on Patrick's shoulder. "I've checked Trish's room twenty times since dinner last night to be sure she hasn't run off again to look for him. I've even thought about going after him myself."

"Me, too. But we've got to trust law enforcement. And the P.I. They've got the resources. We don't."

"You're right. I know you're right."

"But this is going to be tough on her."

"It's going to be tough on all of us."

Patrick stroked her hair. "I've got a confession."

"What's that?"

"I really like that boy."

After a second's pause, Susanne burst into tears. She dropped her face in her hands. He turned her and pulled her into his arms.

"Me, too," she said. "When does this parenting thing get easier? First, they were babies, and I thought they'd break if I dropped them or squeezed them. They wouldn't sleep, so I couldn't sleep. It was so hard. But now that they're older, it's their hearts. Their *hearts*. This is harder, Patrick. This is much, much harder."

He couldn't disagree with anything she'd said. But there was something she'd left out. "The greater the risk, the greater the reward."

"What do you mean?"

"As a parent. You risk it all to love these little creatures, and the reward is exponential."

She sniffled. "Yes, but—"

"Right now, with the stakes just getting higher and higher, this is when we forge the adult relationships with them that will last the rest of our lives. Trish is becoming a young woman. We need to be there for her, no matter how hard it is. Then, God willing, some day, she won't need us to be anymore."

Susanne pulled back and gave him the evil eye. "She'll always need us. Perry will, too."

He laughed. Over Susanne's head, he saw snowflakes the size of dimes falling outside the window. Dendrites, maybe? But it didn't matter what they were. They were just beautiful. "Yes, probably. And someday, we're going to need them."

"I don't want to ever put them through anything like this. This pain. These feelings." She wiped her eyes.

"Even a woman as determined as you can't hold back the tides." He wriggled a little. His broken ribs were hurting. An injury that wouldn't have happened if he were younger and more malleable. But as much as he had loved his youth, he loved his life now and the people in it. His mind flashed on an image of the buck in the park, at the moment Abraham had been sharing his secrets with Cyrus and

Patrick. Patrick didn't want to be like that lonely stag in the wilderness, even if the price was broken ribs or a broken heart.

What small things those were, compared to all he had.

***

Next up: There's more **Patrick Flint** and family coming in *Sitting Duck*. Get yours at https://www.amazon.com/dp/B09BDFWFLF. A killer blizzard has hit tiny Buffalo, Wyoming, where Dr. Patrick Flint is trapped inside the hospital with his family, trying to save the life of a prominent local citizen. An injured drifter shows up at the door, and Patrick takes him in. When the power and communications go out that night, people start dying, and the drifter is nowhere to be found. Patrick is caught between his duty to his patient, his loyalty to his family, and his fear for all of their lives. With the storm still raging, will there be any survivors left in the hospital when help finally arrives?

Or you can adventure on in the *What Doesn't Kill You* super series mystery world:

Want to stay in **Wyoming**? Rock on with Maggie in *Live Wire* **on Amazon** (free in Kindle Unlimited) at https://www.amazon.com/Live-Wire-Maggie-Romantic-Mystery-ebook/dp/B07L5RYGHZ.

Prefer the **beginning** of it all? Start with Katie in *Saving Grace* on **Amazon** (free to Kindle Unlimited subscribers), here: https://www.amazon.com/Saving-Grace-Doesnt-Romantic-Mystery-ebook/dp/B009FZPMFO.

Or **get the complete WDKY series** here:
https://www.amazon.com/gp/product/B07QQVNSPN.

***

And don't forget to snag the **free** *What Doesn't Kill You* **ebook starter library—including a Patrick Flint short story—**by joining Pamela's mailing list at https://www. subscribepage.com/PFHSuperstars.

To Clark, the son who makes me question myself in the best possible ways.
And to Eric, the husband who convinces me he loves me just the way I am, past, present, and future states.

ACKNOWLEDGMENTS

When I got the call from my father that he had metastatic prostate cancer spread into his bones in nine locations, I was with a houseful of retreat guests in Wyoming while my parents (who normally summer in Wyoming) were in Texas. The guests were so kind and comforting to me, as was Eric, but there was only one place I wanted to be, and that was home. Not home where I grew up, because I lived in twelve places by the time I was twelve, and many thereafter. No, home is truly where the heart is. And that meant home for Eric and me would be with my parents.

I was in the middle of writing two novels at the time: *Blue Streak,* the first Laura mystery in the What Doesn't Kill You series, and *Polarity,* a series spin-off contemporary romance based on my love story with Eric. I put them both down. I needed to write, but not those books. They could wait. I needed to write through my emotions —because that's what writers do—with books spelling out the ending we were seeking for my dad's story. Allegorically and biographically, while fictionally.

So that is what I did, and Dr. Patrick Flint (aka Dr. Peter Fagan— my pops—in real life) and family were hatched, using actual stories from our lives in late 1970s, Buffalo, Wyoming, as the depth and backdrop to a new series of mysteries, starting with *Switchback* and moving on to *Snake Oil, Sawbones, Scapegoat, Snaggle Tooth, Stag Party,* and *Sitting Duck,* with more to come. I hope the real life versions of Patrick, Susanne, and Perry will forgive me for taking liberties in creating their fictional alter egos. I took care to make Trish the most annoying character since she's based on me, to soften the blow for the others. I am so hopeful that my loyal readers will enjoy them, too, even though in some ways the novels are a departure from my usual stories. But in many ways they are the same. Character-driven, edge-of-your-seat mysteries steeped in setting/culture, with a strong nod to the everyday magic around us, and filled with complex, authentic characters (including some AWESOME females).

Each book starts with a memory of something incredibly, well, *dumb*, that my dad did. It's amazing how each of us, no matter how brilliant, is still completely fallible, with our blind spots and bad decisions. With *Stag Party*, that mishap was the time my dad broke a few ribs riding a horse he shouldn't have, despite my mother's stringent objections. How this story evolved from there is the magic of imagination, I guess!

I had a wonderful time writing these books, and it kept me going when it was tempting to fold in on myself and let stress eat me alive. For more stories behind the actual stories, visit my blog on my website: http://pamelafaganhutchins.com. And let me know if you liked the novels.

Thanks to my dad for advice on all things medical, wilderness, hunting, 1970s, aeronautical, and animal. I hope you had fun using your medical knowledge for murder!

Thanks to my mom for printing the manuscripts (over and over, in their entireties) as she and dad followed along daily on the progress.

Thanks to my husband, Eric, for brainstorming with and encouraging me and beta reading the *Patrick Flint* stories despite his busy work, travel, and workout schedule. And for moving in to my parents' barn apartment with me so I could be closer to them during that time.

Thanks to our five offspring. I love you guys more than anything, and each time I write a parent/child (birth, adopted, foster, or step), I channel you. I am so touched by how supportive you have been with Poppy, Gigi, Eric, and me.

To each and every blessed reader, I appreciate you more than I can say. It is the readers who move mountains for me, and for other authors, and I humbly ask for the honor of your honest reviews and recommendations.

Thanks mucho to Bobbye Marrs for the fantastic *Patrick Flint* covers.

Patrick Flint editing credits go to Rhonda Erb, Whitney Cox, and Karen Goodwin. The proofreaders who enthusiastically devote their time—gratis—to help us rid my books of flaws blow me away. Thank you all!

SkipJack Publishing now includes fantastic books by a cherry-picked bushel basket of mystery/thriller/suspense writers. If you write in this genre, visit http://SkipJackPublishing.com for submission guidelines. To check out our other authors and snag a bargain at the same time, download *Murder, They Wrote: Four SkipJack Mysteries*.

p.s. My dad is defying his diagnosis and doing fantastic now. It's my prayer we'll be collaborating on this series for many years to come.

BOOKS BY THE AUTHOR

Fiction from SkipJack Publishing

THE *PATRICK FLINT* SERIES OF WYOMING MYSTERIES:

Switchback (Patrick Flint #1)

Snake Oil (Patrick Flint #2)

Sawbones (Patrick Flint #3)

Scapegoat (Patrick Flint #4)

Snaggle Tooth (Patrick Flint #5)

Stag Party (Patrick Flint #6)

Sitting Duck (Patrick Flint #7)

Spark (Patrick Flint 1.5): Exclusive to subscribers

THE *WHAT DOESN'T KILL YOU* SUPER SERIES:

Act One (WDKY Ensemble Prequel Novella): Exclusive to Subscribers

The Essential Guide to the What Doesn't Kill You Series

Katie Connell Caribbean Mysteries:

Saving Grace (Katie #1)

Leaving Annalise (Katie #2)

Finding Harmony (Katie #3)

Seeking Felicity (Katie #4)

Emily Bernal Texas-to-New Mexico Mysteries:

Heaven to Betsy (Emily #1)

Earth to Emily (Emily #2)

Hell to Pay (Emily #3)

Michele Lopez Hanson Texas Mysteries:

Going for Kona (Michele #1)

Fighting for Anna (Michele #2)

Searching for Dime Box (Michele #3)

Maggie Killian Texas-to-Wyoming Mysteries:

Buckle Bunny (Maggie Prequel Novella)

Shock Jock (Maggie Prequel Short Story)

Live Wire (Maggie #1)

Sick Puppy (Maggie #2)

Dead Pile (Maggie #3)

The Ava Butler Caribbean Mysteries Trilogy: A Sexy Spin-off From *What Doesn't Kill You*

Bombshell (Ava #1)

Stunner (Ava #2)

Knockout (Ava #3)

BOX SETS:

(50% off individual title retail)

The Patrick Flint Box Set Series

The Patrick Flint Series Books #1-3

The Patrick Flint Series Books #4-6

The What Doesn't Kill You Box Sets Series

The Complete Katie Connell Trilogy

The Complete Emily Bernal Trilogy

The Complete Michele Lopez Hanson Trilogy

The Complete Maggie Killian Trilogy

The Complete Ava Butler Trilogy

Juvenile Fiction from SkipJack Publishing

Poppy Needs a Puppy (Poppy & Petey #1)

Nonfiction from SkipJack Publishing

The Clark Kent Chronicles

Hot Flashes and Half Ironmans

How to Screw Up Your Kids

How to Screw Up Your Marriage

Puppalicious and Beyond

What Kind of Loser Indie Publishes,

and How Can I Be One, Too?

Audio, e-book, and paperback versions of most titles available.

Patrick Flint and Katie Connell also available in hardcover and large print.

ABOUT THE AUTHOR

Pamela Fagan Hutchins is a *USA Today* best selling author. She writes award-winning romantic mystery/thriller/suspense from way up in the frozen north of Snowheresville, Wyoming, where she lives in an off-the-grid cabin on the face of the Bighorn Mountains. She is passionate about hiking/snow shoeing/cross country skiing with her hunky husband and pack of rescue dogs (and occasional rescue cat) and riding their gigantic horses.

If you'd like Pamela to speak to your book club, women's club, class, or writers group by streaming video or in person, shoot her an email. She's very likely to say yes.

You can connect with Pamela via her website
(http://pamelafaganhutchins.com)
or email (pamela@pamelafaganhutchins.com).

PRAISE FOR PAMELA FAGAN HUTCHINS

2018 USA Today Best Seller
2017 Silver Falchion Award, Best Mystery
2016 USA Best Book Award, Cross-Genre Fiction
2015 USA Best Book Award, Cross-Genre Fiction
2014 Amazon Breakthrough Novel Award Quarter-finalist,
Romance

The Patrick Flint Mysteries

"Best book I've read in a long time!" — Kiersten Marquet, author of
Reluctant Promises
"*Switchback* transports the reader deep into the mountains of
Wyoming for a thriller that has it all--wild animals, criminals, and one
family willing to do whatever is necessary to protect its own. Pamela
Fagan Hutchins writes with the authority of a woman who knows
this world. She weaves the story with both nail-biting suspense and a
healthy dose of humor. You won't want to miss *Switchback*." -
- Danielle Girard, *Wall Street Journal*-bestselling author of
White Out.
"*Switchback* by Pamela Fagan Hutchins has as many twists and turns
as a high-country trail. Every parent's nightmare is the loss or injury
of a child, and this powerful novel taps into that primal fear." -- Reavis
Z. Wortham, two time winner of The Spur and author of *Hawke's
Prey*
"*Switchback* starts at a gallop and had me holding on with both hands
until the riveting finish. This book is highly atmospheric and nearly
crackling with suspense. Highly recommend!" -- Libby Kirsch, Emmy
awardwinning reporter and author of the *Janet Black Mystery Series*

"A Bob Ross painting with Alfred Hitchcock hidden among the trees."
"Edge-of-your seat nail biter."
"Unexpected twists!"
"Wow! Wow! Highly entertaining!"
"A very exciting book (um... actually a nail-biter), soooo beautifully descriptive, with an underlying story of human connection and family. It's full of action. I was so scared and so mad and so relieved... sometimes all at once!"
"Well drawn characters, great scenery, and a kept-me-on-the-edge-of-my-seat story!"
"Absolutely unputdownable wonder of a story."
"Must read!"
"Gripping story. Looking for book two!"
"Intense!"
"Amazing and well-written read."
"Read it in one fell swoop. I could not put it down."

What Doesn't Kill You: Katie Connell Romantic Mysteries

"An exciting tale . . . twisting investigative and legal subplots . . . a character seeking redemption . . . an exhilarating mystery with a touch of voodoo." — *Midwest Book Review Bookwatch*
"A lively romantic mystery." — *Kirkus Reviews*
"A riveting drama . . . exciting read, highly recommended." — *Small Press Bookwatch*
"Katie is the first character I have absolutely fallen in love with since Stephanie Plum!" — *Stephanie Swindell, Bookstore Owner*
"Engaging storyline . . . taut suspense." — *MBR Bookwatch*

What Doesn't Kill You: Emily Bernal Romantic Mysteries

"Fair warning: clear your calendar before you pick it up because you won't be able to put it down." — *Ken Oder, author of* Old Wounds to the Heart

"Full of heart, humor, vivid characters, and suspense. Hutchins has done it again!" — *Gay Yellen, author of* The Body Business

"Hutchins is a master of tension." — *R.L. Nolen, author of* Deadly Thyme

"Intriguing mystery . . . captivating romance." — *Patricia Flaherty Pagan, author of* Trail Ways Pilgrims

"Everything about it shines: the plot, the characters and the writing. Readers are in for a real treat with this story." — *Marcy McKay, author of* Pennies from Burger Heaven

What Doesn't Kill You: Michele Lopez Hanson Romantic Mysteries

"Immediately hooked." — *Terry Sykes-Bradshaw, author of* Sibling Revelry

"Spellbinding." — *Jo Bryan, Dry Creek Book Club*

"Fast-paced mystery." — *Deb Krenzer, Book Reviewer*

"Can't put it down." — *Cathy Bader, Reader*

What Doesn't Kill You: Ava Butler Romantic Mysteries

"Just when I think I couldn't love another Pamela Fagan Hutchins novel more, along comes Ava." — *Marcy McKay, author of* Stars Among the Dead

"Ava personifies bombshell in every sense of word. — *Tara Scheyer, Grammy-nominated musician, Long-Distance Sisters Book Club*

"Entertaining, complex, and thought-provoking." — *Ginger Copeland, power reader*

What Doesn't Kill You: Maggie Killian Romantic Mysteries

"Maggie's gonna break your heart—one way or another." *Tara Scheyer, Grammy-nominated musician, Long-Distance Sisters Book Club*

"Pamela Fagan Hutchins nails that Wyoming scenery and captures the atmosphere of the people there." — *Ken Oder, author of* Old Wounds to the Heart

"I thought I had it all figured out a time or two, but she kept me wondering right to the end." — *Ginger Copeland, power reader*

BOOKS FROM SKIPJACK PUBLISHING

FICTION:
Marcy McKay

Pennies from Burger Heaven, by Marcy McKay

Stars Among the Dead, by Marcy McKay

The Moon Rises at Dawn, by Marcy McKay

Bones and Lies Between Us, by Marcy McKay

R.L. Nolen

Deadly Thyme, by R. L. Nolen

The Dry, by Rebecca Nolen

Ken Oder

The Closing, by Ken Oder

Old Wounds to the Heart, by Ken Oder

The Judas Murders, by Ken Oder

The Princess of Sugar Valley, by Ken Oder

Gay Yellen

The Body Business, by Gay Yellen

The Body Next Door, by Gay Yellen

Pamela Fagan Hutchins

The Clark Kent Chronicles, by Pamela Fagan Hutchins

Hot Flashes and Half Ironmans, by Pamela Fagan Hutchins

How to Screw Up Your Kids, by Pamela Fagan Hutchins

How to Screw Up Your Marriage, by Pamela Fagan Hutchins

Puppalicious and Beyond, by Pamela Fagan Hutchins

What Kind of Loser Indie Publishes,

and How Can I Be One, Too?, by Pamela Fagan Hutchins

Marcy McKay

When Life Feels Like a House Fire, by Marcy McKay

Ken Oder

Keeping the Promise, by Ken Oder

FOREWORD

Stag Party is a work of fiction. Period. Any resemblance to actual persons, places, things, or events is just a lucky coincidence.

CPSIA information can be obtained
at www.ICGtesting.com
Printed in the USA
BVHW030933310821
615688BV00001B/53